W9-BCM-654

"I don't think I can love anybody,"

he said at last. "There's something missing inside me. I like people, but there's a distance between them and me. I don't feel it so strongly with you, but it's always there, and it might always be there."

Olivia swallowed hard. "Why do you want to marry me, then?"

"I can see things very clearly. I know exactly what I want in a marriage, and I know the woman who can give it to me. We'll get married for the right reasons, all the right reasons. I'll be faithful and supportive, and I'll put you and the children first. But I can't give you what I don't have to give."

Olivia sensed how hard this was for Brett to talk about, and she loved him more for being able to say it. He was a man yearning for all the things she knew she could give him. He was right; he had chosen well.

PERU PUBLIC LIBRARY

Paperback Exchange

Please Return

Dear Reader,

Sophisticated but sensitive, savvy yet unabashedly sentimental—that's today's woman, today's romance reader—you! And Silhouette Special Editions are written expressly to reward your quest for substantial, emotionally involving love stories.

So take a leisurely stroll under the cover's lavender arch into a garden of romantic delights. Pick and choose among titles if you must—we hope you'll soon equate all six Special Editions each month with consistently gratifying romantic reading.

Watch for sparkling new stories from your Silhouette favorites—Nora Roberts, Tracy Sinclair, Ginna Gray, Lindsay McKenna, Curtiss Ann Matlock, among others—along with some exciting newcomers to Silhouette, such as Karen Keast and Patricia Coughlin. Be on the lookout, too, for the new Silhouette Classics, a distinctive collection of bestselling Special Editions and Silhouette Intimate Moments now brought back to the stands—two each month—by popular demand.

On behalf of all the authors and editors of Special Editions,
Warmest wishes,

Leslie Kazanjian
Senior Editor

EMILIE RICHARDS
All the Right Reasons

Silhouette Special Edition

Published by Silhouette Books New York

America's Publisher of Contemporary Romance

SILHOUETTE BOOKS
300 East 42nd St., New York, N.Y. 10017

Copyright © 1988 by Emilie Richards McGee

All rights reserved, including the right to reproduce
this book or portions thereof in any form whatsoever.
For information address Silhouette Books,
300 East 42nd St., New York, N.Y. 10017

ISBN: 0-373-09433-7

First Silhouette Books printing February 1988

All the characters in this book are fictitious. Any
resemblance to actual persons, living or dead, is
purely coincidental.

SILHOUETTE, SILHOUETTE SPECIAL EDITION and colophon
are registered trademarks of the publisher.

America's Publisher of Contemporary Romance

Printed in the U.S.A.

Books by Emilie Richards

Silhouette Romance

Brendan's Song #372
Sweet Georgia Gal #393
Gilding the Lily #401
Sweet Sea Spirit #413
Angel and the Saint #429
Sweet Mockingbird's Call #441
Good Time Man #453
Sweet Mountain Magic #466
Sweet Homecoming #489
Aloha Always #520
Outback Nights #536

Silhouette Special Edition

All the Right Reasons #433

Silhouette Intimate Moments

Lady of the Night #152
Bayou Midnight #188

EMILIE RICHARDS

grew up in St. Petersburg, Florida, and attended college in her home state. She also fell in love there, and married her husband, Michael, who is her opposite in every way. "The only thing we agreed on was that we were very much in love. We haven't changed our minds about that in the sixteen years we've been together." They now live in New Orleans with four children who span from toddler to teenager.

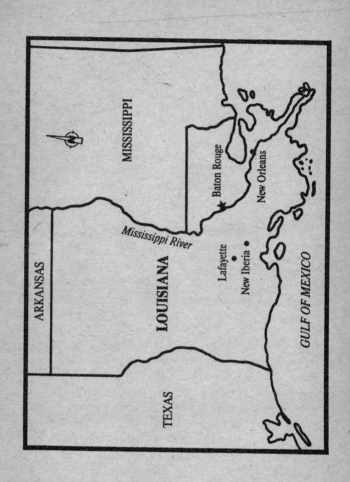

Chapter One

Brett Terrill was tired—no, more than tired. He was exhausted. But exhaustion was to be expected since he hadn't really planned to run more than one lap around the two-mile circular pathway at New Orleans's Audubon Park. Unfortunately, he hadn't counted on Drew Sherwood's zeal. After a lifetime of leisure, forty-five-year-old, rapidly graying Drew had recently converted to running the way some people converted to religion—and for the same reasons. Drew wanted eternal life, and he expected a long daily run to give it to him. Now, he was trying to convert Brett. They were on their second lap.

Drew's efforts weren't working; Brett hadn't experienced the thrill of conversion. He just wanted to finish the lap and collapse with a cold beer and a mind too numb from fatigue to contemplate anything more important than the nineteen-inch screen on his boob tube.

Drew's conceited chuckle disturbed Brett's fantasy. "I can't believe you, Terrill. Thirty years old and you're puffing and panting like a hound dog in the summer sun."

Brett wondered just how long it had taken Drew to come up with the analogy. He guessed at least half a mile. "Listen," he said, trying not to sound out of breath, "this was never my idea. You said a little jog around the park. How was I to know you were planning a marathon?"

"You've let yourself go since you broke it off with Kate."

Brett slowed a little, waiting for the familiar stab in his gut—or his ego, if he were really going to be honest. When the only things he felt were the cold trickle of sweat down his nose and the crisp, autumn air burning his overworked lungs, he decided that running wasn't a waste of time after all. If it could help deaden him to the end of a two-year relationship with the woman he'd planned to marry, maybe he'd do another lap after this one.

Drew openly contemplated his friend as they continued down the tree-shaded asphalt path, skirting skateboarders and a pair of Tulane University coeds walking a Doberman. Brett kept his eyes straight ahead. He hardly noticed when the girls, two fresh-faced Southern beauties, followed him with their eyes. Brett knew he attracted women. Kate had told him once that it was his classic good looks combined with a reticence, a mysterious something, that made every woman who met him want to be the one to find out what went on inside his broad-shouldered body and perfectly shaped head.

Every woman except Kate Parsons herself.

"I saw Kate today," Drew said, still watching Brett.

Brett betrayed no reaction. "That's hardly a surprise. You're an attorney; she's an attorney."

"You're an attorney, too. Have you seen her?"

"Why are we talking about Kate?"

"I've always admired your ability to cut through to the heart of a conversation." Drew turned his eyes straight ahead. "We're talking about Kate because as far as I can tell, you haven't talked about her since you moved out of her apartment three months ago."

"That's right."

"It's time, Brett."

Brett thought privately that the time was probably long past. He'd needed someone to talk to the day he'd moved out and for weeks afterward, too. But there had been no one he'd trusted enough to share his confusing feelings with. Now the confusion seemed to be gone.

"There's not a lot to say," he said cautiously. "Kate's going up in the world. I wanted a wife; she wanted a political career. According to her, the two wouldn't go together right now. I finally gave the words 'right now' their proper interpretation."

"Never?"

"That's right." Brett realized he'd speeded up as he told his story. He forced himself to slow down. "Kate'll always find an excuse to avoid commitment. She's too political to tie herself permanently to one man when she might have more to gain as a free agent."

Brett knew Drew wouldn't dispute his words. Drew knew Kate Parsons was perfectly capable of selling her favors if the right occasion arose. They would be sold with class and style, but the word for it was the same.

The two men had gone another quarter of a mile before Drew spoke again. "Why did you stay with her so long?"

Brett realized this part of the story still hurt. "Damned if I know," he said lightly, as if he were laughing at himself. But he did know. There was a little boy inside him, a little boy he'd been trying to exorcise all his adult life. That little boy wanted a home, a family—something he had never had. For two years Kate had led him to believe that someday they would make that home, have that family, together. He'd been a fool.

"You sold yourself pretty short, didn't you?"

Brett knew he had sold himself short. He'd thought he knew what he wanted, but his desire, his dream, hadn't been focused. Kate had not been the woman for him, but the proof of it had taken two long years, seven hundred and some odd days of learning about his own needs. He wouldn't sell himself short again. Now he knew exactly what his goal was. He knew exactly what he was looking for. "Next time I'll know better," he told Drew and meant every word.

Drew grinned. "You're in better emotional shape than you know if you're already thinking about next time. Are you looking around?"

"It's not quite that premeditated."

"Meg would love to fix you up with one of her friends."

Brett laughed, and the laughter felt good. He had talked about Kate, and he was fine. He realized he must finally be over the worst of his failure. He ought to circle the day in red on his calendar.

"Shall I tell Meg you laughed at the idea?"

Drew and his wife, Meg, were two of the few people in the world Brett cared enough about to worry about alienating. He shook his head. "Tell Meg I love her, but I don't want one of her feminist friends."

"Oh, she'll love that. Brett Terrill, social activist, knight in shining armor to the downtrodden, champion of every cause Meg holds dear, doesn't want to meet a feminist."

"Tell Meg if she divorces you, I'll make an exception." Brett noted the spot where their run had begun and slowed to a walk. "What I don't want is another Kate."

Drew slowed, too, wiping the sweat from his forehead on the sleeve of his jogging-suit jacket. "In your newfound wisdom, exactly what kind of woman are you looking for?"

That was tough. Brett's answers ran deep. He wasn't sure how to verbalize them, or even if he wanted to. Then, suddenly, the answer was in front of him.

"See the woman in the distance with the two little kids?"

Drew shook his head, reaching inside his jacket for the glasses he always wore unless he was running. He waited for his nearsighted eyes to focus. "The dark-haired one wading in the lagoon? You like crazy women?"

"We passed her twice. I noticed her both times. She adores those children. Last time around she was down on the ground wrestling with the little boy. Now look at her. I'll bet she's wading in that freezing water to get something for one of them. I want a woman like that, someone who puts her family first, someone who's more interested in romping in the park than getting ahead in the world."

Drew took off his glasses and wiped them on the hem of his jacket before replacing them. They had fogged up immediately the first time, but this time they remained clear. "Too bad she's not free."

"Women like that seldom are. Some man snaps them up before they're old enough to vote."

Drew's restrained laughter was in his voice. "Yes, sir, it's too bad. If she were free, you could walk right up and introduce yourself, tell her you like the way she handles kids and ask her to marry you."

Brett was trained to pick up nuances in conversation. The ability to hear the grain of truth inside the most outrageous statement had helped him beat down more than one witness. "What are you getting at?" he asked. "What do you know that I don't?"

"Nothing important." Drew turned to his friend and clapped him on the back. "Only for once, I noticed something you didn't. Those two kids are Lenny Broussard's youngest, Trey and Lucy. And that's not Cherry Broussard with them."

Brett was intrigued. "Then who is she?"

"Their nanny," Drew said triumphantly. "They hired her almost a year ago. Cherry was overwhelmed trying to do everything by herself. You know the Broussards have four teenagers, too. I don't think Lucy and Trey were exactly planned.''

Lenny Broussard was one of the senior partners at the law firm, Broussard, Carrington and Sherwood, where Drew and Brett both practiced. Although Brett had seen the Broussard children, he could not have identified the blond boy and girl from a distance. It made sense that Drew could, however. The Sherwoods and the Broussards had been close friends for a decade.

"A twentieth-century Mary Poppins." Brett examined the small, curvy brunette with interest as they got closer.

"A wet and cold Mary Poppins," Drew amended. "I wonder what she's doing in the lagoon."

"Whatever it is, I think I owe it to Lenny to see if she needs help." Brett veered off the path in the young woman's direction.

"Only because you owe it to Lenny!" Drew called after him in humorous agreement. "You know, suddenly I feel like an old man of forty-five." He pivoted away from Brett, picking up his pace until he was jogging once more. "I have a feeling this is a job for someone younger. I'd better do another lap if I'm going to turn back the clock." But his words were lost on Brett, who was covering the distance between the path and the shore of the lagoon like a man refreshed and ready for anything.

"Trey, please stop crying. See? I've just about got it. It's not going to sink, I promise."

Olivia LeBlanc tried to ignore four-year-old Trey's screams along with the squish of lagoon-bottom mud seeping in through the tops of her tennis shoes. When another student at the Hopkins Academy for Nanny Development in Baton Rouge had taught her to make boats out of newspaper, Olivia had never thought to ask what happened if the boats sailed beyond reach. Now she knew, and she was sorry she did.

"Fish git it."

"No, Lucy. Fish don't eat boats." Olivia imagined that the Audubon Park fish probably thrived on richer fare, like Dixie beer cans or Popeye's chicken boxes. If they didn't, the city of New Orleans should train them and save a fortune on trash collection.

Two more steps and Olivia calculated she'd have the boat—depending, of course, on whether there were any horrible surprises lying in wait under the murky water. She summoned up her courage, calling on generations of Cajun ancestors for help, and took another big step. Now there was only one left. The water couldn't get any colder. As muddy as it was, there were bayous at home in New Iberia that made this lagoon look like a crystal-clear spring, and there couldn't be any species swimming under the surface here that hadn't at one time or another graced the dinner table of the LeBlanc home.

A fresh shriek from Trey forced Olivia to cover the final distance. Leaning as far as she dared, she slapped the water beyond the boat with a dead branch and successfully pushed the boat toward shore. She was wet, cold and cheerfully triumphant. She was also planning a letter to her boat-folding nanny friend to warn her of the activity's pitfalls.

"No, Lucy. Mine!"

Olivia looked up just in time to watch Trey stumble over a tree root at the lagoon's edge and flop headfirst into the water in a race to keep his sister from grabbing the boat.

"Trey!" Horrified, Olivia plunged back toward the shore. She had done the unforgivable. She had taken her eyes off the children for a moment, and disaster had struck. The next agonizing seconds seemed to last for hours. In the midst of them she found herself wondering how anyone ever survived childhood.

She reached Trey at the same time someone else did. Strong arms folded around the little boy and lifted him out of the water. "That was quite a stunt, son," a deep voice chided Trey.

Olivia looked up and saw a warm male smile before she saw anything else. Other impressions followed in the split second that she glanced at him: a long, lean, impossibly perfect body; brown hair; humor-crinkled eyes; a navy blue jogging suit.

She knelt at the water's edge and pushed Trey's dripping hair out of his eyes. "Are you all right, Trey?"

Obviously he was. Trey's face and hair were beaded with water, but his coat was muddier than it was wet, and from the waist down he was barely damp.

"I got it." Trey held up a soggy wad of newspaper for her to see. "It's mine."

"It's nobody's." Olivia pried what had once been a boat out of Trey's hand and tossed it into a trash receptacle. "Look at you! Was an old piece of newspaper worth getting soaked for?"

Trey hung his head and began to cry.

"I suspect he's been punished enough," the man observed.

Olivia looked up ruefully. "You're right. Getting wet in this weather is worse than anything I could come up with if I tried."

"Well, he's not as bad off as he would have been if his whole body had gone in. Lucky for him the water was shallow." The man pulled a small hand towel out of the waistband of his jogging pants and handed it to Olivia to help dry Trey's face and hair.

Olivia accepted it gratefully, mopping up the worst of the damage. "That should help."

"Maybe a little, but with this wind both of you are going to be freezing in a minute. You're wetter than he is."

Between wading and kneeling to check Trey, Olivia knew the man was right. She rivaled Trey for being soaked and muddy. She must be quite a sight. Standing, she met his eyes, adult to adult. "I haven't said thank-you."

"You don't need to. You'd have had him out in a second yourself."

"Yes, but you were quicker."

"I wasn't taking a stroll in the middle of the lagoon."

Olivia rested her hands on Trey's shoulders and turned her attention back to him. "Come on, Trey, we're going to have to race back to the car to keep you warm. No more tears. Your face will freeze."

Brett assessed the Broussards' nanny as she consoled the little boy. She was younger than Brett—he'd guess twenty-two or so, although even that might be giving her the benefit of the doubt. Her hair was long and glossy black, a true blue-black that was rare, even in the exotic melting pot of Louisiana. The intensity of it was startling against her rose-tinted complexion. Her eyebrows were straight, highlighting long-lashed dark eyes, and her features were even, almost pert, with only her full bottom lip hinting at the woman just maturing.

He'd begun to compare her with Kate in his conversation with Drew; now he succinctly and silently finished. Kate was tall and blond, as fashionable as Princess Di and just as slender. This woman was petite and curvaceous. Kate would probably say she was overweight; Brett thought lush would be a better word. There was nothing fashionable about her emerald-green sweatshirt with the statement, "I'm a Hopkins Academy Nanny," embossed on its front. Her dripping rolled-up jeans were serviceable, unadorned denim, and the tennis shoes that had just emerged from the lagoon were mud-encrusted and much the worse for wear.

The most obvious comparison had struck him when they had exchanged that one brief glance. In those few seconds Kate would have sized up this strange male, judged his potential and signaled her interest. This woman had done none of those things. The only emotions Brett had been able to read in her velvet-dark eyes were shyness and perhaps just a hint of embarrassment that she hadn't prevented Trey's fall.

Brett's analysis was interrupted by a whimper. Lucy, who had missed out on all the excitement and all the consolation, was contorting her tiny face like a wind-up toy being primed to perform. Without thinking, Brett bent and scooped up the little girl, jostling her to quell the flood of approaching tears.

Olivia looked up to see the tall, handsome stranger with his arms around Lucy. Perhaps she hadn't been careful enough to keep Trey from taking a dunk in the lagoon, but there was one thing she was always careful about. "Excuse me," she said softly, "but I'm trying to teach the children not to let strangers touch them."

In the rush to rescue Trey and comfort both children, Brett hadn't thought to introduce himself. Now he grinned. The Broussards' nanny was inches shorter than he was, but he had a feeling that if he persisted in holding Lucy without identifying himself, he'd know what it felt like to be attacked by an outraged mother hen protecting her chick.

He tried to put her at her ease as he set Lucy on the ground. "I'm one of the attorneys in Lenny's office, Brett Terrill. I jogged by here earlier with Drew Sherwood, the Sherwood in Broussard, Carrington and Sherwood, and he recognized the children. I've met Lucy and Trey, but I doubt they remember me."

Olivia hid her eyes, bending to roll down the legs of her jeans. "I'm Olivia LeBlanc. The children's nanny." When she straightened, the shyness she'd tried to hide had magnified. How humiliating to have suspected one of Mr. Broussard's colleagues of something as heinous as child molesting. "I'm sorry," she started to apologize.

Brett held up his hand to stop her. "Don't be sorry. I'm impressed. You were doing your job and doing it very well."

"It's just that in a big city, you can never be sure who to trust." Her voice trailed off.

For the first time Brett really listened to the musical cadence of her speech. He placed it immediately. She was from southern Louisiana, and she was probably Cajun.

"Wanna carry." Lucy held up her arms for a repeat performance, this time from Olivia.

Olivia bent to sweep the little girl off her feet. Lucy fit perfectly on her hip, and Olivia brushed her strawberry-blond curls behind her ear in an affectionate gesture. "You always wanna carry," she scolded. "At least put your arms around my neck and warm me up."

Lucy did as requested, nestling her head against Olivia's shoulder.

"Are you cold?"

Olivia was surprised that Brett Terrill hadn't wandered away. In her year with the Broussards she'd almost become one of the family, but she was still used to their friends treating her like nothing more than a highly paid servant. Brett's warm interest was a surprise. She had seen enough of him to confirm her first impressions and add a few more. He was absolutely gorgeous, with hair the color of dark roasted coffee beans and strong, regular features, including a mouth that would set any woman's mind to wandering. Men with his looks and charm were seldom this concerned about others.

"I'm fine," she murmured. "With Lucy's help I'll warm up. It's Trey I'm worried about. We've got to get back to the car."

"He can have my jacket." Before Olivia could refuse, Brett had stripped off his fleece-lined jogging-suit jacket and draped it around the little boy's shoulders. "Is that better?"

Trey hugged it gratefully around him, and his tears trickled to a halt.

Olivia managed a tentative smile. "Thank you, Mr. Terrill..."

"Brett." His voice insisted.

"Brett. But now you'll be cold."

"After running four miles? I won't be cold for a long, long time."

Olivia decided that continuing to object would be sillier than just accepting the jacket. Trey could use it, and she wasn't wearing one to give him herself. She realized she hadn't yet looked directly in Brett Terrill's eyes. Now she saw that they were the darkest of blues, and they were staring at her. The expression in them gave her a bigger jolt. She recognized it as blatant, masculine interest. She hadn't had many such predatory looks aimed in her direction, but she'd seen just enough not to mistake this one for anything else. Olivia's stomach immediately settled at the base of her spine.

"Which way to the car?" he asked.

Olivia inclined her head toward St. Charles Avenue, and Brett slipped his hand over Trey's and began to lead the little boy along the path.

Brett measured the distance to the avenue and the speed at which they were covering it. He probably had two minutes to get to know Olivia. He wished he had a better opportunity to find out about her, but he suspected it would take more than a few minutes to put her at ease enough to discover anything important.

He decided not to waste time. "Do you enjoy being Trey and Lucy's nanny?"

"I love children." Olivia wondered if she could have said anything more obvious, but Brett seemed to like her answer.

"So do I. Sometimes I don't think many people do."

"Where I come from, everybody loves children, and in a town that's mostly Catholic there are a lot of children to love."

"I didn't think you were from New Orleans. Where's home? Bayou Lafourche? Lafayette?"

She smiled, revealing even, white teeth. "Close. New Iberia. I haven't lost the accent?"

"No, and I hope you don't. It's lovely. Do you speak French as well?"

Olivia shook her head sadly. "I understand it perfectly. But we were never allowed to speak it at home. French was for the grown-ups. Now when I try, no one understands a word I say."

"I'm cold, Livvy."

"I'm not surprised, Trey," Olivia told the little boy gently. "I'm afraid you're just going to have to walk faster. If I carry you and make Lucy walk it will take the rest of the day to get to the car."

"Trey, would you like me to carry you?" Brett offered.

Olivia hugged the dozing Lucy tighter against her full breasts as a sudden gust of wind blew over the lagoon. "You're very kind, Brett," she warned, "but Trey's such a mess, he's going to ruin your clothes if you do."

"They'll wash." Brett lifted Trey, who seemed to be deciding if he should let this stranger have the dubious honor of assisting him. Then, with a sigh, Trey settled against Brett's warm body and stuck his thumb in his mouth.

Olivia glanced at Brett again and saw that he was still watching her. Brett Terrill with the tantalizing mouth, broad-shouldered physique and charming manners was the stuff dreams were made of. As a girl she'd had dreams of meeting and marrying a man exactly like him. As she'd grown older she'd become more realistic. Men like Brett had eyes for glamorous, high-powered career women. They didn't look for shy young nannies whose only career aspirations were to take care of other people's children. That didn't mean that the right man wasn't out there waiting for her somewhere. It only meant that the right man wasn't someone like Brett.

"I hate to take you out of your way," she said softly, her eyes stealing back to his.

"You're the only one who hates it. Besides, Trey and I need to have a man-to-man talk about forcing lovely young nannies to go wading in the lagoon."

"It was the lesser of two evils," Olivia assured Brett. "Trey wanted to go after the boat himself. Of course, he ended up doing that anyway."

"Well, at least it gave me an excuse to meet you."

Olivia felt strangely uneasy, like someone who has walked into a crowded, noisy party at the moment the room falls silent. She was sure she had missed something. Why did Brett want to meet her? She was acutely aware that in spite of having been rolled up, her jeans were wet to the knee and tight in places they shouldn't be, her hair was slipping out of its casual braid, and her shoes were sloshing noisily as she walked.

Brett broke the silence. "So how do you like New Orleans?"

Since nothing scintillating came to mind, Olivia settled for the truth. "I like it."

Brett wondered when he had last encountered such a shy female. He imagined it had been in high school. Olivia's shyness wasn't the adolescent variety, though. His impression was that it reflected a sweetness of spirit instead of a low self-esteem. Olivia didn't think badly of herself; she probably just didn't think much about herself at all.

He was thoroughly intrigued. "Tell me about New Iberia."

"Well, it's an oil town, and you know what that means now that oil prices have dropped. A lot of men are out of work; a lot of people have moved away. It's very sad."

"And that's why you're working in New Orleans?"

Olivia smiled at him, and Brett privately classified this first really full-blown smile as the most remarkable he'd ever seen. It transformed her girlish face into mature beauty. He revised his guess about her age. She was older than he'd thought by several years.

"Hopkins Academy nannies are in demand all over the country, but they aren't in demand in New Iberia," she said with a husky laugh. "Besides, I'm related to almost everyone there. Who would pay me to do what a good cousin should do for free?"

"Are you really related to almost everyone in New Iberia?"

"No." She laughed again. "Just all the Cajuns."

Brett tried to imagine what that would be like. "Is your life your own?"

"Is anyone's?" Olivia adjusted the sleeping Lucy's head so that it rested more comfortably.

On St. Charles Avenue Olivia stopped at a brown Toyota and handed Brett her keys so that he could unlock the doors. Then she carefully placed Lucy in her car seat and buckled her in as Brett helped Trey in beside her. She checked Trey's seat belt, too, before she straightened and faced Brett.

"It was nice to meet you, Brett. Thank you for rescuing Trey and helping me get him to the car." Olivia gave Brett a tentative smile. "I'll have your jacket cleaned and sent back to you."

"My pleasure." Before she could move away, Brett touched her arm. "I'll be seeing you again."

Olivia had the feeling that he wasn't referring to the possible crossing of their paths because of their mutual connection with the Broussards. She nodded, at a loss how to respond.

"Unless there's a reason not to," Brett probed.

Olivia was thoroughly confused. "We might see each other. You do work with my boss."

Brett's eyelids dropped a fraction, and the eyes beneath them flickered with humor—and something much more powerful. "I wasn't talking about accidents, Olivia." He liked the sound of her name—four musical syllables adding up to a word that perfectly conveyed the sweet ripeness of the woman standing in front of him. Olivia.

She tried to joke. "Accidents? I didn't think you planned to run me down with your car."

He smiled, and the smile answered any questions she might have had about his intentions. Olivia knew that if a smile could seduce a woman, she was no longer innocent.

"I hope I don't have to run you down at all," he said, the smile growing more provocative by the moment. "But I've never refused a chase if the prize was worth having." Reluctantly he lifted his hand. "Soon, Olivia."

He turned and started down the sidewalk. Long after she'd pulled into the heavy traffic on St. Charles Avenue, Olivia was sure she could still hear Brett's confident whistle.

Chapter Two

Olivia was halfway to the Broussards' Garden District home before she convinced herself she had taken Brett Terrill too seriously. He had been passing the time with her just as charming men had passed the time for all recorded history. He had been flirting, probably to keep his skills sharp and ready for a time when he'd really need them. And she suspected a man as attractive as Brett Terrill would need them often.

Convincing herself that Brett wasn't really interested in her left Olivia with conflicting emotions. She was relieved she wasn't going to flounder around in a flirtation that was way over her head, but at the same time she was disappointed. Brett was every secret fantasy she'd ever harbored, then abandoned as impossible. To find a man as attractive, as charming as Brett, even to know one existed in the real world, was a cruel trick of fate.

Olivia knew she was a romantic, but she liked to believe she balanced that part of herself with good common sense.

At night, however, when the world was quiet and her body was filled with strange, restless yearnings, she had doubts about how realistic she really was. At such times it wasn't the down-to-earth, everyday men she knew that she longed for. It was someone like Brett, someone who reminded her of all the good things life was said to offer. Someone whose gaze could send sensations dancing along her nerve endings until her body was a magnificently choreographed ballet.

More and more, lately, she'd begun to wonder if any man could do that to her. Now she no longer had to wonder. She only had to worry that she had found a totally unattainable man to teach her that she, too, could fall victim to that thing called sexual attraction.

"I'm cold, Livvy," Trey whined from the back seat.

"I've got the heat on, Trey. We'll be home in a minute. Pull the jacket around you some more."

That was another thing about Brett Terrill. Continuing her internal monologue, Olivia swerved into the right lane to turn down Louisiana Avenue for the last leg of the trip home. Brett Terrill was more than a wonderful face and body. He was a considerate human being. He had been as concerned about Trey and Lucy as she had. It was almost the style now for men to profess interest in children, but Brett's interest had been more than a living demonstration of some article from *Cosmopolitan*. Brett genuinely liked children, and he didn't like to see them unhappy.

He was altogether too perfect. It was a shame.

"My shoe has mud on it," Trey observed.

"Your pants have mud on them; your coat has mud on it; your nose used to have mud on it." Olivia peeked at Trey in the rearview mirror. "Still does, in fact."

Trey giggled and rubbed his nose on his sleeve, compounding the problem. Then he sneezed.

Olivia groaned.

Red-haired, eternally cheerful Cherry Broussard was waiting on the first-floor gallery of her two-story Greek revival home when Olivia pulled into the driveway. As always, Olivia patted herself on the back for choosing the Broussards to work for.

The Broussard family was not the first to offer Olivia a position as their nanny. The Hopkins Academy for Nanny Development—acronym H.A.N.D., because so many mothers needed an extra one—was the most notable of all nanny-training programs in the United States and as good or better than its British counterparts. Hopkins Academy nannies were sought after, fought over and bribed with salaries and benefits that rivaled those of many a young executive. The reason was simple. Hopkins nannies were handpicked, highly trained and devoted to their jobs. Having one was as prestigious as owning a Rolex or a Jag. When Olivia finished her two years of training, she, like the other new graduates, had been immediately offered her choice of several different placements.

There had been no contest in Olivia's mind. After interviews with three other families, she had taken one look at the Broussards—one look at the obvious love between parents and children—and she'd known she had found her place.

Olivia had never regretted her decision, although sometimes she did wonder what it would have been like to accept her first offer and spend her days pushing an heirloom-quality Silver Cross pram down the sidewalks of Beverly Hills. The Broussards had no pram. Lucy and Leonard III, or Trey, were thriving toddlers when she'd arrived to take over their care. Cherry had put her life on hold to raise her two new babies, and they'd been raised well. But Cherry, devoted mother that she was, had older children and a husband who also needed her. Olivia's job was to help provide the loving care Cherry didn't always have time to give. Together she and Cherry were an unbeatable team.

Today Cherry threw open the car door to hug Trey and a just-waking Lucy before Olivia had turned off the engine.

"How did the boat sailing go?" Cherry took a closer look at Trey and bit her lip to keep from laughing as he described Olivia's impromptu wade and his own fall from grace.

Olivia came to stand beside Cherry, her muddy shoes in one hand. She was glad, as always, that she had picked an employer who was so relaxed with her children. About now, half the women who could have employed her would have been delivering a blistering lecture. Cherry had enough experience to understand that sometimes things didn't happen as they were supposed to, no matter how careful a nanny was.

"Well, what would you have done?" Olivia asked when Cherry had finally given way to laughter. "Poor old Trey was heartbroken at the thought of losing his boat. You can see he couldn't even wait until I got it back to shore."

"It was just newspaper," Cherry chided the little boy gently. "Poor Olivia."

"Poor Trey," Olivia said, faintly chagrined. "He was sneezing on the way home."

Cherry shook her head in mock exasperation. "You're usually so firm with them. What convinced you to go wading in that awful water?"

Olivia heard the teasing in Cherry's words. Olivia was not always firm enough with the children. It was her one failing as a nanny. She hated confrontations and preferred to find ways to bypass problems. If she had to be strict, she could be, but she worked very hard to avoid it. "Well, it really had nothing to do with Trey's boat," she began. "It was such a warm day, my feet were hot. I went wading to cool off."

Trey's mouth dropped open. "It wasn't hot. It was freezing. She waded 'cause I screamed a lot!"

Olivia threw up her hands in defeat. "Out of the mouths of babes."

"Screaming over paper boats now, smoking in the boy's room when he's a teenager," Cherry said sanctimoniously.

Then both women burst into laughter. When they had quieted, Cherry gave Trey orders to head upstairs and undress for a hot bath. Affectionately she patted the little boy's bottom as he ran by.

"I see Trey still has his rescuer's jacket. Did you get his address so we can return it after it's washed?" Cherry bent to unbuckle the belt on Lucy's car seat.

Olivia's answer was as forcibly nonchalant as a faked yawn. "Actually, you know the man. It was Brett Terrill. He says he works with Lenny."

Cherry straightened with Lucy in her arms and turned back to Olivia. "Brett? That's a coincidence."

"He was jogging at the park and recognized the children. He was on his way over to say hello when Trey tripped and fell."

"Then it was a lucky coincidence." Cherry watched thoughtfully as Olivia brushed off the seat and closed the door. "Actually, I'm surprised Brett would bother saying hello to the children. He's only seen them once or twice."

"He seems to enjoy kids. He was very good with Trey. He even carried him to the car to help keep him warm."

"I wonder if he was interested in more than the children."

Cherry's comment was a surprise. Olivia dropped her pose and decided to be frank; it wouldn't hurt to have another opinion about what had happened. "I'm sure it was the children he was interested in. But he is a flirt. I guess it comes naturally to him. It's probably something he does if he has any woman around as an audience."

"You couldn't be more wrong." Cherry started toward the house, and Olivia followed her as far as the porch. "Brett keeps to himself. Women flirt with him, not vice versa. Of course, he may have changed since..."

Olivia caught Cherry's hesitation. "Since what?"

"Well, Brett's been seriously involved with a woman for the past couple of years. They broke up a few months ago. Maybe he's looking for someone new."

That explanation fit with Olivia's theories. The man was just flexing his muscles. She had been interesting to practice on, nothing more. "He must be desperate if a woman standing in the middle of a muddy lagoon looked good to him," she joked.

"Brett? Desperate?" The sound of Cherry's laughter, like the sound of Brett's whistling, remained in Olivia's ears long after it should have died away.

Sometimes Olivia thought that the only way a stranger could tell she wasn't a member of the Broussard family was by the color of her hair. The Broussards' locks ranged from the pale strawberry blond of Lucy and Trey to the fiery red of Cherry Broussard, with the four teenage girls covering the full gamut in between, depending on how much peroxide or henna they used in their rinse water.

Olivia's black hair might set her apart, but from the moment Cherry Broussard had tactfully told her that her Hopkins Academy uniform ought to be relegated to the back of her closet, Olivia had been treated like one of the Broussard kids. She was respected and trusted, but she was also teased and shamefully manipulated.

So it should have been no surprise to her a week later when she came down for Sunday dinner to find Brett Terrill sitting at the dining-room table.

Olivia immediately understood why Cammie and Mimi, the fourteen-year-old Broussard twins, had insisted she change into her prettiest red dress. Apparently Olivia was the only household member who hadn't known that Brett was invited.

"And you've met Olivia," Lenny said as Brett stood when she entered the room.

"Yes, I've had that pleasure," Brett said, his deep blue eyes smoldering with warmth. "Hello, Olivia."

Olivia tried not to show her surprise. After her conversation with Cherry she had thought about Brett more than she wanted to admit. Her job kept her busy, but thoughts of him had come to her at the oddest times. She was at the point of being irritated with herself. No matter how often she faced the fact that she was being ridiculous, Brett Terrill was still alive and well in her fantasies. Now the real man—definitely alive, well and even more wonderful than she'd remembered—was standing right in front of her. Farewell, fought-for peace of mind.

"Hello, Brett." Olivia moved toward her regular seat next to Lucy's high chair, but Cherry waved her to one at Brett's side.

"I promised Lucy I'd sit by her tonight," Cherry explained. "It was the only way I could get her to take her allergy medicine."

"Allergy medicine and sitting beside her now, good grades and trips to Europe when she's a teenager," Olivia murmured, moving toward her new seat. She wasn't fooled a bit by Cherry's explanation. Cherry had admitted more than once that if Olivia only handled mealtimes with the children, she would still be worth more than they paid her.

"Olivia and I try to keep each other from spoiling Trey and Lucy silly," Cherry explained to Brett. "It doesn't work."

Brett was standing behind Olivia's chair when she reached it, and she let him seat her. It was truly unfair. He had been memorable in his jogging outfit and T-shirt, but in a superbly tailored gray suit, white shirt and scarlet tie, he was even better. His fingertips rested on her shoulder as he pushed in her chair, and Olivia felt the warmth from the casual caress spread to far more interesting parts of her body. There was something about Brett that made her respond with the maturity level of Cammie and Mimi.

Brett sat, too, and Mrs. Ware, the Broussards' part-time cook, served the first course, a spicy turtle soup that filled the dining room with exotic, mouth-watering smells. Olivia let the conversation flow around her as she ate. She tended to be quiet normally. Today she was too busy trying to figure out how Brett's presence had been arranged to participate at all.

Brett joined in the conversation easily, but he watched Olivia from the corner of his eye as he did. He seldom paid attention to the colors a woman wore, but Olivia in red was an extraordinary sight. Her dress contrasted sharply with her beautiful white skin and the blue-black of her hair, which she wore hanging straight down her back in a shining, silken fall. He had thought her girlish and sweet when he'd met her at the park, but today, in the red dress with her hair loose, those adjectives seemed inappropriate.

He'd also thought her shy, and that observation seemed to have been correct. She hadn't really looked at him once, nor had she spoken much. After the annoying chatter of the few dates he'd had since his breakup with Kate, Olivia's silence was peaceful yet intriguing. He decided that there was something nice about having to uncover her secrets layer by layer. It gave him something to anticipate.

"Olivia, Brett told me about running across you at the park last week," Lenny said, when the soup was half finished.

Olivia smiled tentatively. "Did he tell you what I said to him?"

Lenny laughed. "He did. I'm glad you're careful with my children."

Cherry cocked her head, puzzled. "What's this about?"

Lenny gave a significant glance in Trey and Lucy's direction. "I'm afraid Olivia suspected Brett here might not have the children's best interests at heart. That was before she found out who he was. Brett told me all about it when he invited himself to dinner."

Olivia silently asked for forgiveness for the evil thoughts she had aimed at Cherry. Cherry hadn't been matchmaking; Brett had invited himself. Now Olivia only had to figure out why.

"Lenny, you make it sound as if we didn't want him here," Cherry chastised her husband. "I've been inviting Brett for months."

"They've been busy months for me," Brett said smoothly. "I'm just glad the invitation was still open."

The meal progressed to salad. Olivia listened to the conversation, answering politely when she was spoken to. She was acutely aware of Brett sitting so close to her. Apparently he was left-handed, because their arms touched frequently, and each time it happened, she was unnerved. Even though she tried to ignore him, his movements caught her eye. She noticed the breadth of his hands, the lean length of his fingers, the way his cuff slid back when he lifted his arm to reveal a gold watch fastened around his hair-sprinkled wrist. By the last bite of lettuce she would have given anything for even the twins' level of sophistication.

Brett was mesmerized by the unstudied grace of Olivia's movements. Every motion she made was fluid, unhurried. She had none of the frantic energy of so many women he'd known. Olivia wasn't moving toward a goal; each curiously delicate gesture she made was an end unto itself. He wondered if she was ever awkward.

He studied her profile as they waited for the stuffed veal to be served. She was smiling at something one of the twins had said, and her upward-curving lips fascinated him. He wanted to know their taste, to find if they changed in passion, softening, heating, forming whispered, broken pleas. Olivia in the midst of passion, Olivia in his arms, was a thought he'd savored since first meeting her. Like the spicy, sensuous dinner they were being served, the thought was to be relished, imbibed slowly and thoroughly delighted in.

"Let's have dessert in the living room," Cherry suggested when everyone had finished.

"Trey and Lucy, too?" Olivia asked. She had gotten through the meal, although she'd felt tongue-tied and awkward the whole time. At least now she had no worries about Brett's intentions. After her performance during the meal, he couldn't have any interest in her. "Or would you like me to take them up to the playroom for theirs?"

Cherry cut off Olivia's escape, standing to take the tray off Lucy's high chair as she did. "No, I think it will be good for them to stay with the grown-ups this time. We'll all go into the living room." The words were unmistakably an order.

The Broussards rose and moved into the other room, and Olivia and Brett stood, too. Olivia, careful not to collide with Brett, began to follow the others until Brett's hand on her arm stopped her. "Olivia?"

She had spent so much time during the meal noticing his hands that she felt completely undone to have one of them casually touching her. She swiveled a little to face him, trying to appear nonchalant.

"I promise I don't bite," he told her.

She sighed and considered the wisdom of pretending she didn't understand. Instead she made her eyes meet his. "I didn't think you did."

"Are you always this quiet?"

Only when her tongue felt firmly glued to the roof of her mouth. "Not always."

"Prove it." Brett hadn't dropped his hand, and now he caressed her wrist in gentle circles with his thumb. "Come dancing with me after dessert."

Her wrist felt so sensitive she was sure he had bypassed her skin entirely and gone right for the nerve endings. "Dancing? At six on a Sunday?"

"Say yes and I'll provide the place."

She hadn't imagined his interest. She had been reading Brett's signals correctly. It hardly seemed possible.

Brett could read the surprise in Olivia's dark eyes. He had rarely come across a woman who was this unaware of her own charms. Some male instinct he hadn't even known he possessed surged through him. He wanted to put his arms around her and keep her safe; he wanted to slay dragons for her.

"I'm usually not off on Sunday evenings," Olivia said finally. She was sure he knew she was hedging. "The Broussards may have plans."

"They don't. I asked."

So everybody but Olivia herself had known Brett's intentions. "It seems it's all been arranged," she said softly.

"Only if you say yes."

Why did she feel as if she was being asked for something more important than a simple date? Olivia realized she had progressed, or possibly digressed, to a point where she really knew very little about what was going on around her. She was going to have to go entirely on instinct. And her instincts were very clear. If she told Brett no, that would be the end of that. She wouldn't have another chance to say yes. And despite what she knew and didn't know, she didn't want to lose this opportunity.

She nodded uncertainly. "Then yes."

"Good."

Olivia looked down at her clothes. "Shall I change?"

"I like that dress." Brett touched her sleeve. "You look lovely in it."

Olivia murmured her thanks as they went to join the Broussards in the living room. She was still trying to figure out what had just happened when she took her place on the sofa. Her attention was quickly diverted by Trey, who settled in her lap and leaned back to survey the room with the benign arrogance of a king on his throne. When dessert and coffee were finished he had to be bribed to get down so she could get ready to leave. Guiltily Olivia promised she'd bring him a surprise, since she'd be missing his bedtime story that night.

"Surprises now, the keys to the car when he's a teenager," Cherry said sweetly.

"But by then I'll be living in Beverly Hills and you'll have to undo my spoiling by yourself," Olivia reminded her.

"Beverly Hills?" With Olivia settled beside him Brett guided his black BMW out of the driveway to creep down the narrow Garden District street.

Olivia watched him drive. She admired the way his hair had tumbled onto his forehead. She held on to that small imperfection like a good-luck charm. "I throw that up to her at least once a day. I turned down a job for a movie producer and his wife so I could work for the Broussards."

Brett was impressed. "Why did you choose the Broussards instead?"

"Well, they wanted a nanny. Mrs. Producer wanted a Hopkins Academy uniform. It seemed like an easy choice."

Brett let his eyes flicker over her. There was something about the thought of Olivia in a classic British nanny's uniform that stirred his libido. "You have a uniform? Does it go with the sweatshirt you were wearing at the park?"

"No, Mary Hopkins would die if she saw that. In the South, the uniform's a seersucker dress and maroon blazer. Cherry gave me the sweatshirt as a gag since she won't let me wear my uniform anymore. She says it intimidated her to be around such a flagrant status symbol."

Brett laughed, but he was impressed that Olivia's training was so well thought of.

Olivia continued to watch Brett, even though they both fell silent. His broad hands with the long, elegant fingers rested lightly on the steering wheel. His posture was casual but watchful, as if he were aware of the potential power of the car but content just to have it available if he needed it. She suspected that in the same way he was a man who was fully aware of his own power and only made others aware of it when it was necessary.

"How long have you been with Broussard, Carrington and Sherwood?" she asked when the silence had extended just a bit too long to be comfortable.

"A little over two years. Before that I was a public defender in St. Bernard parish. I met Drew when I was defending a fairly controversial character. The case went on for months and got a lot of publicity. Drew used to come watch the trial when he had the time. When my defendant was found not guilty, Drew asked me to join the firm."

Olivia knew enough to realize what a huge change it must have been to go from defending indigents to defending some of the city's most prestigious citizens. "Do you like what you're doing now better?"

"I like the money I'm earning better," he said bluntly. "The cases aren't always as interesting or as important. I try to make up for it by taking an occasional client I'm interested in defending whether they can afford me or not."

"Then you're a busy man."

He swung the car into a parking space, shutting off the engine before he turned toward her. The expression in his eyes made the meaning of his next words clear. "Not too busy."

Not too busy for what? For breaking the hearts of unworldly nannies? Olivia realized Brett's expression had made her shiver, but it was fear as well as sexual attraction. She was no match for a man like Brett Terrill.

She might be twenty-four, but she had hardly wiggled her toes in the waters of male-female relationships. She'd had a steady boyfriend in high school who ended up married to the class floozy—as much from frustration at Olivia's refusals to frequent the back seat of his dad's Chevrolet as from true love. After high school she'd worked in Morgan City as the secretary to a kindly, married oil executive before going to the Hopkins Academy, and Joe had protected her from all advances, welcome or unwelcome, from any man on his crews. At the academy she'd had a reputation to maintain and a full study schedule. Lined up and totaled, her love life was a big, hollow zero.

Sometimes Olivia imagined herself going into old age with nothing but the pictures of children she'd cared for to keep her company. It was the tear-jerking script of a bad movie, and twenty-four was a bit premature to worry about it. Still, Olivia did worry. She was pretty in a Renaissance madonna sort of way, but how many men were looking for a quiet young woman with a face Raphael and Michelangelo would have loved?

Now, with Brett's blue eyes trained on hers and her pulse rate speeding, Olivia wanted the safety of being alone again. Apparently she was being pursued by an expert who was so far out of her league there was really no contest at all. Worse, she had a feeling that when Brett tired of her, she was going to be lonelier than she'd ever known she could be.

Olivia's feelings were clear to Brett. He reached over to release the catch on her safety belt, then raised his hand to touch the hair falling over her shoulder. "You don't have anything to be afraid of," he told her.

"Yes, you said you wouldn't bite."

His smile was lazy and very, very male. "I did say that, but perhaps I shouldn't have. It's a promise I'm not sure I intend to keep."

Chapter Three

Tipitinas, with its renovated sailor's bar charm and ear-numbing sound system, was exactly the place to bring Olivia. Brett congratulated himself on the instinct that had made him choose one of New Orleans's best-loved jazz clubs as the scene of their first date. The fact that on this particular Sunday Tipitinas was featuring a Cajun band hadn't hurt, either. He wanted to make Olivia comfortable, and he was beginning to think that making Olivia comfortable wasn't going to be easy.

She was afraid of him. He'd played the male-female game enough in his thirty years to know that the fairly mild signals he'd been sending out should only have stepped up the awareness between them. This revised version of the game didn't seem to be working that way. There was something in Olivia's eyes that made him feel like the big bad wolf. Despite his teasing, if Olivia was Little Red Riding Hood, he'd much prefer to be thought of as her woodcutter savior.

Regardless of what she seemed to believe, he didn't want to hurt her. In fact, he was beginning to think he might want to marry her.

"This is wonderful." Olivia faced Brett, her shyness temporarily forgotten. "I haven't been here before."

"Are you talking to me?" he asked with a grin, one hand cupped behind his ear.

She smiled the smile that totally fascinated him and pointed to a table in the corner. "That's the only one left."

"We'd better grab it."

They settled in the corner while Bruce Daigrepont and his band wailed mournful French from the stage to the accompaniment of an accordion, fiddle, drums and a triangle. Olivia had watched the dancers for only thirty seconds before she realized she and Brett were overdressed. Brett solved his part of the problem by stripping off his jacket and tie, but there was little she could do except plan to wear her best jeans if she ever came back.

"I've never done Cajun dancing," Brett admitted during a rare lull between songs. "What about you?"

"I hope you're kidding." There was something about being in a place like many she'd been to with her family and childhood friends that had put Olivia at ease. True, here the crowd was distinctly young-professional, while at home she would have been surrounded by older couples who had grown up doing the dances these people had probably learned in a night class. But the music, the atmosphere and the enthusiasm were the same, and soothing.

"Then you're going to teach me?"

Olivia sipped the beer Brett had bought her and thought how nice it would be to be able to teach him something. She knew that if their relationship continued, she was undeniably going to be the student most of the time. "You're on."

Brett stood and held out his hand. When it closed around hers Olivia stiffened. She was much too old to be experiencing this intensity of sensation at such a simple act. But she had put her sexuality on hold for years; now it was pushing to the surface like a newly germinated plant seeking the sunlight. Brett's hand clasping hers wasn't cause for rejoicing; it wasn't the catalyst for a love poem, the inspiration for a symphony. It was a casual gesture. She was losing her mind.

Brett had wondered if Olivia's skin would feel as soft, as pliant and warm, as it looked. Her hand nestled in his was better than his imaginings. He hadn't been to bed with a woman since he'd ended his relationship with Kate. Now the months of repressed longings bore down on him until he wondered if he could trust himself to hold her close. He was losing his mind.

Olivia knew they'd better begin to dance, that she'd better do something to explain the color rising in her cheeks. She took Brett's other hand.

"This dance is a two-step," she said loudly enough so he could hear. "Cajun dances are either two-steps or waltzes."

Brett was grateful he'd been spared the waltz lesson first. At least in the two-step he could stand far enough away from Olivia to keep from scaring her to death.

"You have to keep one leg fairly straight and the other leg bent so you can bounce." She demonstrated, then laughed as Brett tried to follow her instructions.

"Not quite, huh?"

"Not quite," she said diplomatically, "but just keep trying. Once we get the beat, I'll show you some of the twists and turns."

Brett had a natural sense of rhythm and a physical grace that took over on their third try.

"I'm impressed," Olivia told him. "Now hunch over a little and stick out your bottom."

"Pardon me?"

"Is this the first time a woman's asked you to do something so provocative?"

He was delighted that she could tease him. On the dance floor Olivia's shyness was forgotten, left back at the table with her purse and his jacket. He did as she'd suggested, surprised that the change in posture made the bouncing rhythm simpler.

By the fifth dance Olivia had taught him a few easy twirls and holds that broke the monotony of the steps. By unspoken mutual consent they'd sat out the waltzes, but when the next dance turned out to be slow and dreamy, Brett pulled Olivia into his arms and began to waltz her around the room.

Cajun women did not drape themselves all over their men, but neither was there anything that said a third party should be able to walk between partners. Olivia settled her body an inch from Brett's, but she refrained from resting her head on his shoulder. She could have. The top of her head came just to the bottom of his earlobe, and the fit seemed perfect to her.

Brett was torn between pulling her closer and possibly setting their relationship back to pre-Audubon Park, or maintaining the distance between them and silently going crazy. He couldn't remember ever wanting to feel a woman against him this badly, not even when he was a randy teenager and women were all he could think about. There was a lushness, a voluptuousness, about Olivia's body that cried out for the strong, hard lines of a man to mold it. There was something definitely pagan about his feelings. They weren't the feelings of a twentieth-century man intellectually dedicated to the principle that women and men were created equal.

"How about another beer?" Brett pulled away from Olivia when the waltz ended. It was a relief in a way to have his decision made for him. No music, no cuddling on the dance floor. And now that this one was over with, no more waltzes unless the beer succeeded in cooling his ardor.

"Not for me." Olivia watched Brett wend his way to the bar. How he could remain so collected while her own body was becoming unhinged, cell by cell, was a mystery. Did he have any idea what that last dance had done to her? Obviously twenty-four years of repression had been breeding a monster inside her. The first magnificent, fascinating man who took her into his arms had unleashed it, and he was obviously unaware he had done so. Olivia silently said a short battery of prayers designed to make sure he remained that way.

"Are you having a good time?" Brett asked when he returned. The band was taking a well-deserved break, and the wonderfully shabby room was filled with the buzz of conversation and the sizzling energy of single men and women looking each other over.

That was a hard question to answer. She was having a confusing time, a time filled with distinct, unfulfilled yearnings and frustration at her own inability to offer him a fascinating conversation. No, it wasn't a good time, but it was a time she wouldn't forget or trade for any other.

"I like being here," she said, because she had to say something. "It reminds me of home a little."

"Are you homesick for New Iberia?"

"No. It was time to get out on my own. Time to grow up."

"And have you?"

"Have I what?"

"Have you grown up?"

If the sensations still dive-bombing back and forth through her body were any indication, she was growing up before his eyes. Olivia smiled a little. "What do you think?"

"In some ways you seem more like eighteen than twenty-four. Not immature, just..." His voice trailed off.

The word was "innocent," but Olivia wasn't about to supply it for him. "How do you know I'm twenty-four?"

"Lenny told me."

"What else did Lenny tell you?"

"Do you really want to know?"

"I asked."

"He said that you were completely dedicated to your job, as far as he knew you didn't have a boyfriend, and if I hurt you in any way I could forget about becoming a partner at the firm."

Olivia's gaze dropped to the table, then flicked back up to his. "And you still came to dinner?"

"I got tired of jogging. You didn't show up at the lagoon again." Brett reached across the table and covered one of her hands with his.

"I steered Lucy and Trey toward the sandbox in the back yard," she murmured. "It's drier."

"Do you know your eyes sparkle when you talk about the Broussard kids?"

Privately Olivia thought that if her eyes were sparkling it had more to do with Brett's hand on hers than with Lucy and Trey. "They're wonderful children. I love them."

"Isn't it going to be hard to leave when the Broussards don't need you anymore?"

"Well, I'll miss them, but I'm their nanny, not their mother. There'll be other children. And I'll keep in touch, even if I make it to Beverly Hills next time."

"Do you plan to continue being a nanny?"

Olivia wondered what Brett was really asking. Was this the inevitable "Aren't you going to do something more important with your life?" question?

"I'm taking it one step at a time. But I don't have a more important career in mind, if that's what you mean. Nannying is an honorable profession; I'm paid well, and I love it."

"It's a single woman's career, though, isn't it? Would a nanny leave her children with a nanny so she could go out to work herself every day?"

Olivia laughed at the prospect of an endless chain of nannies taking care of the children of nannies who were taking care of the children of nannies. "I'm only twenty-four," she said softly. "I'll just wait and see."

The band came back up to the stage, and Olivia and Brett danced several more two-steps. The night air was cool when they finally left. Olivia wasn't sure why, if it had been the drinks or the music or just getting to know Brett better, but she was soaring high, her shyness temporarily forgotten. Lifting her hair off her shoulders, she let Brett slip on her coat. Then she pointed to the sky. "Look, I think there's going to be a full moon."

"Do you need to get home soon, or shall we drive around for a while until it comes up?"

Olivia sighed. "I miss the country on a night like this. There's nowhere really peaceful to go in a city. The parks are too dangerous, and there are streetlights everywhere, so you can't see the stars. At home we live close enough to Bayou Teche so I can go there sometimes to listen to the sound of the water at night. That's where I'd like to watch the moon."

Brett was convinced that the only way he and Olivia would ever approach any sort of intimacy was if he moved so slowly he appeared to be standing still. But her wistful expression undid his best intentions. She wanted the moon over a bayou, and he could give it to her with no difficulty. Perhaps it wasn't wise, but how often had wisdom gotten any man his heart's desire?

"I know a place like that in New Orleans," he said casually. "Maybe not quite as isolated, and there are lights. But you can pretend."

"Where?"

"My place."

Brett's place was an apartment on Bayou St. John, not far from where it flowed into Lake Pontchartrain. The apartment was at the back of a large home, and it had originally been intended for the owner's mother-in-law. It was well designed, with an entrance so private an experienced burglar might have had difficulty locating it. Best of all, it had a courtyard overlooking the water, with a weathered cypress fence surrounding it.

Brett hadn't been in the apartment long enough to put his own stamp on it, but in the few short months he'd been leasing it he had grown addicted to the absence of city noises and the presence of several ducks who visited every morning and evening for their twice-daily dole.

There was little furniture inside the apartment, but Brett had bought patio furniture the day he'd moved in, and even though it was now November, he spent every available moment outdoors watching the ever-changing panorama from his courtyard.

There had been no question in Brett's mind that Olivia would like his apartment and his view. The only question had been how to convince her that he intended her no harm. Men usually didn't invite women home at the end of their first date with anything as casual as moon watching on their minds. Either she'd been too unsophisticated to think of that herself, or far more eager for his company than he'd suspected. Whichever it was, Brett had been surprised at her enthusiastic yes.

Olivia had been a bit surprised, too. She hadn't wanted the evening with Brett to end, and she'd jumped at the chance to make it last a little longer. But they were in his car heading away from the heart of the city before she fully realized that Brett was taking her to his apartment. She wasn't so virginally paranoid that she expected to have to fight for her virtue because she'd said yes, but she hadn't really thought her action through, either. Brett's apartment would be quiet; he lived alone. What would they say to each other?

"I was lucky to find this place," Brett told her as he turned onto the street paralleling Bayou St. John. "It hadn't even been advertised. A friend told me about it."

"Have you lived here long?"

"Just a few months."

Olivia put that fact together with Cherry's statement about Brett's recent past. She wondered if he had been living with the woman Cherry had mentioned before he'd moved here. What had happened to that relationship? Had Brett decided he wanted to play the field?

Brett went on. "The people who own the house are away a lot of the time. I have more privacy than I know what to do with."

"Do you like it? I've never had enough privacy to know whether I would or not."

Brett pulled into the carport beside his apartment and turned off the engine. "Privacy is highly overrated."

Olivia wondered exactly what he'd meant as she waited for him to come around and open her door.

Brett extended his hand, and Olivia gave him hers as he helped her out of the car. She was surprised when he didn't drop it. Holding hands with Brett took on an intimacy it never had with anyone else. Something flowed between them, something as powerful as sexual attraction and as unifying as shared dreams. For two people as different as they were, the almost spiritual connection between them seemed impossible.

Brett led her down a path shaded by two giant magnolia trees. Then, reluctantly, he dropped her hand to unlock the door and usher her inside.

The apartment was obviously not yet a home. As Brett hung up her coat in the living-room closet, Olivia assessed what she could see. The furniture had the unmistakable stamp of having come with the apartment. It was in a style she thought of as Early Landlord, unmatched bits and pieces scrounged from someone's attic.

There were no pictures on the institutional white walls except for an outdated calendar hanging at the bar dividing the living room and kitchen. The wall-to-wall carpeting was new and nondescript, designed to match everything and nothing, and the only light was from an outdated fixture on the ceiling in the center of the room.

"What do you think?" Brett asked, coming back to stand beside her.

"I think you don't spend much time here."

"Not inside, anyway. Would you like a drink?"

"Coffee, if you have it."

Olivia followed him into the kitchen and sat at the table as he filled the coffee maker. The kitchen was much like the living room. Brett's entire apartment brought out Olivia's nesting instincts. It was possible he was one of those men who never noticed his surroundings, but she rather doubted it. Brett seemed entirely too sensitive to live this way and not be affected by the bleakness of it. Perhaps, like many men, he just had no idea what to do.

"Milk? Sugar?"

"Black as goddamn," Olivia said without thinking.

"Black as goddamn?"

She laughed, surprised at what she'd said. "I'm sorry. It's a family joke."

Brett leaned against the counter, waiting for the coffee to finish dripping. "Tell me."

"Well, my grandfather spoke French mostly, Cajun French, of course, and sometimes he had big trouble trying to translate his thoughts into English. He was visiting this Baptist preacher who lived down the bayou from his house one afternoon, and the preacher asked him how he wanted his coffee. Grand-père tried to think of a way to explain that he only drank it black and strong enough to melt the spoon, but his tongue wouldn't work correctly. Black as goddamn was the best he could do. Of course the preacher understood immediately."

Brett smiled. "He made his point."

"Better than that. They were friends till they died." Olivia took the cup that Brett passed her and sipped it as he poured himself one and joined her.

"I have a feeling you have a wealth of stories like that."

"Doesn't everybody? The only problem is that they're never very interesting to anyone outside your own family."

"Families interest me."

"Tell me about yours." Olivia met Brett's eyes over her coffee cup, and she was surprised at the shadow turning them from blue to gray.

"Which one?" he asked lightly. "I had five, no, make that six."

Olivia sipped her coffee and tried to puzzle out his meaning. "Do you want to explain?" she asked finally.

Brett liked the way she'd asked her question. She didn't demand an answer; she didn't seem embarrassed that she'd touched on something that might be sensitive. She just wanted him to know she would listen if he wanted to talk. He felt soothed by her presence. He had never met a woman so undemanding, so easy to be with.

"I was a foster child," he said, no self-pity in his voice. "My real mother was always in the background, but my families were the people I lived with, the people who took care of me when I was sick and fed me when I was hungry. The people I could count on."

"And you couldn't count on your mother?"

"She flew in and out of my life like some sort of migrating bird, always promising to rescue me from the people who were trying to give me what she never could. It was hard on everybody. I think that's why I was moved so often."

There was something so final about Brett's last sentences that Olivia had the feeling she'd heard just about everything she ever would on the subject of his childhood. How had it shaped him into the man he was now?

"You must have put yourself through college and law school," she said tentatively.

"Actually, that was one thing my mother did for me. She was well off, even if she wasn't a good parent. There was plenty of money when I needed it to go to school."

Olivia set her coffee cup down. "It doesn't sound like it was easy."

"Did you study child psychology at the Hopkins Academy?"

Olivia nodded.

"Then you know that kids can live through all kinds of things and still turn out fine."

Olivia also knew that someone like Brett could turn out fine on the surface and still have a gaping hole deep inside him that might never be filled, even if he was someday loved with a single-minded devotion. She wondered if he knew that, too.

Brett stood and extended his hand to her. "I want to show you the moon over the bayou. Shall I get your coat?"

"It's not that cold."

Outside Olivia was instantly enchanted with Brett's courtyard. Here were all the signs that Brett planned to stay a while. The furniture on the brick patio was light wood with bright, comfortable cushions on the chairs. There were huge Mexican pots along the fence waiting to be planted with shrubs of colorful annuals, and there was an extravagantly expensive bird feeder filled with sunflower seeds. Best of all, there were life-size bronze statues of a mother cat and four kittens playing under a small leafless tree in the corner.

"They're darling." Olivia stooped to run her fingers along the mother cat's intricate curves. She touched each kitten, as if to let them know none had been singled out for special favor.

Brett watched her. "I wanted a dog when I moved here, but I'm not home enough to take care of one. Then I thought about getting a cat, but I was afraid it might disturb the ducks. Matilda and her babies were my compromise."

"Matilda?" Olivia stood, cocking her head to examine the cats again. "Yes, it's perfect." She twirled to face Brett. "And ducks? You keep ducks?"

"Doesn't everybody?" He grinned at her, and the grin was so boyish, so free of anything except pleasure at her approval, that Olivia's heart turned over. Deep inside Brett there was a kind of shyness, too, a secret place that surpassed anything she had ever felt herself. For all his strength and intelligence, Olivia knew there was still a little boy inside Brett who yearned for the things he'd been denied.

There was a woman inside Olivia who suddenly knew that she would be the one to give them to him.

"I'll show you my ducks," he said, the grin curving into something more seductive.

She lifted her eyes to his, unafraid. "Is that like showing me your etchings?"

He was surprised by the warmth in her gaze. The shy, uncertain Olivia he'd been trying to work around was momentarily gone. Facing him was a woman who seemed to have discovered something important about herself. "If you'd like it to be," he told her.

She shook her head slowly. "Not yet."

No two words had ever seemed more provocative. His hand breached the slight distance between them and settled on her hair. "I can wait."

She rested her hand on his shoulder, sliding her fingers up to touch the visible pulse in his neck. "And how good are you at waiting, Brett?"

"I suspect we'll both find out." He inched her closer.

"I've waited a lifetime," she said, warning him. "That's a very long time."

"Did you think I didn't know?"

She smiled, closing her eyes as he bent to kiss her. There were no doubts, no restraints. There was only the feel of Brett's body hard against hers and the taste of his lips. There was only the sensation of offering her softness to him to protect and to be protected, and the undeniable feeling of belonging completely to another person.

Chapter Four

There was little to distinguish the suite of offices that was Broussard, Carrington and Sherwood from other, similar law offices in the central business district of New Orleans. If a visitor paid close attention, he might notice that the paneling was solid mahogany, and that select pieces of the Duncan Phyfe Federal furniture were not reproductions. If the visitor was really perceptive he might smell old money, Louisiana politics and social status—New Orleans style—in the air.

Brett was never quite sure how he had ended up working for the most prestigious law firm in the city. He suspected that in an attempt to bring Broussard, Carrington and Sherwood into the twentieth century, the three senior partners had scoured Louisiana for someone whose reputation was more liberal, more populist, than their own. Why they hadn't settled on one of the many other young lawyers with established practices and social ties that would have brought them more business was a question Brett had asked himself repeatedly.

The answer he had finally accepted was simple. Lenny Broussard, Robert Carrington and Drew Sherwood liked him, respected him and knew he could handle the business they already had. More business was unthinkable anyway.

Besides, Brett's views on most issues differed only in degree. In any argument they were all usually on the same side, although Brett was always more adamantly progressive. He had brought in cases the firm never would have been asked to take, and he had added a certain life, a certain vitality, that had shaken them all out of their complacency.

In exchange Brett now had more money than he knew what to do with and a prestige in the community that sometimes made him chuckle. The child who had never belonged anywhere suddenly belonged with a vengeance.

There were other attorneys in the city who would have given almost anything for Brett's position. Kate Parsons was one of them. Brett had lived with her for six months before he'd discovered that she had been Broussard, Carrington and Sherwood's second choice. That knowledge had done peculiar things to their relationship. Brett had begun to wonder just how much their living arrangement had to do with her professed love for him, and how much of it was vicarious enjoyment of the job that she believed should have been hers. At the end, the answer had been clear. Kate's words of love had been worth less than the air she exhaled with them.

If that still hurt, one thing made up for it. Brett had not loved Kate, either.

The difference, of course, was that he had never told Kate he loved her. He'd wanted to marry her, to share her life, to grow old together. But he had never loved her. Brett knew he was incapable of love. There was something missing inside him, something that couldn't grow because he had never seen enough love to imitate it. He and Kate were alike in that way. Neither of them was capable of strong emotion. Only in that had they been a good match.

The Friday after his date with Olivia, Brett faced Kate over the elegant, massive desk in his office and wondered why they had wasted two perfectly good years playing house.

"My client refuses your client's offer for settlement," Kate said, pulling out several typed pages to set them on the desk in front of Brett.

"Since when have you been representing Mary Jane Atkinson?" Brett briefly glanced over the pages, then folded his hands over them.

"Since she decided a woman would understand her claims better than a man. Frank sent her to me."

Frank was one of the senior partners at Kate's firm, a firm with slightly less prestige than Brett's. It was a large firm, with plenty of young, hungry attorneys vying for recognition. Brett had no doubt that Kate would keep her place at the head of the pack.

He examined Kate idly as he pretended to think about Mary Jane Atkinson's greed. Kate was as lovely, as perfect, as always. Living with her, he had found she was one of those women who woke up in the morning looking just as good as she did after makeup and a cup of coffee. Even in the midst of their lovemaking, she had always looked untouched by their mutual passion, as if the perfect shell of her beauty couldn't be marred by something as physical as desire.

"Well?" she asked finally.

"Well, I'll present it to my client. But you know as well as I do that he won't consider these kinds of extravagant demands."

"My client won't consider less."

"Then we'll see each other in court. Another messy divorce for someone else to decide." Brett stood as Kate did. "I'll walk you out."

"At least when you and I parted we didn't have to go through something like this," Kate said with a smile that didn't extend to her eyes. She reached behind her ear to settle a comb more firmly in her faultlessly arranged blond curls. "We were much too civil for this kind of cat fighting."

"But then there was nothing to fight about. Neither of us had anything to lose." Brett opened the door to usher her out of his office. He didn't miss the assessing glances of the firm's trio of secretaries as he and Kate passed by. He wondered if they had been listening for raised voices.

"Well, I'll wait to hear from you," Kate said when they reached the door going into the corridor.

"I'll let you know what Harry Atkinson says." Brett paused, then added, "You're looking well, Kate. Take care of yourself."

"I always do, Brett." She smiled the only kind of smile she seemed capable of and disappeared down the hallway.

"She does have a sort of icy charm."

Brett turned to face Drew, who had come up silently behind him. "She does have that."

"Not much to base a relationship on."

"Not nearly enough."

Drew patted Brett on the arm, reassured by his friend's serenity. Obviously Brett was recovering from the upheaval in his life that had been called Kate Parsons. "Lenny tells me that you and the wading nanny are seeing each other."

"Obviously I should have settled on someone less public."

"Settled on?" Drew lifted his eyebrows. "That sounds fairly serious."

"It's about as serious as it can get," Brett said quietly. "Someday soon I'm going to ask her to marry me."

* * *

Olivia relived Brett's kiss for the better part of a week. Nothing that had ever happened to her compared with it. Nothing that had ever happened to her had been so right.

Afterward she knew she had retreated back into shyness. What did one say to a man who kissed you that way, a man who knew every pressure, every movement, every intimacy you desired and gave it to you like the most precious of gifts?

As if he had understood, Brett had taken her down to the water, and they had waited silently in the moonlight until a duck and two drakes came to eat the dried corn she and Brett threw to them. Brett had teased her about not going into the water after them, and she had laughed with delight when one of the drakes tried to follow them back into the courtyard.

They had both been quiet on the way back to the Broussards'. Created by the memory of their shared intimacy, the silence had been deliciously seductive. When Brett left her on the Broussards' doorstep, just touching her bottom lip with his finger, Olivia had wanted to sing or shout her happiness.

Instead she had gone to bed, checking on Trey and Lucy before getting under the covers to remember the feel of Brett's body against hers and his lips teaching her lessons she wouldn't soon forget.

Now it was Saturday, and Olivia had an entire day to herself. She had not spoken to Brett since Sunday, but sometime during their drive home, he had told her that his week was going to be very busy. He had left her with the impression that he would call as soon as his time was his own again. Olivia was content to wait.

To fill her day off, Olivia headed for the interstate to make the hour-and-a-half trip to Baton Rouge.

Olivia might be relatively timid around people she didn't know well, but on the highway, she was a demon. She was sure it had something to do with the places where she had learned to drive, country roads with nothing to slow her down except a nagging respect for the law and an occasional cow. She couldn't drive that way in the city; anyone trying those stunts in New Orleans was as good as dead, since New Orleans was full of high-flying drivers just like Olivia. Instead she saved her lane-switching, speed-limit-destroying, double-dare-you tactics for those long stretches of interstate leading in and out of the city.

Today, in her old Toyota, she made the trip to the Hopkins Academy with fifteen minutes to spare.

The school was a modern complex sitting back from a peaceful avenue on the outskirts of Baton Rouge. Mary had bought ten acres when land was still cheap enough to be a good investment. With uncanny insight she had sat quietly by and watched the land increase in value until the time was right to sell half of it. With the money she received she built the first of four buildings that were to become the attractive complex Olivia was visiting today.

Through the years Mary hadn't stinted on any of the things that made the academy the peaceful, eye-pleasing refuge that it was. The landscaping was subtropical, designed to provide something in flower during every season; the buildings, though constructed over the period of a decade, combined similar vast expanses of glass and gray brick. Doors and trim were natural cypress, which weathered and grew more charming as the years passed.

Olivia had loved her two years at the school. She had lived in the small dormitory, doing clerical work for Mary to help pay her room and board. She had been Mary's special favorite from the moment she had entered the front door, but only she and Mary had ever known why.

The reason had been one of those simple, unconsidered acts of heroism that make wonderful newspaper stories—if the newspapers find out about them. Six months before entering the academy, Olivia had been on her lunch break from her secretarial job, waiting to cross the street to her car.

A woman pushing a stroller had stopped on the other side of the crosswalk. As Olivia had watched, the woman had turned and taken off her shoe to empty it. The toddler in the stroller had leaned forward; his mother had lost her grip, stumbling backward and bumping the stroller hard as she fell. The stroller had rolled into the street, right into the path of a speeding truck.

Olivia had shouted, dashed between cars to throw herself against the stroller in time to keep the child from getting hit. She had felt the whoosh of hot air against her stockinged legs and the frantic swirl of her dress around her knees. With calm detachment she had handed the stroller back to the weeping mother and bent her head to her waist to keep from fainting.

The toddler was more than all right. He was the son of Carl Younger, vice president of the oil company Olivia worked for. Neither the grateful mother nor father would take no for an answer. Olivia had to be rewarded, and the reward had to be substantial.

Olivia woke up one morning with a brand-new Oldsmobile in her driveway.

Until that moment, attending the Hopkins Academy had been a dream. Olivia could not afford to spend two years pursuing a career that in the long run might not be any more lucrative than her present secretarial job. Suddenly she could. She sold the car, returned the money to the Youngers and then promptly asked them to loan it back to her.

Carl Younger himself made sure that Mary Hopkins knew just exactly what kind of student she was getting.

Olivia and Mary had stayed in close touch after Olivia's graduation, and Olivia visited whenever she could. Mary had been a tireless, vital force during Olivia's years at the academy, but in the past months Olivia had been worried about her friend. Mary had always seemed younger than her seventy years, but recently she'd begun to show signs that she felt seventy and then some. Although she hadn't taught more than an occasional seminar since Olivia had known her, Mary had still managed a large share of the school's administration. Now she rarely left her third-floor dormitory apartment, preferring to let her staff take care of more and more details. The only thing she had remained responsible for was interviews with prospective students.

Today Olivia took the stairs to Mary's suite two at a time, eschewing the elevator that had recently been installed for Mary's use. She knocked, waited, then knocked again. It took Mary a long time to answer.

"So you remembered an old woman."

"I don't remember an old woman, but I remember Mary." Olivia leaned over to kiss Mary's cheek. Mary's silver hair was precisely arranged, and her clothes were neat and practical, as always. But Olivia didn't miss the fact that Mary seemed to have lost weight, or that she'd grown subtly older. She wondered if after the pleasantries were over she could safely broach the subject of Mary's health.

"Come in, Olivia. I fixed tea for us."

The apartment, though spacious and well-lighted, seemed grimly unpleasant this morning. Olivia longed to open the windows and freshen the musty, heavy air, but she knew it was too cold outside. Mary was bundled up in a sweater and a shawl, even though the room felt as if it were at least ninety degrees. Mary would obviously not welcome a breeze.

"Tea and crumpets?" Olivia asked, wandering around the living room looking at Mary's pictures as the older woman set out dishes.

"I can't get crumpets in Baton Rouge anymore. I had Millie make us blueberry muffins."

"I'll bring crumpets the next time I come. There's got to be someplace in New Orleans where I can get them for you." Olivia watched the slow pace of Mary's movements. She knew her friend suffered from arthritis, but surely it couldn't be making this much difference in Mary's health. She'd had arthritis for years.

"I'm fine without them, child. I adjusted to this heathen diet when I moved to Louisiana. I'll trade crumpets for redfish any day."

Olivia turned back to the pictures and smiled. Half of Mary's life had been spent in her native England, and half of it had been spent in Baton Rouge. She had come as the nanny to a wealthy Louisiana politician, and she had stayed for some mysterious reason known only to her. Trained in England's most prestigious school for nannies, Mary had seen an immediate need for a similar school in the United States. The rest had been nanny history.

Mary had often joked that with a name like Mary Hopkins, her career had been determined from birth. She never danced with chimney sweeps on rooftops, nor had she ever opened an umbrella to soar through the clouds. She did have Mary Poppins's sense of humor, however, and there was magic in the way she could make even the most contrary child behave. Best of all, Mary seemed to understand instinctively what made people tick and what they needed to keep ticking. Mary was a legend in her field.

"Do you miss England, Mary?" Olivia asked.

"Missing things takes too much time. You understand that as you grow older."

Olivia seated herself at the small table in the dining room and watched Mary pour tea into delicate china cups. "Sometimes when the Broussard children are driving me crazy, I think about these times with you and wish I could lock the kids away somewhere and come back for a cup of your tea."

"Children never drive a Hopkins Academy nanny crazy."

"How can you say that with a straight face?" Olivia stirred her tea while a sugar lump in it dissolved.

"Are you still glad you chose that position?"

"Supremely." Olivia thought about Brett and smiled.

"And, of course, that's what's put the light in your eyes."

Olivia's spoon clanked loudly against the side of the cup. "You notice everything."

"So do you. That's why I've always found you so refreshing. Half the people I know aren't even aware that their nose is in plain view."

Olivia was pleased with the compliment. Mary didn't give them easily. Olivia pressed her advantage. "Well, I'll tell you about the light in my eyes if you'll tell me how you're really feeling."

Mary leaned against the back of her chair as if she were too tired to maintain any pretenses. "I'm not feeling well. But old people aren't supposed to feel well. They're supposed to feel this pain or that pain and complain about it until everyone flees screaming into the night."

Olivia didn't know how to hide her concern. "You know that's not true. And when did you start talking about yourself as old?"

Mary's shrug was almost imperceptible. "It happens to us all, child. I've made my peace with it. I'm lucky that I'm still well enough to live here. I just take one day at a time. Today I feel better than I did yesterday. Tomorrow? Who knows?"

"And, of course, you've seen a doctor."

Mary's smile fleshed out the gaunt shadows in her face. "I've seen one. He's confirmed my diagnosis."

"Which was?"

"Old age."

Olivia knew she wasn't going to get any more information out of her friend. Perhaps Mary was right, anyway. Perhaps after a lifetime in which she'd accomplished more than any other two people Olivia knew, Mary was just tired. Perhaps the years had finally caught up with her.

Mary reached across the table and touched Olivia's hand. "Your turn."

Olivia felt suddenly shy. "Well, I've met this man."

"I thought as much."

"Did you now?" Olivia laughed a little. "And what else did you think?"

"I think that you'd better take it slowly, child. You have a lot of living you need to do."

Olivia was more than surprised at Mary's words. She was baffled. "And I can't do that living with a man?"

"You're talking about living with him?"

"You know what I meant!" Olivia held out her cup for more tea.

"What I think is that you're selling yourself short again. You always have, you know. You're such a sweet little thing, and that's all most people see. But I know how much more there is inside you. You're like a rose just beginning to open to the sun." Mary covered Olivia's hand with hers, and her flesh felt waxen and cold. "Don't get so involved with this man that you don't reach your full potential."

Olivia shook her head. "There are many ways to grow, Mary."

"Try them all, child. Don't settle for the first way that comes along."

But Olivia thought about Brett and the kiss they'd shared and knew that the words "settle for" hadn't been invented with Brett Terrill in mind.

The drive back to New Orleans took the full hour and a half. Olivia found herself with too much to think about to concentrate on lane hopping. She and Mary had spent a quiet morning together; then Olivia had taken her to a nearby restaurant for lunch. Mary had eaten little, picking at her food politely. She had seemed almost grateful to return to her apartment, and Olivia had left earlier than she'd planned, aware that Mary needed to rest.

Back in New Orleans, Olivia stopped by Uptown Square to shop for play clothes for Trey and Lucy. Outfitting the children was one of the delights of her job, and she browsed carefully through piles of colorful shirts and jeans to find good quality at a decent price.

It was after five when she pulled into the Broussards' driveway. Right beside Brett's BMW.

Olivia's hands went to her hair. She had pulled it back into a simple knot at her nape, and it made her look as old-fashioned as the sculpture on a cameo. Her high-necked white blouse and dark skirt did little to conceal the ten pounds she was always sure she needed to lose. She wondered if she could sneak in the back way and change before seeing Brett.

"I was just about to give up on you." Brett appeared in the doorway, Trey hanging on to one hand and Lucy the other.

Resigned, Olivia slid out from behind the steering wheel and took out her packages, closing the door behind her. "I didn't know you were coming. I'd have been home sooner if I had."

"Did you buy me something?" Trey left Brett's side to grab for Olivia's packages.

"Uh-uh." Olivia held the bags high, shaking her head at her tiny charge. "That's no way to ask."

Trey stamped his foot, and his eyes gleamed with tears. "I wanna see!"

"You may see, Master Trey, when your manners improve," she said in her best no-nonsense Mary Poppins voice.

Trey threw himself on the ground and began to kick his feet. Olivia stepped over him and climbed the porch stairs. Lucy was watching her brother's tantrum with interest. Olivia blocked her view, picking up the little girl and stroking her curls.

"Are you just going to leave him there?" Brett asked, surprised by Olivia's callousness.

"Well, if he's not finished by dark, I might have to let him continue it in his room. The mosquitoes get bad about dusk."

"This is the same woman who went wading to save a newspaper boat?"

"An occasional tearful plea is acceptable, Brett, but bad manners are unforgivable. Trey's got to learn."

"How can you stand to listen to him?"

Olivia smiled at the genuine distress in Brett's voice. He looked wonderful today, dressed in a bright blue T-shirt covered with a wool sport coat. His hair was rumpled, probably from roughhousing with the children, and he was more attractive because of it. She wanted to kiss away his concerns.

"I can stand to listen to it because that's what I'm paid to do, just like you're paid to solve people's legal problems. If I spoiled Trey and allowed him to do whatever he wanted, I wouldn't be worth a plugged nickel." She touched his arm, tilting her head toward Trey as she lowered her voice. "Besides, I can guarantee that sometime in the next minute, he's going to get up, dust himself off and find something better to do."

"Livvy, can I please see what's in the bag?" he said, fulfilling her prophecy.

Olivia set Lucy down and held out her arms to the little boy on the ground. He climbed the stairs and flung himself against her. "Do you know those pants Jason has, the ones with all the pockets?" she murmured in his hair.

Trey sniffed in affirmation.

"Well, I got you two pairs, one brown and one blue. But yours have snaps on the pockets so nothing can ever fall out."

"Can I see?"

Olivia gave Trey the bags and patted his bottom as he and Lucy ran into the house.

"Do you do that for all the men in your life?"

Olivia stood. "Do what?"

"Make them toe the line, then reward them with that kind of unreserved affection?"

"There aren't so many men in my life," she said with a half smile.

Brett reached out and tucked a strand of hair behind her ear. "You do realize there's one more than there used to be, don't you?"

Despite Mary's warning, Olivia had to admit that she had realized exactly that. And the realization was wonderful.

Chapter Five

If my mother knew where you took me tonight!''

Olivia took Brett's hand and led him to the side garden that distinguished the Broussard home from the other beautiful houses on Prytannia Street. The garden was Lenny Broussard's pride and his only form of recreation. It was not unusual for cars to slow down, then stop to enjoy the seemingly unrestrained tangles of wisteria, magnolia, crepe myrtle and bougainvillea. Only Lenny and his gardener knew that under the verdant, untrammeled growth was a formal design that kept the garden from reverting to jungle.

Olivia loved to sit on the tree-shaded benches to enjoy the rich, fermenting smell of the earth and the perfume of moisture-dewed blossoms. Tonight it was not as private as Brett's courtyard had been. Cars whizzed by, and the music from a neighbor's party spilled into the air. Still, under cover of the trees she and Brett weren't visible to anyone, and Olivia hoped that might just be important.

"And why would your mother disapprove?" Brett asked as he settled beside her on a stone bench.

"Well, when she heard I was coming to New Orleans she warned me about three things. Sailors, Bourbon Street and ptomaine poisoning from little hot-dog carts shaped like hot dogs."

Brett laughed, surprised at how easy laughing was and how good it felt. There seemed to be nothing inside him blocking it anymore. "If that's all your mother warned you about, then she was remiss. But how'd we manage to hit all three of your prohibitions tonight?"

"It was your idea. When you said you were taking me out to dinner, I expected something different."

Brett had planned something different, too, but once they were alone in his car, Olivia's retreat into shyness had called for drastic measures. Walking Bourbon Street to enjoy its naughty honky-tonk had been the perfect solution.

"You know you loved it," he chided her. "You had two hot dogs before I could get you near a restaurant."

"You had two hot dogs first! I only ate mine to keep up with you!"

Brett took her hand between his and began to play with her fingers. "It seems to me, Miss LeBlanc, that your second hot dog was eaten to negate the effects of the Hurricane you made me buy you." Privately he suspected that a third hot dog might have been in order, too. The potent New Orleans specialty of fruit juices, rum and God knows what else had proved too much for Olivia.

Olivia was irate. "Made you buy? You practically poured it down my throat."

"If I did, it was to lessen the shock the barker gave you when he steered you into the nightclub to see the all-male revue."

"Nightclub? Strip joint! And was it the barker who steered me in there? I thought it was you."

"Actually, I think you were pushed in by those Greek sailors." Brett threaded his fingers through hers and stood, pulling her up, too. "I think they took one look at you and tried to separate us."

"I doubt it. I'm afraid I'm not nearly as well endowed as the men in that revue were."

"Says who?" Brett pulled her closer.

"Said one of the sailors. In Greek."

"You don't speak Greek."

"It was unmistakable."

Brett laughed and kept pulling until her body was flush against his. "How a shy little thing could handle herself with such aplomb in a packed strip show of female impersonators is beyond me. The expression on your face was priceless."

"You were laughing too hard to notice my expression!"

"Ah, Olivia, you make me laugh. No one has made me laugh in a long, long time." Brett threaded his fingers into her hair, dislodging hairpins as he did. "And you make my heart beat faster, and my day worth getting up for and my whole life seem brighter."

"Brett?"

Brett's lips stopped inches from hers. "Yes?"

"Is that you or half a Hurricane talking?"

"Me. And it was only one-third of a Hurricane. You drank more than your share."

"I can hold my liquor. You, on the other hand..."

"Go on."

"You get mushy."

Brett exploded into laughter, hugging her as tightly as he could. He was only just getting to know Olivia, but each time he was with her he discovered a different woman. This slightly woozy one was a total delight.

"Kiss me, Brett."

Obliging her was no hardship. Brett finished pulling the pins from her hair and tangled his fingers in the long mass.

He urged her closer and began to bestow tiny, nipping kisses along her hairline. Her skin was perfect, the kind of skin destined to have made enemies for her during adolescence. It had the fresh taste of warm cream, and it was soft and untouched by cosmetics.

The laughter that had been bubbling inside both of them settled like the effervescence of expensive champagne into something dark and full-bodied that became an anticipation of more delights to come. Olivia relaxed against Brett. She didn't have enough energy to hold herself away from him. Why should she deny either of them what they wanted? And she knew he wanted the softness of her body. She could feel his arousal, and she knew her own power.

"O-liv-i-a." Brett murmured the syllables against her cheek. "Perfect." His mouth approached hers. "Perfect."

"Brett." She turned her mouth to meet his, felt the smooth, hard surface of his lips graze hers, then retreat.

"Do you want more?"

"Much more." Her lips parted slightly this time, and he took advantage of the movement, slipping his tongue inside, then retreating once again.

She stirred in his arms, restless. She was just beginning to know the feel, the shape, the taste of his mouth. She wanted to know it all.

"More?"

"Much, much more."

Triumphantly he held her still, plunging his tongue into her mouth to mate with hers. She moaned a little and wrapped her arms around him, holding him as tightly as he held her. Her breasts seemed to swell and harden against his chest, just as his flesh was swelling and hardening against her. For the first time she understood the pain a man endures when release is denied him.

Brett continued to hold her close, but he pulled his mouth from hers and rested his cheek against her hair. "So sweet," he said softly. "So very, very sweet."

"It might get sweeter if you keep kissing me," she said tentatively, in invitation.

Brett laughed and kissed her hair. "Olivia, are you really twenty-four?"

"I am."

"Then you should know it doesn't get sweeter. It gets...different."

"How will I know if I don't find out for myself?"

He groaned, moving away a little so that she wouldn't find out too much, too soon. "I think we'd better save a few surprises for another night."

Olivia sat down on the bench and looked up at him forlornly. "Even as a child I hated surprises."

Brett squatted in front of her, putting his hands on her knees. "Shall I make love to you then? Here in the Broussards' garden? Because we were fast getting to that point."

"Is it always this fast, Brett? We've seen each other exactly three times, and yet I feel like saying yes."

He wondered if they were doubling the rum in Hurricanes these days. "It's not always this fast," he explained with patience. "There's something very potent between us."

Olivia could hear her own words, but she couldn't believe she was saying them. "I don't understand it. Why me, Brett? Why me of all the women you could choose from?"

"Don't you know how attractive you are?"

"Look at me. I'm home and family and mother love. I'm chocolate-chip cookies and milk and a lap every kid wants to sit on. Are you sure you can see what you're getting into here? I don't want any more out of life than a man to love and children of my own to raise. I'm hopelessly old-fashioned, Brett."

"You're also just a tiny bit tipsy."

She shook her head, and it was suddenly amazingly clear. "No, I don't think I am. I just had to warn you."

"I see what you are. Who you are. I like what I see. I like what I feel when you're in my arms." He framed her face in his hands, and in the dim light from the street lamps he could see that her cheeks were flushed and her eyes as sparkling as diamonds. He pulled her face to his and kissed her tenderly.

Olivia could only sigh.

"I'm going to be busy for most of the coming week," Brett told her when he moved away. "But Thursday is Thanksgiving, and I understand the Broussards are going up to Shreveport for the holiday. Are you going, too?"

Olivia shook her head. "I'm going down to New Iberia to be with my family."

He felt a strong surge of disappointment. He had hoped to spend the day with her. "That's too bad. I wanted to take you out for dinner."

"You can't eat Thanksgiving dinner in a restaurant. It's un-American." She realized suddenly that he had no other place to eat it, no family to eat it with. The knowledge chilled her. She couldn't imagine being that alone, that rootless. Even if her parents died, there were dozens of relatives who would welcome her. She would never celebrate a holiday by herself. She didn't want Brett to, either.

Olivia lifted her hand to stroke his cheek. "It's presumptuous of me, I know," she said, and she heard the sounds of Acadiana deepen in her voice as she plunged on nervously, "but would you like to come home to New Iberia and spend the holiday with my family? I can promise you'll be more than welcome."

"I couldn't impose that way."

"It wouldn't be an imposition." She traced his lips with one fingertip. "It would be a pleasure."

"How much of a pleasure?" He kissed her fingertip.

"As much as we can get away with under the noses of a houseful of Cajun men."

"I'm assuming said house comes equipped with a yard with at least one tree we can hide behind."

"It does."

"Then I'll come." He didn't smile, but his eyes were shining. "I hope you don't regret this in the morning."

"I think you should save that line," Olivia said serenely. "The rate things are going, you may need it for a more important occasion."

Early Thursday morning Olivia could hardly remember her own name. What on earth had possessed her to invite Brett to meet her family? Details of their night on Bourbon Street were hazy, but when she remembered bits and pieces of their conversation, she couldn't believe them.

Had they really discussed their growing attraction? Had she really warned him that she was looking for a husband and father for her children? Had she practically laid her body at his feet? Good Lord, what would Mary say if she knew?

Olivia had been raised on wine and beer like most of her friends. Liquor wasn't the big deal for her that it had been for kids raised in more restrictive homes. She'd been lovingly guided to learn her limits, and Olivia knew her limits were well over half a Hurricane. She'd been flying high that night, but had it been rum or just being with Brett? Perhaps the combination was lethal. Just in case, from now on when she was with him, she was going to stick to orange juice and an occasional beer.

Olivia had finished her packing the night before. As she waited for Brett to arrive, she put together a picnic breakfast. There would be a noticeable dearth of places to eat once they got out of New Orleans, and even though the sun wasn't up yet, the weather promised to cooperate if they wanted a quick meal outside.

When the front doorbell rang, she took a deep breath, reminded herself that she was not going to act embarrassed and went to answer it.

"Pardon me, but is this the Shady Lady Revue? Home of the famous All-Male Extravaganza and the largest Hurricanes in Louisiana?"

Olivia hid her face against Brett's chest, and he wrapped his arms around her. She could feel the rumble of laughter against her forehead. "A gentleman wouldn't remind me of that," she said in a muffled voice.

"Then do I get to remind you of all the things you said later?"

"No!"

Brett's hands traveled down her back to bring her closer. "Kiss me and I'll promise to drop the subject."

"Blackmail!"

"I love it. You love it. Happy Thanksgiving, Olivia."

She turned her face up to his and received the gentlest, most achingly tender kiss she could ever have imagined. Brett knew exactly how to break the ice.

The trip to New Iberia passed in a blur. They decided to take the interstate as far as the turnoff to Donaldsonville, then to cross the Mississippi River to take the more scenic back roads to the coast. They passed vast expanses of marsh, fields of sugarcane and sprawling eyesores of factories along the river, chatting as they went about Brett's job and the Broussard children.

At Pierre Part, they slowed down to admire the sleepy little Cajun town nestled on both sides of a narrow, winding bayou. They pulled over at the first opportunity and sat in the warmth of the newly risen sun to eat cinnamon rolls and drink coffee from a thermos.

"I ran away to Pierre Part once," Olivia told Brett after they'd finished eating.

Brett couldn't imagine Olivia doing anything that willful. Maybe there was yet another Olivia he hadn't met. "Most kids run away to the city, not the smallest town in the world." Brett stretched out and put his head in her lap.

Olivia wondered if he realized how his head nestled in that very intimate place was affecting her. "I was twelve. I wanted to go to a party, but most of the kids there were going to be older than me. My brothers found out and told my mother. Of course she refused to let me go. My grandfather had a cabin here, and a cousin of mine was coming up to do some fishing, so I told him I'd been invited to spend the weekend with another cousin of ours and hitched a ride."

"How many LeBlancs are there in the world?" Brett asked with interest.

"There aren't enough zeros to tell you," she teased. "Anyway, I got here, but by then I'd lost my nerve. I kept thinking about how worried my mother would be and how mad my father would get." She laughed. "Cajun kids grow up in fear of the loup-garou, but by the time we're old enough to be over that we're terrified of our mothers' tears and our fathers' anger."

Brett's face grew serious. "Your father didn't beat you, did he?"

Olivia brushed the hair off his forehead. "Never in my whole life. Not even when I got my cousin to take me back home that night. I'll never forget it, though. He was sitting on the front porch holding an old fishing pole that he'd been trying to repair. When I climbed the steps, he just looked at me. Then he took the pole, snapped it in two like it was a little twig and dropped it at my feet. He never said a word."

"And you never ran away again."

"I certainly didn't."

"What's the loup-garou?"

"Your fantasy life has been sadly neglected."

He captured her hand and kissed the palm. "Not since I met you."

Olivia felt her cheeks heating. "The loup-garou is half man, half beast, a bit like your werewolf."

"My werewolf? This is getting interesting."

"Yours, meaning American, not Cajun."

"Cajuns aren't American?"

"Do you like to fluster me?"

"Very much."

"I'll sic the loup-garou on you if you don't watch out."

"I like what I'm watching already, thank you."

She tried to ignore the cat-with-a-mouse expression on his face. "The loup-garou prowls around hoping to catch bad little boys and girls. I used to see him in my dreams."

"I'm jealous."

"You're incorrigible." Olivia wiggled her knees so Brett would sit up. "We'd better go. I promised my mother we'd get there in time to shell the shrimp for the jambalaya."

"Jambalaya? Are we going to have anything as normal as turkey?" Brett sat up.

"Wild turkey, stuffed with oysters. Don't worry, you'll like it." She paused. "You do like seafood, don't you? You have to like seafood."

"Or the loup-garou will get me?"

"Or my mother will get you."

Brett did like seafood. Better yet, he liked Olivia's parents, her three brothers, her numerous aunts and uncles and "coo-zans" and the endless stream of other people who wandered in and out of the brick ranch house perched in a residential section not far from Bayou Teche.

He wasn't sure what he'd expected; something more ethnic perhaps, a cypress house leaning out over some churning waterway or at least an authentic Cajun cottage surrounded by moss-draped live oaks. Instead, for all practical purposes Olivia had been raised in suburbia. Only the shrimp boat in her driveway and a garage filled with fishnets and nutria traps hinted at the unique flavor of this particular suburb.

"So, how long you've known my daughter?" Etienne LeBlanc sat on the front porch and peered at his guest over a beer and a bowl of freshly boiled shrimp that Olivia's mother had just placed in front of them.

Brett wondered how much more he was expected to eat before the meal actually began. In the hour since he and Olivia had arrived he'd been served more food than he normally ate in a whole day. Still, he wanted to make a good impression. He reached for a shrimp.

"Just a few weeks."

Etienne lifted his dark, bushy eyebrows, obviously considering this new piece of information. He was a short man, with a body as strong and barrel-chested as a bull's. His strength and stamina were facts of local renown. He had little education, but he'd worked his way up through the ranks to become a production foreman with a big oil company, and even though South Louisiana was in the midst of a depression, Etienne had held on to his job. Etienne Le-Blanc was not a man anyone wanted to lose.

"Livvy's my only girl," Etienne observed unnecessarily.

Brett understood immediately. "And you protect your own."

"I do. I do that."

"So do I." Brett leaned back in his chair and peeled the shrimp slowly.

"Then I can stop worrying?"

"You can stop worrying." Brett dipped his shrimp in the spicy tomato sauce on the table between them. "Unless you want to worry about whether she says yes when I ask her to marry me."

Etienne was quiet for a while. "I grew up with Livvy's mother. Myriam was my cousin, way, way back. Her brother was my best friend."

"Two weeks hardly compare," Brett said, reaching for another shrimp.

"Nah. I didn't ever look at Myriam, she was like my sister. Then one day she walked by and I looked. We got married as soon as her mama said she could. Myriam, she was a lot like my Livvy is now.''

"Then she was beautiful.''

"Yeah.'' Etienne narrowed his eyes as Brett reached for another shrimp. "Don't they feed you in New Orleans, son?''

Brett suddenly noticed that Etienne hadn't eaten a single thing. "Not like this.''

Etienne shook his head. "You keep eating, and Myriam's gonna keep bringing you food. You'll be as stuffed as the turkey by the time dinner gets here.''

Chapter Six

"My family is crazy about you." Olivia reached for Brett's hand and wove her fingers through his.

"Your family is wonderful."

Olivia's smile was a thoroughly contented one. "They are, aren't they?"

Brett looked out over Avery Island's Bird City and felt Olivia's hand sheltered warmly in his. In the four days they had spent together at her parents' house, she had shed much of her shyness. But then who could remain shy with a houseful of bantering men? Olivia was everybody's darling, but as the only girl in the family she was also fair game to be teased unmercifully.

"I like your brothers. When Richard finishes college, I'm going to see if I can get him to study law."

Olivia heard more than small talk; she heard plans for their future. Richard was only a sophomore at the University of Southwestern Louisiana in Lafayette. It would be at least two years before he thought about graduate school.

"Look, Brett," she said, quickly changing the subject. She pointed to a lone snowy egret who had left his perch on a man-made nesting ground raised on stilts above the waters of a small, quiet lake. "Look at the way he sails. So effortless, so graceful. I wish I could fly like that."

"Where would you go?"

Since there was nowhere she wanted to be except right beside him, Olivia shook her head. "I don't know. I'd just be content to be able to fly, I guess, even if I didn't go anywhere in particular."

"So if you were an egret, you'd stay close to your nest."

"And if I didn't have nestlings of my own, I'd take care of someone else's so she could fly far and free. An egret nanny."

"It would be a shame if you didn't have nestlings of your own."

"I guess I'd have to hope there was a male egret who felt the same way." Olivia smiled as Brett squeezed her hand in response.

"I'd wiggle my plumes for you."

"I'd be impressed. Very impressed. You'd have very beautiful plumes."

They watched the birds strut and flap their wings. There were few compared to the number that would come back in the spring. Avery Island was a wildlife sanctuary, a semitropical jungle on a vast mound of salt deposited by the waters of the Gulf of Mexico. The salt mines had been strategically important during the War of 1812 and the Civil War, but now it was a different seasoning altogether that gave the island its fame. Avery Island was the home of Tabasco sauce.

Bird City had come later in the island's history. Edward Avery McIlhenny had begun it on the smallest possible scale as the nineteenth century merged with the twentieth. The snowy egret was in danger of extinction, and "M'sieu Ned," anxious to do something, captured eight tiny egrets and caged them on a platform in a dammed-up pond. When fall came and the time for migration occurred, the cage doors were opened, but it took the destruction of the cages and the cold winds of winter to convince the young egrets to fly away.

Six returned that first spring, and now thousands returned each year to build their nests out of materials supplied by Avery Island workers. Other species of birds came, too, and the area was a mecca for tourists, a feathered monument to one man's foresight and concern.

Olivia faced Brett. "Did you know that the able-bodied egrets won't touch the food in the pond? They leave it for the young and the elderly. Even the mothers and fathers feeding their hatchlings make long trips back and forth for food."

"The fathers feed the young, too?"

"Egrets heard about women's liberation long before humans did. Mama egret stays with the babies during the night, but then at dawn, Papa egret comes flying back to the nest with breakfast. He baby-sits while Mama forages for herself. They take turns all day."

"It's humiliating to be enlightened by birds."

Olivia laughed softly. "Egrets are almost more human than bird. I think they even fall in love. When they were still hunted for their plumes, the hunters would kill one, then wait by its nest because they knew the mate would always come back, no matter how much danger he or she sensed. When the mama and papa egret see each other after a separation, they spread their plumes, put their bills together and make soft noises, almost like doves cooing."

"Like this?" Brett bent his head and rubbed his cheek against hers, making an approving sound deep in his throat.

Olivia sighed with pleasure. "I think I'm glad I'm not a bird. Your skin is nicer than feathers."

"Have you noticed that since we got to your house on Thanksgiving Day there hasn't been time to act like egrets?"

Olivia had noticed. She'd expected to have little time alone with Brett, but this was the first time in four days that they hadn't had her relatives nearby. Even when she'd taken Brett to view the magnificent Shadows-on-the-Teche plantation house on Friday and on a walking tour of downtown New Iberia on Saturday, someone had tagged along.

"What are they afraid of?" Brett asked, lifting a long lock of her hair to dangle it over her breast.

"My family? They're not afraid of anything. They just like your company."

"O-liv-i-a." He smiled a wicked smile. "You can do better than that."

She should have known Brett would see right through her perpetual escort services. She focused her eyes on his smile. "They're afraid you'll look at me like you're looking at me now."

"Cajuns are smart," he said, bending toward her.

"There are people coming down the path behind us," she warned before he could kiss her.

"Then I think we should give them a clear view of the egrets without bothering them." Brett put his arm around Olivia's shoulders and turned her in the direction of another path leading through a dense stand of bamboo. "Let's explore."

The morning was chilly, although the bright sunshine warmed whatever it could touch. Once they were out of the dark forest of bamboo they wandered through the luxuriant gardens, enjoying their time alone together.

Even though she'd been relentlessly chaperoned, Olivia was surprised at how much more she knew about Brett than she had before Thanksgiving Day. He drank his coffee with sugar but his tea plain, exactly the opposite of her own tastes. His early-morning manners were as good as his late-afternoon ones. He was addicted to the evening news, and he was a staunch Democrat, a loyalty he shared with her father. He seemed to prefer blue to any other color, and he was most comfortable in jeans and casual shirts.

There were other things she had learned, too, things much more important to know. Brett thrived on family life. He bloomed under the familiar give-and-take that seemed so everyday to her. He liked sitting with her father on the front porch snacking on the endless variety of foods her mother provided for them. He liked teasing her brothers and being included in their impromptu fishing trips or even their trips to the store for milk and bread. He basked in her mother's warmth to the point of asking Myriam to leave Etienne forever and marry him.

Brett had captured all their hearts. Hers most of all. Olivia knew she was unashamedly in love, an emotion so powerful that she worried how she could contain it. The woman who had wondered if love would ever happen to her no longer had to wonder. It had happened, and although she wasn't ashamed, she was concerned. She had no defenses against Brett, and she knew she needed them. Love didn't blind her to reality. And reality was that she was Olivia LeBlanc, and Olivia LeBlanc was not the right woman for Brett Terrill.

"What are you thinking about, bright eyes?" Brett stopped beside a small creek and pulled her close. Secluded from the road by huge magnolias, they were completely alone.

She felt an instant intimacy with him at the affectionate nickname. Still, her thoughts couldn't be shared. "Nothing important."

"Then I'll tell you what I was thinking about." His hands traveled down her spine. "I was thinking that someday I'm going to bring my children here to see the egrets and the gardens."

"I didn't know you wanted children."

"Very much."

"You'll be a wonderful father."

"And?"

"And what?"

"And what kind of husband would I be?" he prodded.

Olivia searched his face. "The best kind, Brett. The kind any woman would be lucky to have."

"I'm glad you think so." Brett bent to join his lips to hers.

Olivia settled her body against him, aware that her heart was speeding. Somehow just admitting that she had fallen in love had increased the intensity of her reaction to Brett until she felt dizzied by it.

Brett felt dizzy, too. Being with Olivia day in and day out and not being able to touch her had been a brutal test. He suspected Etienne had set it up just that way. Now Brett settled his hands on the seat of her jeans to guide her fully against him. He wanted her to believe his next words.

"I want you in my bed, Olivia," he whispered against her cheek. He stilled her answer with another kiss. His hands crept up beneath her sweater and stroked the smooth skin of her back, inch by silken inch. He loved the way she felt. He loved the resilience of her skin, the cozy warmth against his fingertips.

Her hair smelled like the crisp, clean air of an autumn morning. He buried his face in it as his hands moved slowly upward, coming to rest at the clasp of her bra. He released it easily, and her breasts pressed against his chest. His thumbs caressed the sides of them, and he smiled as he felt her shudder.

"I want to fall asleep with you at night and wake up with you in the morning," he whispered.

Her answer was husky and totally incoherent. Brett gently slid his hand between them as his other hand held her still. He took the weight of one breast in his hand and began to massage it. Her face turned to his and her lips parted. He felt her response in the kiss and in the blooming of her nipple.

Olivia wrapped her arms around Brett's neck, silently asking him for more. Satisfied, he responded by stroking both breasts, learning their contours until he could feel her whole body tremble.

Brett could feel a trembling begin deep inside him, too. He couldn't remember being so moved by a woman's response. He felt all-powerful. He felt as if Olivia's life, Olivia's future, was his to stroke and mold as he was molding her soft flesh. He was ready for the responsibility, more than ready. But was she?

Reluctantly his hands glided to her back to hook her bra and then down to her waist. Just as reluctantly he pulled his mouth from hers.

"Can you see how it would be?" he asked, his voice rough with feeling. "It would be perfect."

She nodded, afraid to speak. Lovemaking with Brett would be perfect. Of that she had no doubt. But how perfect would it be to give her body and heart for his pleasure? How perfect would it be to watch him walk away?

Brett could see the confusion in Olivia's eyes. He understood it. He was asking for too much, too soon. And yet, he didn't seem to be able to wait. The more he was with her, the more he wanted her, not just in his bed, but in his life, forever. She was exactly the kind of woman he needed, the kind of woman he'd given up hope of finding. She was everything he'd ever dreamed of having in the woman he married. She was everything that Kate Parsons hadn't been.

As Brett watched Olivia's battle for self-control, he reached up to smooth away the worry lines in her forehead. "I know you won't give yourself easily," he said. "I can wait for you, and I can even pretend to like it. Just don't ever think I don't want you, because I do. More than anything in the world."

Etienne saw the flush on his daughter's cheeks and the brightness of her eyes as she and Brett walked up the steps of the front porch to say goodbye before their trip back to New Orleans. He saw the proprietary way Brett put his hand on Olivia's back to guide her and the possessive expression on his face.

Etienne nodded, satisfied. He liked this young man. Brett was the first man he'd met who seemed good enough for his daughter. He doubted there were many as good—after all, he'd been a young man once himself. He should know.

Best of all, Brett had already declared his intentions. And to a father who had one foot planted in a culture rich in traditional values, Brett's declarations had just been a modern way of asking for Etienne's permission. What point was there in waiting any longer to give it?

"So when you gonna marry my daughter and make this thing legal?" Etienne asked, leaning back in his chair and crossing his arms over his massive chest.

"Papa!"

Brett threw back his head and laughed, both at Etienne's nerve and Olivia's dismay, but his arm tightened around her waist as she tried to break free. "Whoa there," he said, sobering. "Where are you going?"

"I'm going to tell my mother goodbye!"

"She's going to tell her mother what I said," an unrepentant Etienne told Brett. "Those two, they stick together."

"Don't you want to hear my answer?" Brett asked casually.

"I certainly don't." Olivia tried to pull free. "I'm embarrassed enough already. I apologize for my father's bad manners."

"He was just stating the obvious." Brett felt Olivia stiffen against him. She wasn't ready for this, and he hadn't intended to ask her so soon. Less than an hour ago he'd stood with her at Avery Island and begun a serious courtship. Etienne's timing wasn't good.

"What does that mean?" Olivia was still rigid beside him.

Brett had planned to lead up to proposing marriage by slower stages. But the commitment had been made now. There was nothing to do except continue.

"Etienne knows I'm going to ask you to marry me," he explained. "He just thinks I should ask you now instead of dragging this out. I think he's right."

"Marry you?" Olivia faced Brett, her father forgotten. "You hardly know me. You can't marry me."

"If you agree I certainly can." Out of the corner of his eye, Brett saw Etienne nodding his head.

She was wide-eyed with disbelief. "Why, you're as crazy as my father is!"

"Being compared to your father is a compliment." He saw Etienne nod once more.

Myriam LeBlanc came out to the porch, wiping her hands on a dish towel. "Who's comparing you and Brett?" she asked her husband, leaning against his chair.

"Brett wants Olivia to marry him."

Mrs. LeBlanc was quiet for a while, mulling over her husband's words as she examined the shell-shocked expression on her daughter's face. "Well," she said finally, "I like Christmas weddings. We'll have to see if we can get the church for Christmas or Christmas Eve. Livvy? Do you care which?"

"This is not the way to the Broussards' house."

Brett grinned at Olivia's stilted tone. "Hey, I wasn't sure you could still talk."

Olivia sat up straighter and stared out the window. "Where are you taking me, Brett?"

"We're going to my place to talk this through."

"I want to go home."

"We're going to my place, and we're almost there."

"If you wanted to talk, we could have spent the last two and a half hours talking," she pointed out, still refusing to look at him.

"I want to look you straight in the eye when we settle this."

"There's nothing to settle."

"Well, the last I heard our wedding date was still up in the air."

"That's easy. The date is never. Now take me home."

"I've been getting to know all the Olivias in the past weeks, but I haven't seen this one before. You've got a temper." Brett swung his car into the right lane and turned. One more turn and he was on his own street, Bancroft Drive. It had been a long, silent trip back to New Orleans. He was glad to be home.

Brett pulled his car into his driveway and turned off the engine. "Come inside with me, Olivia. Let's settle this."

Short of hitchhiking to the Garden District, Olivia realized she had little choice. She opened her own door and stood by the side of the car until Brett was safely ahead of her. Then, reluctantly, she followed him into his apartment.

"I'll make us something to drink."

"Please don't bother." Olivia sat on the sofa, as close to one end as she could get without sliding off.

It was a mistake. If she'd thought that Brett would opt for symmetry and choose the other end of the sofa, she was wrong. He sat next to her and draped his arm over her shoulder. She had no place to go without ending up on the floor.

"Why are you so offended that I want to marry you?" Brett put his hand under Olivia's chin and turned her face to his. "Believe it or not, there are women in this world who would be happy if I proposed to them."

"We've never even talked about marriage, Brett."

"What did you think we were talking about at Avery Island today?"

She stared into his eyes. "Seduction."

"And that would be better than marriage? You're planning to begin a long series of affairs and I was supposed to be the first?"

Despite her best intentions, a smile flickered across Olivia's face. "I can't think straight when you badger me this way."

"Then just tell me what you feel."

She took a deep breath. "I feel hurt."

Brett stroked her hair. "Why?"

"You don't want to marry me. You've known me for a little over two weeks and for some reason right now you find me attractive. You want me in your bed. Maybe you're tired of the dating game and the idea of marriage to someone sounds appealing; I don't know. But you don't want to marry me, Brett. You just want to marry somebody, and I'm available."

He continued to stroke her hair, letting her words settle between them. "And?" he said finally.

"And what?"

"What else hurts, Olivia?"

She shut her eyes. "Nothing."

"You're in love with me, and you're afraid my feelings for you are so shallow they're hardly even there."

She couldn't have said it better, so she said nothing.

"You're wrong." He touched her cheek. "Look at me."

Olivia opened her eyes and met his reluctantly.

"You fell in love in two weeks. You never expected that to happen, did you?"

She still refused to answer, but Brett went on. "Well, I looked up from my jog at the park two weeks ago and I saw a woman who appealed to me tremendously. She was out in the middle of a lagoon, rescuing a paper boat, and I thought: any woman who cares that much how a little boy feels is someone I want to meet. Then I met you, and you were everything that I'd hoped and more."

"You don't marry someone because of the way she treats little boys, Brett."

"No, you marry someone because you know that you want to live with her, to make a home with her, to raise a family with her. You marry her because you know she'll be easy to grow old with, because you feel comfortable being around her, because you know that in twenty years or thirty you'll still want to hold her in your arms."

"What about love?" Olivia searched his eyes. "You say I'm in love with you, but you've said nothing of your love for me."

"I care very much about you, Olivia. I'll be a good husband, and I'll cherish you deeply. Isn't that what love is all about?"

She shook her head. "No. What I feel for you is so much more than that."

"Then you love me?" His smile was warm.

She still refused to acknowledge it openly. "You've as good as said you don't love me."

His face grew serious, and he grew silent. He continued stroking her hair as he searched for a way to tell her the truth. "I don't think I can love anybody," he said at last. "Not the way most people mean when they talk about love, anyway. There's something missing inside me, I guess. I don't feel those things other people say they feel. I like people, I care what happens to them, but there's a distance between them and me. I don't feel it so strongly with you, but it's there, and it might always be there."

Olivia swallowed hard. "Why do you want to marry me, then?"

"Without those blinders called love I can see things very clearly. I know exactly what I want in a marriage, and I know the woman who can give it to me. We'll get married for the right reasons, all the right reasons. I'll be faithful and supportive and I'll put you and the children first. But I can't give you what I don't have to give."

Olivia sensed how hard this was for Brett to talk about. She could see the tremendous effort he was making to be honest with her. In spite of what he was saying, she loved him more for being able to say it. He was a man yearning for all the things she knew she could give him. He was right; he had chosen well.

"There was another woman." Olivia abandoned all attempts at tact. She had to know everything. She deserved to know. "Did she want more from you than you could give?"

Brett was surprised someone had mentioned Kate to Olivia. If they were going to have a relationship, however, it had to be built on the truth. "Her name was Kate," he said simply. "And she didn't want anything from me."

"You were together a long time."

"We lived together for two years."

"Why didn't you marry her?"

"Kate didn't want marriage. She didn't want a home or a family."

"So you broke up with her and went searching for a woman who wanted those things. And I was the first one who caught your eye."

"The last year Kate and I were together, things got steadily worse between us," he said carefully, trying to feel his way. "By the time I moved out, it had been apparent for a while that our relationship was over. I know lots of women, and more than one of them made it clear during that year that they'd love to help me readjust to the swinging single life. It's not as if I left Kate and you were the first woman I saw."

"You were still on the rebound."

"If that means that I'd had a bad experience and learned exactly what I needed from it, then maybe I was," he told her. "But that's not bad. It doesn't diminish what we could have together. It doesn't diminish what I feel for you. It just makes me believe in miracles. I was beginning to think a woman like you didn't exist, and then, there you were, up to your knees in a muddy lagoon.''

"Love at first sight, only you don't love me.''

"I can't pretend to feel what I'm incapable of feeling. But I don't have to pretend this.'' His arm tightened around her and he moved her closer. "I want you, Olivia. I meant what I said today at the island. But I don't want a one-night stand or even another two-year affair. I want you for keeps.'' He smoothed the hair back from her face and sought her lips with his own.

Olivia tried to remain passive, tried to keep the most essential part of herself separate, but the tenderness of the kiss, the yearning inherent in it, were her undoing. She turned in his arms to slip hers around his neck. If Brett had just wanted her as a possession, as the perfect robot wife, she could say no to him and to this kiss. But she knew, even if he didn't, that Brett needed much more. He needed her love, because only love as strong as the love she felt for him could open his heart.

He groaned and parted her lips, deepening the kiss until she was falling apart inside and her thoughts were a delirious jumble. Pushing her back against the sofa, he smoothed his hand along her neck and shoulder to take her breast. Two weeks against a lifetime of careful judgment, but all she could think about was how much she wanted his hands on her bare skin, how much she wanted to give herself totally to him, how little she cared about propriety anymore.

"I wouldn't have mentioned marriage so soon if your father hadn't brought it up,'' he said, breaking away to sit on the edge of the sofa.

Olivia could see the rapid rate of Brett's breathing. His lips were moist from their kiss, and his tanned cheeks couldn't hide the telltale flush of passion. Most of all, his blue eyes smoldered with the desire that he had never fully unleashed, a desire that could conquer her completely if he wanted it to.

Both of them knew it.

"I'm not going to insist on anything," he said finally. "Just think about it. We'll spend time together; I'll give you time. Just know that I've already waited my whole life for you, Olivia. And I won't keep waiting forever."

Chapter Seven

Cherry Broussard opened the door to Lucy's bedroom and grimaced in sympathy. Lucy was asleep in Olivia's lap, and Olivia was almost asleep herself. The white wicker rocker holding them was still. Cherry crossed the room and lifted Lucy from Olivia's arms. "You've got a long-distance phone call," she whispered as Olivia opened her eyes. "I'll tuck her in."

Olivia checked her watch. It was late, too late for anything except an emergency. She was only up herself because Lucy was cutting a tooth and had awakened from the pain.

Since the closest phone was in the children's playroom, Olivia took the call surrounded by giant building blocks and stuffed animals. After she hung up she sat on the rug hugging a ragged giraffe.

"Olivia?" Cherry came to sit beside her. "Is everything all right?"

Olivia wiped her eyes. "Not really. That was the Hopkins Academy secretary. Mary is very sick. They had to take her to the hospital tonight, and they wanted me to know."

Cherry touched her shoulder in sympathy. "Do you want to go on up there now?"

"She can't have visitors. They're trying to get her stabilized. Sara said I should come early in the morning. Mary's asking to see me."

"I'm sorry. You've seemed so worried the last few days. Is that what's been bothering you?"

Olivia felt a stab of guilt. Since returning from New Iberia she'd been so troubled over Brett's proposal that she had hardly even thought about Mary. "I didn't know Mary was this ill," she admitted. "I knew she didn't look well the last time I saw her, but she insisted she was just getting older."

"Is she very ill?"

"Very."

"Did this Sara say what Mary's chances for recovery are?"

Olivia nodded bleakly. "She's not going to get any better, Cherry. If they can get her stabilized, the most we can hope for is that she'll live a couple of months. And that's if we're really lucky."

Olivia hadn't been expecting to find Mary so ill. She had tried to prepare, telling herself over and over again that Mary was dying and that the grim reaper sowed the path before him with devastation. But the Mary lying in the narrow hospital bed with multiple tubes connected to her was not the Mary Olivia had known. It was hard not to back away in horror.

"Mary?" She approached the bed, looking for signs of the woman she loved. "Are you awake?"

Mary's eyes opened and her head turned. "Olivia." Her voice was weak, but it was unmistakably Mary's.

"Don't try to talk. I'll just sit with you for a while." Olivia covered Mary's hand with hers.

"I wanted to see you."

"I'll stay just as long as they'll let me." Olivia pulled a chair beside the bed and sat, taking Mary's hand again.

"You're my daughter."

Olivia wasn't sure she had heard Mary correctly. She just squeezed her hand to let her know she was still there.

"Not my real daughter, of course," Mary went on after a few seconds. "But you're the daughter I always wanted and never had."

"And you've been like another mother to me," Olivia said soothingly. "But, Mary, you mustn't talk. It's going to tire you too much."

"I don't care. I'm about to get a long, long rest."

Olivia smiled despite the truth of Mary's words. She realized she might as well stop trying to keep Mary quiet. No one could make Mary Hopkins do anything she didn't want to. Even the specter of death couldn't frighten her into submission.

"I'm prepared to go, you know," Mary said after a few minutes. "I've lived my life the way I wanted. The academy has been my life."

"It's a wonderful school."

"I couldn't have it all. I made the right choices. I know I did."

"I know you did, too."

The door opened, and the nurse Olivia had spoken with at the desk bustled in. "That's long enough," she said softly to Olivia. "Miss Hopkins must rest now."

"Olivia, tell her I'm going to bloody well die right here on the spot if she doesn't get out," Mary said clearly.

"I think she means you," Olivia told the nurse with an apologetic smile.

"Two more minutes." The nurse bustled out.

"She's so utterly efficient." Mary shut her eyes. "I made the right choices, Olivia."

"You've lived a good life." Olivia felt frustrated. She knew Mary was trying to tell her something important, but she couldn't understand what, and she didn't want to question her. Mary was quickly getting exhausted.

"I could have married Arlen. He wanted me to. I stayed in Louisiana to be wth him." Mary's sentences were coming in fits and starts. "But I couldn't have him and my dream of the academy. I loved the academy more."

Olivia was surprised. She didn't know anyone named Arlen, but obviously he had once been important to Mary. So Mary had given up her man to found her school. "You did what you knew was best," Olivia assured her.

"Arlen, he . . . he didn't understand. He wanted me to be a wife and nothing else."

Olivia squeezed her hand again.

"Don't let any man do that to you, Olivia. This young man of yours, be sure he understands you have to grow."

Olivia didn't want to remind Mary that they were nothing alike. Olivia had no dreams other than those that involved being a wife and mother. Mary had had a vision, a vision of a school that would train men and women to provide the highest quality of child care. That vision had ruled her life.

"I'm not going to stop growing," she promised. "Brett wouldn't want me to stop growing." As she said the words, she wondered if they were true. Yes, they had to be. If she told Brett she would marry him, they would do their growing together.

"Good." Mary was quiet for a while, and Olivia thought she'd fallen asleep. Then Mary opened her eyes and turned her head so she was looking straight at Olivia. "I made the right decision," she said softly. "But sometimes, sometimes I was so lonely."

* * *

Brett stood at the Broussards' back door and watched Olivia with Lucy and Trey. Lenny Broussard had told him about Olivia's late-night phone call. Brett hadn't seen her since Sunday night, when he'd brought her home from her parents' house. Now he wondered why she hadn't called him to share her sorrow.

As he watched she sat down on the edge of the children's sandbox and deftly turned Lucy so that she and Trey were no longer competing for the same patch of sand.

He wanted Olivia to raise his children. He wanted to make them with her, although with her hair hanging in two long braids across her shoulders, she looked like a child herself and hardly a candidate for motherhood. That didn't matter. He knew what a woman she was.

He pulled the door toward him and stepped out on the back porch. Olivia looked up, and he could clearly read her emotions. She was glad to see him; she was also frightened.

"I was at work when I suddenly got a terrific urge to play in the sand. Is this sand available?"

Olivia watched Brett walking toward her. Today his suit was navy blue and his tie the deep sky blue of his eyes. "Aren't you a little overdressed?"

"What's a dry-cleaning bill?" Brett sat on the edge across from Olivia and ruffled Trey's curls. "How's it going, partner?"

Trey took the question seriously. "Lucy picked up her shovel and there was a bug in it."

Brett frowned. "What kind of bug?"

"A big black one with a hundred legs."

Brett shook his head. "Did you get rid of it for her?"

"She tried to eat it."

"Lucy didn't have much lunch," Olivia explained. "She's cutting a tooth."

Brett grinned, and Olivia smiled back at him. For a moment they were the only two people in the world.

"Livvy made Lucy put it on the ground so it would be okay."

Brett turned his attention back to Trey. "That was good. Most bugs are important, and we don't want to hurt them."

Trey nodded. "You know what?"

"No. What?"

"It crawled over there—" Trey pointed with his shovel "—and a bird ate it. Lucy coulda had it after all."

Brett erupted in laughter, and he heard the sound of chuckles from the other side of the sandbox. When he was calm again, he met Olivia's eyes. "What am I supposed to say to that?"

"Mary Hopkins's firm rule is that if you don't know what to say, say nothing at all. That's why I'm so quiet most of the time."

"I heard about Mary. I'm sorry, Olivia."

"Thank you."

"Are you going back up to see her tonight?"

"She told me she has other people to see, and she's only allowed one visitor at a time. The hospital will call if there's any change."

"Then come with me for dinner. I'll fix it. You can just relax."

An evening with Brett sounded perfect except for one thing, and Olivia didn't have the energy to be tactful about that. She stood Lucy up and began to brush the sand off her overalls. "I haven't made any decisions," she warned Brett. "Were you expecting an answer?"

"I'm expecting to make you dinner. Nothing more."

"I'll have to check with Cherry. I usually have Thursday evenings off, but I was gone this morning."

"Cherry says there's no problem."

"Then I'll run and change." She lifted Lucy and headed toward the house.

Half an hour later she was in Brett's car with her eyes closed listening to mellow rock music on the radio. Brett seemed to understand her mood. He had asked no questions, just made sure she was settled comfortably before he pulled out into traffic.

The drive to Brett's apartment almost put her to sleep. Between Lucy's tooth and the news about Mary, she had slept very little the night before. Then she had gotten up early to drive to Baton Rouge to the hospital, and as soon as she'd known she could do no more good there, she'd headed back to New Orleans to take over Lucy and Trey's care. She was exhausted.

"Are you awake?"

She was, but just barely. Olivia opened her eyes and tried to smile to reassure Brett that she was all right. "Are we there?"

"We are."

Brett came around to open her door, and Olivia welcomed his arm around her. Inside he pushed her gently to the sofa. "I want you to take a nap while I get dinner ready."

"Can't I help?" They both knew she was just being polite.

Brett brushed the palm of his hand across her eyes to make her close them. "Dinner's nothing exciting. All I have to do is pop it in the oven. You rest." He wasn't sure, but it seemed to him that she was asleep before he'd finished speaking.

In the kitchen Brett turned on the oven and put two frozen dinners inside. No one did frozen dinners better than he did. When he and Kate had lived together, he'd been in charge of the frozen dinners and she'd been in charge of making sure they had cartons of salad from the supermarket deli. Idly he wondered if the daughter of Myriam LeBlanc had ever even eaten salad from a carton.

He passed Olivia twice as he went back and forth to his bedroom, once to change his clothes and once on some pretext, just so he could look at her again. She had unbraided her hair and it covered her shoulders and back like a raven's wing. Her skin was rosy and her lips parted slightly, as if in invitation. She had never seemed more desirable.

As he watched, she turned over and frowned in her sleep. He knew she couldn't be comfortable; the sofa was narrow and hard. He checked his watch; the dinners had forty minutes to go. Without weighing the consequences, Brett leaned over, scooped Olivia up and took her to his bedroom.

Olivia awakened in the middle of a dream where she was floating in buoyant, warm water. For a moment she didn't know where she was, nor did she care. She only knew that she felt safe and rested and happy. As she came more fully awake she realized she *was* floating. The bed beneath her was rocking gently with each movement she made.

She turned her head and saw Brett lying next to her. "You have a water bed."

"Do you like it?"

"I like it. Why am I in it?"

"Because I've been imagining you in it for two and a half weeks."

"That doesn't explain a lot."

"I brought you in here. You looked miserable on the sofa."

She turned her head to stare up at the ceiling. "How do you get up in the morning?"

"With great difficulty. If you were sleeping next to me it'd be even harder."

She knew he'd moved closer by the ripples coming her way. "This is a handy thing for a bachelor to have in his apartment. What woman could resist?"

"I think I'm going to find out." Brett smoothed his hand along her jawline, turning her head to him as he did. "I didn't bring you here to seduce you." He brushed his fingers across her lips. "At least I don't think I did."

"I studied Freud in psychology class at the academy. We both know what he'd say." Olivia reached up and wove her fingers through his hair, tugging his head toward hers. "Let's not worry about why I'm here. Just kiss me."

He resisted for a moment, memorizing the way she looked against his sheets and pillows. Poised half over her, he felt like the conqueror in a gladiator film. She seemed so young, so unprepared for where this could lead. He wanted to protect her from everything, including himself. "I'm not sure this is a good idea," he admitted, but even as he said the words his mouth was descending to hers.

One touch and she was addicted. She hadn't realized how much she had needed the comfort of Brett's body. This, and only this, could drive away the reality of Mary's illness. This, and only this, could hold at bay the fear that she was going to lose Brett forever if she delayed her decision.

The weight of his body drove her deeper into the mattress and they rocked together, arms around each other and mouths united. She pulled his shirt out of his jeans to explore the warm, smooth skin of his back. She could feel the subtle padding of muscle and the sensuous stretching of his body as she caressed him. It felt so good, so right, to be this intimate.

She parted her lips, waiting for their kiss to deepen. When it didn't, she made her own delicate forays into his mouth, coaxing him to respond. He accepted her explorations, but held back, wondering how far she would go, how bold she could be.

She moaned a little in frustration. Her seduction skills were undeveloped, at best. When Brett settled on his back and pulled her on top of him to become the aggressor, she knew she was way out of her league.

"Just do anything you want to," he said, holding her face in his hands. His smile was reassuring, but there was a dark, male gleam in his eyes that dared her to take the lead.

"Brett, I don't know how...."

"You have to learn sometime."

"Why now?"

He gathered her hair in his hands and pushed it over one shoulder, running his lips over the edge of her exposed ear. "Because if I do it, you won't leave this bed a virgin," he told her bluntly.

"And what if that doesn't matter?"

"It matters to me." He stroked his fingertips down the smooth column of her neck.

"It's important for you to marry a virgin? Was that one of the reasons I appealed to you?"

"No!" His answer was sharp, and he didn't tone down his explanation of it, either. "I couldn't care less. Do you think I look forward to hurting you the first time we make love? It would be easier for us both if you weren't. But you are, and I won't have you making your decisions backward."

She was sure her cheeks were flushed. He was right. If they made love in the heat of passion tonight, that ultimate of intimacies would prompt her to say yes to his proposal. It would be the easy way out. She rested her head on his shoulder. "I'm sorry. I didn't even realize that's what I wanted."

Brett's arms tightened around her. "I know this is a hard time for you. Let's not make it any harder. Forget about everything else. Let's just learn what pleases each other."

"You please me," she said against his neck. "You're considerate and caring and . . ."

"Finished talking. Definitely finished talking." Brett found Olivia's mouth and silenced her. His hands slipped between them and closed around her waist. It was small, flaring out into ample hips and full breasts, a figure to please a man but not a fashion designer. He explored it, slipping his hands down to caress the softer flesh tapering down to her bottom.

Olivia drew her breath in sharply. If this wasn't a preliminary to lovemaking, she wondered what would be. She was igniting under the practiced movements of his hands. With her hands on his shoulders she kissed his cheeks, his nose, his eyelids. Her breasts grazed his chest, and she moaned with pleasure when he unclasped her bra to take the full weight of them with his hands.

He made no attempt to undress her, letting her clothing provide the semblance of a barrier between them. He wanted to see her, to learn every gorgeous inch with his eyes and his mouth, but he knew once he'd done that, nothing would stand in the way of final consummation.

Olivia had no such compunctions. Awkwardly she unbuttoned his shirt with trembling fingers and exposed his chest. He was perfect, well-muscled with a sprinkling of brown hair tapering toward the snap of his jeans. She stroked her hands the length and width of his chest, learning its textures and shape. Then she let her mouth follow where her hands had been. With her ear against his chest she could hear his heart thrumming in double time.

When the tension became unbearable for Brett, he rolled her onto her back, half covering her as he kissed her the way he had yearned to kiss her from the beginning. One hand stroked her breasts, and finally, with a groan of surrender, he pulled her sweater just high enough so that they were flesh to flesh.

They lay that way for a full minute, neither daring to move. Olivia's body was awash in sensation. Nothing had ever felt this good. Nothing had ever made her feel so complete.

Brett knew only how good more would feel. He wished he hadn't been so magnanimous, so self-righteous about his plans for the evening. He wanted her with a passion that had nothing to do with what was right for either of them.

The oven timer buzzed.

"Saved." In spite of his exclamation, Brett couldn't move. He was filled with fears. What if Olivia said no to his proposal? What if this was the last time they were together, the last time he touched her? He didn't want to lose her. She was no longer just someone he wanted to set up housekeeping with, someone he wanted to help him raise his children. She was Olivia, and he desired her more than any woman he'd known.

"Does the oven turn itself off?" Olivia lifted her hands to stroke his hair, but the movement twisted her body under his and shot quicksilver through her bloodstream.

"Maybe there'll be a power failure."

"Maybe you forgot to pay the electric bill."

"Maybe the dinners will just self-destruct if I leave them in there."

"You feel so warm against me."

"You're so soft, so perfect. I want to kiss every inch of you." Brett could see the effect his words had on her. She wanted the same thing, but there was still a hint of shyness in her eyes. She was a gloriously sensual woman who was terribly unsure of her own charms. He teased her. "Do you want me to?"

"Um..."

He laughed at the sound that could have meant anything. "Do you know what else I want to do?"

"I'm afraid to ask."

"I want to bury myself so deeply inside you that we never come apart, never separate. I want us to be one."

She wanted the same thing, and she had never understood it more clearly. "Um," she said a little louder.

He laughed, moving his legs off hers. If they were going to part, it would have to be by degrees. Anything else would be too wrenching. "I want..."

"No more!" She pulled his head to her shoulder to muffle his words. "If you tell me one more thing you want, I'm going to dissolve, evaporate, incinerate..."

"All of the above?" he asked, nipping the wool of her sweater with his teeth.

"Simultaneously."

"There are better things to do simultaneously." He finished moving away from her.

Olivia pulled her sweater down, wishing as she did that she was pulling it off instead. "I'm glad you want me," she said, feeling suddenly very vulnerable. "I just don't know..."

Brett covered her mouth with his fingers and shook his head. "Don't say anything now. I'm going to get up and turn off the oven. Then we're going to eat and I'm going to take you home. There's still time for answers, bright eyes."

The answers came sooner than Brett had anticipated.

Olivia combed her hair and straightened her clothing, surprised by the bright-eyed woman who stared back at her from the bathroom mirror. Brett's nickname for her certainly made sense since he had come into her life.

In the kitchen she helped him set the table and get the dinner on. Sitting together over dried-out once-frozen chicken and vegetables, she understood finally why Brett wanted to marry her. Even sharing a mediocre meal was special if you were with someone you cared about, someone you could care about forever. It wasn't just the lovemaking, the passion, that counted in a relationship. It wasn't just the words of love. It was the day-to-day sharing. It was the relief from a world full of strangers, the knowledge that there was someone waiting for you who wanted to make your life as easy as possible.

"Mary told me this morning that she's been very lonely sometimes," Olivia said, reaching for the salt.

"She never married?"

"No. She could have, I think. Evidently the man didn't want her to have the academy. He wanted her to himself."

"There must have been compromises they could have made."

"I guess there weren't. Mary's very stubborn. Perhaps the man was, too."

"It's hard to manage a career and a marriage now. It was probably almost impossible then."

"I guess that's what Arlen thought."

"Arlen?" Brett set his fork down. "Arlen who?"

"She didn't say. Do you know an Arlen?"

"I don't know one. But I've heard of one. Arlen Labouisse. He was attorney general of Louisiana after World War Two. They say he was headed for the governor's mansion and then who knows?" Brett shrugged. "There was a big scandal. I remember reading about it when I was studying state history in law school. It seems to me he'd secured the Democratic nomination for governor, and then one day he just resigned and disappeared, leaving everything in chaos. There were rumors of a love affair gone awry. No one ever heard any more about him until years later, when he died in Kentucky and left an enormous amount of money to LSU."

"I wonder if Mary's Arlen and Arlen Labouisse are the same?"

"I wonder if he was lonely, too?" Brett stood to make coffee.

Two wasted lives. Two people who could have found their way together if they'd compromised, worked together for solutions. Olivia knew suddenly that nothing would be worse than letting the same thing happen to her. She was in love with Brett. It had happened too fast to be sensible, and yet hadn't she wanted someone like him her whole life? Someone who would cherish her, care for her and their children, be the husband every woman dreamed of having?

True, Brett didn't love her the way she wanted to be loved. But Brett had to learn to love, and learning would take time. If she married him they'd have time; they'd have the rest of their lives. But if she didn't marry him, they wouldn't have a chance. Only in the intimacy of sharing and living their lives together would love grow and thrive.

Suddenly the decision seemed simple.

"Do you always eat this way?" she asked, addressing the question to his back.

"More often than I should."

"When we're married, I'm not going to let you buy any of these awful dinners. I'm a very good cook."

His hand paused between the coffee can and the pot, but he didn't turn. "So how many more should I buy in the meantime?"

"I'd say enough to last you until Christmas Eve. I'd like to be married about five. In candlelight."

Chapter Eight

I'm sorry, Olivia, but you know as well as I do that any LeBlanc wedding is a big wedding, whether it's planned that way or not." Myriam LeBlanc stood back and examined her daughter. "Exquisite."

"Uncle Dennis saw me in the hall. He wanted to know if he should start carving a cradle. Everyone sitting out there thinks I'm pregnant because Brett and I planned this in such a rush. All two hundred and fifty of them!"

Myriam clucked her disapproval. "They'll see. Besides, only Etienne's side of the family would think such a thing. My side wouldn't dare!"

"Who can tell whose side is whose?" Olivia stepped up to the mirror. Her reflection showed a young woman so innocent, so virginal-looking in pristine white, that no one would dare think she was marrying for any reason other than true love. It did not show the young woman who was wondering if she had made a huge mistake. "The dress is perfect, Mama. Thank you."

"Thank Mrs. Broussard. She's the one who found it."

Olivia smiled, and the radiant bride in the mirror smiled back at her. She was still amazed at the number of people who had hopped on the bandwagon to make sure the wedding took place on Christmas Eve. Cherry, who had shopped for Olivia's dress and bought it as a wedding gift; Myriam, who had done all the alterations so that it would be ready in time; Father Henley, who had found parishioners willing to put the church back in order for midnight mass; friends and relatives who had decorated and assembled floral arrangements and food for the reception.

Secretly Olivia had hoped that if she had the wedding on a busy holiday like Christmas Eve, few people would feel compelled to come. But she should have known better. Everybody wanted to see Etienne and Myriam's little girl walk down the aisle, and they had cheerfully changed their plans to accommodate her.

Even Brett's friends had gotten in the spirit. Everyone from his law office was coming, and a fair number of others had accepted invitations, too.

Olivia had not wanted to be the center of attention. She would have eloped if she could have, but it was clear that Myriam's heart would have broken. Now Olivia straightened the skirt of her dress and examined herself, hoping that what she saw would give her courage to make the impossibly long trip down the center aisle.

The dress was heavy satin in a princess style with no adornment except long, puffed lace sleeves over fitted satin. She had decided to leave her hair down, but she had drawn it back from her face with the top layer in a cluster of long curls. It suited the elegantly old-fashioned dress and the spray of white rosebuds she was wearing in a circlet around a short lace veil.

Her bouquet was white rosebuds, too, with orange blossoms and white iris to set them off. She hoped it was large enough to hide the fact that her hands were shaking.

"What did Miss Hopkins say when she saw the dress?"

Olivia buried her nose in the flowers for a moment, trying to force herself to relax. "She said I'd be the most beautiful bride in the world. She was looking so much better, Mama. I can't believe how she's rallied. They're even talking about letting her go home with a nurse."

"I wish she could have come."

"I don't think she'd have wanted to. She's not happy I'm getting married."

"Did she tell you that?"

"She didn't have to tell me. She has this way of looking straight through you if you don't do what she thinks you should. She was a nanny for a lot of years."

"At least she's well enough to give you that look."

Olivia smiled. "She made me bring Brett to meet her."

"Did she approve?"

"He charmed her socks off. Then she asked him why he couldn't wait to marry me."

Myriam clucked and shook her head. "She's ornery enough to be a LeBlanc."

"Brett told her delayed gratification wasn't his style."

"He didn't!"

"Mary said she wished she could have been his nanny. She would have taught him a thing or two."

"And Brett's still speaking to you?"

"Brett laughed all the way back to New Orleans. He loved her."

The sounds of organ music drifted through the closed doors.

Olivia squeezed her eyes shut. "I can't go through with it. You marry Brett, Mama. He asked you first."

"By tomorrow morning you'll be fine."

Olivia's eyes flew open. "I may not live that long. Listen, you stand at the back of the church and yell 'Fire!' I'll sneak out the front."

"Your grand-père held me up the whole way down the aisle. Then he handed me over to Etienne, and Etienne held me up. Your papa and Brett will do the same for you."

"Mary was right. I'm not ready for this."

"Mary wanted you to be like her. You've got to be yourself. Brett loves you. He'll be a fine husband."

"He'll be a fine husband," Olivia repeated, choosing the only one of her mother's statements she knew to be true.

A knock sounded at the door. "They're ready for you, Myriam," Etienne called.

"Just do what Father Henley told you to do," Myriam instructed. She sniffed, then clasped Olivia to her. "Next time I hug you, you'll be a married woman."

Olivia waited until her mother had gone, then turned back to the mirror. Who was the lovely young woman reflected there? One thing was certain. Whoever she was, she was about to change. Olivia only hoped the change was going to be a good one.

Brett shook hands and murmured thank-yous in a daze. He still hadn't completely accepted the fact that he was a married man. Obviously all these people coming through the informal receiving line thought he was, and he clearly remembered saying "I will" to Father Henley. Then there was the indisputable evidence standing next to him: Olivia in a white dress murmuring the same thank-yous he was.

How could Olivia keep these people straight? He peeked at her from the corner of his eye. She was heart-stoppingly beautiful. He hadn't even known a woman could look like this. He wanted to take her aside and ask her if she felt married.

"Well, you stole my nanny." Cherry Broussard leaned over and kissed Brett on the cheek. "You've played havoc with my sanity. The children are devastated."

"Lucy didn't look devastated when she was skipping down the aisle."

"Did you like the part where she spilled the whole basket of rose petals, then picked them up one by one?"

"She's very meticulous. It didn't matter if the wedding was delayed fifteen minutes."

"You're going to take good care of Olivia, aren't you, Brett?" Cherry asked, her face growing serious.

"The best."

She lowered her voice so only he could hear. "Kate's here."

Brett's eyes were carefully blank, but he stopped smiling. "I didn't invite her."

"She came with Frank Hendricks. His date, I guess."

"Frank was invited," he acknowledged.

"I thought you should be warned."

Brett nodded his thanks.

He shook a dozen more hands before he spotted Kate. Dressed in a chic black-and-white polka-dotted dress and matching white pillbox, she looked as if she belonged in the royal family. He wondered if a prince would have been good enough for Kate, or if she was more ambitious than that.

Olivia leaned over to be kissed once again and peeked at Brett as she straightened to greet the next guest. She wondered if Brett felt married. Right now he was looking wary. She imagined he was as tired as she was of shaking hands and hearing congratulations. He looked as if he wanted it to end.

"Olivia? I'm Kate Parsons, a friend of Brett's."

More than a friend. Olivia focused on the sophisticated woman in front of her and knew immediately who Kate was. She couldn't believe Brett had invited his former live-in lover to their wedding. She smiled mechanically. "How do you do, Kate?"

"It was quite a nice wedding. How did you manage it in such a short time?"

Olivia wanted to believe there had been no sting in Kate's words, but she wasn't that much of an optimist. Kate, with her untouchable blond beauty and her perfect smile, was enjoying this confrontation.

"We worked hard," Olivia said, answering only the most surface level of the question.

"Hello, Kate." Brett managed to pass one of the Le-Blanc uncles off into the crowd in time to come to Olivia's aid. "You've introduced yourself to Olivia?"

"I have. You look wonderful in a tux, Brett. But then you always do."

"Thank you."

"I wish you both the best," Kate said with a cold smile. "I know what being married means, especially to you, Brett."

Olivia tried not to flinch.

"And Brett's any young woman's dream, isn't he?" Kate went on, turning back to Olivia. "You'll be perfect for each other."

"I'm sure Frank is looking for you," Brett said, his voice deathly calm. He put his arm around Olivia as if for protection.

Kate's smile widened. "Take care of her, Brett. But then, you'll enjoy that, I'm sure." She turned and threaded her way into the crowd.

Olivia stiffened and tried to draw away from Brett, but he wouldn't let her. "I didn't invite her," he said quietly as the next person came to greet them. "She came with a friend of mine." He paused. "A former friend."

Olivia nodded. She was glad Brett had told her, and she believed he was telling the truth. The problem was that it didn't matter. Kate Parsons had a face now, and she was more beautiful than Olivia had ever imagined. More important, Kate had sliced right through the reasons for their marriage and exposed them. It was as if Kate had sensed Olivia's deepest, darkest doubts and spoken them out loud like a witch's curse. Olivia wished she could find a quiet place to recover.

There were no quiet places. Food and champagne flowed freely, and even though the next day was Christmas, people stayed to celebrate until well after seven.

Olivia had just finished chatting with Drew and Meg Sherwood when she felt Brett's arm around her waist. "It's time to go. Father Henley suggested we leave so everyone else will follow. He's got midnight mass to prepare for."

Olivia realized she'd been avoiding her new husband. Kate's words and her own anticipation of the night to come had made her shyer than ever before. She didn't feel like a radiant bride. She felt like an unsophisticated, overweight and undereducated country girl who had somehow snagged a wonderful man, a man who was quickly going to lose interest in her when he saw how unskilled she was in bed.

What had possessed Brett to marry her? Did he want a young woman he could mold into the perfect wife? Was he crazy?

"You should see the look on your face."

Olivia jumped. She had been so lost in her own thoughts that she'd forgotten where she was.

"You look like a lamb about to go to the slaughter. I promise tonight won't be that bad." Brett's words were low, husky and entirely for her. "You may even like it," he added.

"I must seem very foolish to you."

Brett realized that his teasing had only made things worse. He tried to reassure her. "You seem very beautiful to me, very sweet, very desirable." He lifted one of her hands and kissed it. "You seem like the woman I just promised to have and to hold until death do us part."

"You do realize that I'm only twenty-four. Till death do us part may be a very long time."

"It's a little late for second thoughts, Olivia." Brett lifted her chin with his fingertips. "Is it tonight you're worried about? I'm sorry I teased you. We can wait until you've had a chance to recuperate from the wedding. We have a whole week alone together and a lifetime after that. There's no hurry." He wished he were a little boy again so he could cross his fingers.

How could she explain that she was afraid he was going to be disappointed in her? That after seeing Kate she realized just how ordinary she really was? Kate had been Brett's first choice. Now Olivia knew what it meant to come in a distant second.

"Throw your bouquet and let's get out of here," Brett said, taking her silence as his answer.

The bouquet went to Mimi Broussard, who promptly pulled flowers out of it for each of her sisters until there was nothing left. Afterward Olivia and Brett ducked out the back door to find a small, dedicated group of well-wishers who had anticipated their exit. Pelted with rice, they raced to Brett's car to drive away to the sound of clanking tin cans tied to his bumper.

"Are you glad it's over?" Brett asked when they were safely away from the church.

"Yes. How about you?"

"I'll never forget how beautiful you were coming up that aisle. I'm glad we'll have photographs."

"Somebody stretched that aisle an extra hundred feet, just for the wedding." Olivia was encouraged by Brett's laughter. "I was sure they were going to have to play 'The Wedding March' six times just to get me to the altar."

"You looked so serene."

"I was saying the rosary." Olivia smiled, and she could feel herself relaxing. Away from the stress of the reception, she might just recover her equilibrium and self-confidence.

"You'll have to teach it to me. I could use it in court." Brett reached for Olivia's hand and put it on his knee. "I'm glad we're not going far."

"How far are we going?"

"I wondered when you were going to ask." Brett slowed down to turn off the highway onto a two-lane blacktop road. "The place was your father's idea."

"Don't tell me we're going to honeymoon on a shrimp boat?"

"Next best thing. You'll see in a few minutes."

Olivia smiled at his secretive manner. Then the full impact of his words hit her. "Brett, this was my father's idea?"

He nodded.

"You never should have let my father know where we were going! I told you this had to be a secret."

"You told me you didn't want to know. You didn't tell me it had to be a secret from your father."

Olivia groaned and hid her face in her hands. "We've both been so busy. I didn't think to warn you. This is all my fault."

"What on earth is the matter?"

"Stop the car. Turn around. We've got to go somewhere else."

"Olivia, it's Christmas Eve, for God's sake. A lot of places are closed for the holidays. Besides, I've already arranged this, and you're going to love it."

"If I'm right, you're not going to love it. I can guarantee it."

Brett pulled off on the side of the road and stopped the car. "What's going on?"

"Have you ever heard of a *charivari*?" She gave the word its French pronunciation.

"No."

"Well, if you're really lucky, you'll get through the next few nights without a live demonstration."

He touched her cheek. "Are you going to enlighten me?"

"It's a Cajun custom, one that's almost died out, I'm glad to say, but my father's family is famous for trying to keep it alive. It happens on the wedding night or some night soon after. A group of men come to the house of the bride and groom and, well, they serenade them with pots and pans and screeching.''

Brett was obviously trying not to laugh.

''I'm glad you think it's funny,'' she said, not meaning a word of it.

''I'm sure they won't do anything that barbaric,'' Brett promised, but his eyes were dancing.

''Maybe they won't be able to find twelve men. They have to have twelve men willing to be the leaders. Custom says we have to invite them in to entertain them afterward or they can keep it up for thirty nights.''

''I'm sure your father wouldn't want to traumatize you that way,'' Brett assured her.

''You'd like it if they did, wouldn't you? I can see it in your eyes.''

He slid his arms around her and pulled her to him. ''I'm going to like it all. I'm going to like everything about being married to you. Even the *charivari* that I'm sure we're not really going to have.''

She was beginning to believe he might just mean it.

Their honeymoon destination was the renovated slave quarters of an old plantation house sitting on the banks of Bayou Teche. With only a week until Brett had to go back to work, they had made a mutual decision to stay in Louisiana. But Olivia hadn't believed Brett would find anyplace so romantic, so perfect.

Inside she wandered through the three comfortable rooms, admiring the cypress paneling and the simple, tasteful furniture. The wavery glass of the windows showed moonlight on water and the thick, gnarled columns of live oaks. Spanish moss was draped from branch to branch, like the dainty patterns of the lace of her wedding veil.

''Do you like it?'' Brett asked, coming up behind her.

''I love it.'' Olivia turned and put her arms around his neck. ''How did you know? It's perfect.''

"I'll give you moonlight on the bayou anytime I can." He rested his hands at her waist. "Are you cold?"

She was, but she hadn't even noticed it. "There's a little fire in the fireplace. The plantation caretakers must have started it a while ago."

Brett nodded. "I asked them to. The heating system in here's about as old as the cabin, but not nearly as interesting. I'll get it going. Why don't you change?"

Change into what? Change into whom? Into someone like Kate, who would know exactly how to act right now? Olivia wanted to tell Brett to forget about the fire. They could snuggle under the covers and make their own heat. Their conversation at the reception, or rather Brett's conversation—she had been almost mute—stopped her, however. Brett had been very kind, but she had also sensed a disinterest in the outcome of this night. They were married; the rest would follow in its own good time. She wondered if now that they were husband and wife she had somehow lost her desirability.

Olivia's arms dropped to her side, and she turned and went into the bedroom where Brett had taken their suitcases. She closed the door behind her.

Brett exhaled forcefully. He hadn't expected this impasse. Olivia was shy, but in the weeks they had spent together, she had warmed up considerably. Now it seemed they were back to square one. He damned Kate for showing up and destroying Olivia's confidence. Kate was better at subtly tearing people to shreds than she was at anything else. He wanted to reassure Olivia, but he was afraid that if he even mentioned the scene at the reception again, it would make it more important than it had been.

He would just have to be patient tonight and not rush her. If worse came to worst, tomorrow he could send to New Orleans for a jug of Hurricanes.

Olivia stood in the bedroom and looked down at the body that now seemed woefully inadequate. She had gained more weight. She was positive she had. When had it happened? What was Brett going to say when he saw her naked for the first time? He'd probably never even seen a woman with breasts like these. And her hips? Maybe they were functionally perfect for childbearing, but how was she to explain that to him?

In the bathroom she took a quick shower and made firm plans not to eat anything for the next week. Maybe she couldn't start off her honeymoon looking like a model, but if she fasted during it, she might end up that way. If Brett saw she was trying, maybe he'd give her the benefit of the doubt. Maybe he wouldn't mind waiting until they were back in New Orleans to consummate the marriage. By then she'd be as skinny as a rail.

"Olivia?"

She dried off and slipped a nightgown and robe over her body, making sure the belt on the robe was tied tight. "I'll just be a minute."

Brett schooled himself not to pounce on Olivia the minute she came out. Admittedly, he hadn't had any practice with shy young virgins, but some inborn chivalrous part of him knew better than to scare her to death. He'd told her they could wait. He'd meant it, hadn't he?

The door opened, and she came out wearing a long, sheer white robe tied tightly around her narrow waist. It emphasized the hips and breasts that he'd been fantasizing about for weeks, and Brett swallowed twice to be sure his voice was calm. "You look as lovely as you did in your wedding dress."

If she'd hoped that the sight of her in her robe would bring him to his knees, she'd been wrong. Olivia swallowed twice to be sure her voice was calm. "Thank you. The water's hot if you want a shower."

He doubted he'd need the hot water.

"Why don't you go sit by the fire? It's heating the room nicely." Brett turned away to find his newly purchased pajamas.

Olivia was glad something was heating the room. Passion certainly wasn't. "I'll do that."

They passed each other with inches to spare.

When Brett came into the living room later, he found Olivia sitting in front of the flames with her arms wrapped around her knees. He imagined her lying back against the thick area rug, her body dressed only in firelight. He imagined himself beside her, on top of her, inside her. He imagined her convulsing around him and crying out with pleasure.

He imagined he needed another cold shower.

Olivia looked up and saw the stricken expression on Brett's face. Was he regretting their marriage already? Was he regretting it before he'd even slept with her? Somehow that possibility made her sit up a little straighter.

"I saw champagne in the refrigerator. Was that for tonight?" She was pleased with the ordinary sound of her voice.

Brett wondered if champagne was a reasonable substitute for Hurricanes. "The whole bottle."

"I'll get it." Olivia stood, and the firelight outlined the voluptuous symmetry of her body through the sheer robe.

Brett reminded his heart to beat. "I'll help."

The kitchen was tiny, with hardly enough room for two. Even so, they managed the champagne and crackers and cheese without touching each other, carrying it back into the living room to sit in front of the fire, the champagne between them.

"To many happy years," Brett toasted her.

"To a marriage like my parents'."

"I'll drink to that." Brett swallowed half his glass in one gulp.

Olivia just toyed with hers. Champagne had calories. She'd almost forgotten. And even though she hadn't eaten anything at the reception, the lure of the crackers and cheese was less than the lure of the perfect body she'd have if she quit eating entirely.

"It's been quite a day," Brett said, pouring himself another glassful.

"Quite a day," she affirmed.

"Don't try to pretend you're not exhausted," Brett said finally. Olivia hadn't taken a sip. His best and last hope for getting her to relax was shattered. "I think we should go to bed. To sleep," he added quickly. "We're both too tired to begin anything tonight."

She didn't know much about it, but somehow she'd believed a man was never too tired for lovemaking. Not if he was with a woman he truly desired. "All right," she said, not meeting his eyes. "I'm sure you know best."

Brett stood, pulling his unfamiliar robe around his unfamiliar pajamas. "I'll bank the fire."

"Then I'll go on to bed." Olivia stood, too. "Am I too tired to be kissed good-night?" She was surprised by the petulance in her own voice.

For a moment Brett wondered if he'd been wrong. She was angry. Olivia was definitely angry. He probed a little. "I don't know. Are you?"

"Probably." She forced herself to calm down and smile. "But that won't stop me." She stood on tiptoe and kissed him, not touching him in any other way.

Brett resisted pulling her close. It would be the end of his self-control. "Good night. I'll be in bed in a little while."

"Oh, don't hurry on my account." She turned, swishing the skirts of her gown and robe, and disappeared into the bedroom.

Chapter Nine

Brett woke up at midnight, which was strange in and of itself. He had to have been asleep to wake up, and he'd been absolutely certain that sleep was going to elude him that night. At first he wasn't sure what had awakened him—the faint baying of a hound in the distance, the brightness of the moonlight tracing distorted patterns through the windows, the absence of Olivia's quiet breathing.

Olivia! Brett sat up and felt the place where she had been lying. It was still warm from her body heat. She wasn't there. He wasn't imagining it. He swung his feet over the side of the bed and went to look for her.

The fire had died in the living room. He'd expected to find her there, but the room was empty. She wasn't in the kitchen, either.

Where could she have gone? Abruptly Brett realized what had disturbed his sleep. A sound, a faint click. The front door closing. He went back to the bedroom to find his jacket, then followed her into the night.

"Olivia." He waited, but there was no answer. He tried again, a little louder. "Olivia!"

"Brett?"

She sounded surprised. He wondered if she'd thought he wouldn't care that she had gone.

"I'm over here," she called.

He followed the sound of her voice toward the bayou. A statue in white stood on the bank gazing at the water. He shook his head and removed his jacket, lifting her tousled hair to drape the jacket around her shoulders. She was wearing nothing more than her gown and robe, and the night was cold.

"What are you doing out here?" he scolded. "You're going to freeze."

"I couldn't sleep. I wanted to see the bayou."

"The bayou will be here tomorrow."

"I was thinking about Evangeline."

"Evangeline who?"

"Longfellow's Evangeline. Only I was thinking about the woman, Emmeline Labiche, whose life the poem's probably based on."

"You couldn't think about it inside?'

"Do you know the story, Brett? It's so sad."

Resigned, he put his arm around her. "No."

"Emmeline was separated from her fiancé, Louis Arceneaux, during the *grand dérangement*."

"When the Acadians were expelled from Nova Scotia?"

"Yes, back in the eighteenth century. She was put on one boat; he was put on another. Emmeline ended up in Maryland, and Louis here, at St. Martinville on Bayou Teche. Louis was certain he'd never see Emmeline again; he didn't even know if she'd lived. But years later Emmeline migrated to St. Martinville, along with her guardian. The first person she saw when the boat docked on the shore of the bayou was Louis. She ran to him, and he reached out to her, but then he turned away. He could never call Emmeline his own. He was betrothed to another. The story goes that Emmeline lost her mind after that. She wandered the banks of the bayou, picking flowers and talking about Louis and how he had been taken away by the British and killed. She finally died of a broken heart.''

"Olivia, why are you thinking such sad thoughts?'' He turned her to him and gathered her against his chest. ''You haven't lost anyone. We're just starting our life together.''

"We haven't started anything. Our marriage isn't real yet.''

He wondered if she could hear his heart beat faster. "Are you afraid we'll be separated before we do? That I'll find another lover?''

"You had another lover. She's already come between us.''

He held her tighter, trying to make sense out of what she was saying. "How has Kate come between us? She came to the reception; she said a few unkind things. But what I had with her has been over for months. How can she affect us now?''

"I saw her, Brett. She's beautiful and sophisticated and probably brilliant. She's all the things I'm not. You wanted her before you wanted me. No wonder you weren't excited about being my lover tonight.'' Her voice broke, and she bit her lip.

Brett couldn't believe what he was hearing. "Not excited? I've never wanted anything or anyone as badly as I've wanted you tonight. I just didn't want to rush you. You seemed so distant, so tired. I care too much about you to make you unhappy.''

"Unhappy?'' She lifted her head. "I couldn't be more unhappy than I've been tonight.''

"Then why didn't you tell me what you wanted? Why didn't you show me? Is that supposed to be entirely up to me?''

"I was afraid to.''

"Afraid of what? Afraid I'd tell you I was dreaming of Kate tonight?" He shook her gently. "I left Kate. I moved out of our apartment; she didn't leave me. I left her because I realized she wasn't what I wanted anymore. Maybe my relationship with you developed at the speed of light, but that doesn't mean it wasn't real or that it was second best. It means that it was so right, nothing could stand in its way. Nothing except your crazy insecurities."

Olivia pushed away from him. "You didn't even try to touch me tonight! What was I supposed to think except that maybe I'd made a big mistake marrying you?"

Brett crossed his arms over his chest and stared at her. "You can stay out here and think what you want," he said finally. "I'm going to bed." He turned and started back toward the cabin.

Olivia shivered and pulled his jacket tighter around her. "Brett?"

"What?" He paused at the cabin door, his back to her.

She wasn't sure what to say. She only knew she had to say something. "This is our first fight."

"Memorable, isn't it?"

"I don't want to fight."

"You could have fooled me."

She cleared her throat, and the sound seemed as loud as a rifle shot. "Do you still want me?"

"What do you think?"

"I love you."

He turned slowly, and in the brightness of the moonlight she thought she could read triumph in his expression. He held out his arms. "Come to bed, Olivia."

She ran to him, and he lifted her and strode across the threshold.

Inside, the cabin seemed warm in comparison to the icy chill of the night air. Brett laid Olivia on the bed and stripped off the jacket and robe. Then he chafed her bare arms to warm them. She shook her head and smiled, reaching up to pull him down on top of her.

"Not so fast, bright eyes," he warned. "Or this is going to be over before it begins."

"I don't care. The suspense is killing me."

He laughed with delight but refused a kiss. "I care. How many firsts do we get to celebrate together?" He smoothed her hair back from her face and gave her a chaste kiss on the forehead. "I want to enjoy them all slowly. The first time I undress you. The first time I see you naked in the moonlight. The first time I learn the feel of your body with my lips. The first time I make you mine . . ."

"I don't know if I'll live through all that," she said breathlessly.

He laughed again and lowered his mouth to her ear. His tongue explored its delicate contours. "You're shivering."

"Believe me, I'm not cold." Tentatively she lifted the fabric of his pajama top and stroked his back.

"Aren't you? Then what could it be?" Brett drew his lips along her neck and over her jawline, still avoiding her mouth. He kissed her cheek, her nose, her eyelids, before he moved to torment her other ear.

Olivia moaned and rotated her hips against his. Her fingertips dug into his warm skin. He moved his mouth lower, finding the pulse beat in her neck, the hollow at the base of her throat, the smooth skin exposed by the low neckline of her gown. "Did you wear this to drive me crazy?" he murmured. "It covers just enough to make me wonder what it's covering and just little enough to keep me from thinking about anything else."

He brushed a hand along her shoulder and nudged the strap of her gown lower, exposing the top of one breast. His mouth followed, lingering to absorb the feel of her against his lips. She turned a little, and the strap fell lower until nothing was covered but the hardened peak of her breast.

He kissed it, then drew it into his mouth to suckle through the cloth.

Olivia arched toward him and gasped at the sensation. Her hands came around to his chest, whether to push him away or hold him to her she wasn't certain. But it didn't matter, because he moved and began to nudge the other strap down her shoulder. For a moment she was imprisoned by the thin bands of cloth, and her hands fell to her side. Then she was free, and she knew Brett was looking at her. She shut her eyes.

"You're more beautiful than any fantasy." Gently he cupped her breasts and lifted them to the moonlight. "Absolute perfection."

She heard the awe in his voice, felt the faint tremor of his hands. She wanted to cry with relief. Instead she cried out with pleasure as he took one breast and then the other into his mouth and laved them with his tongue, washing them with kisses.

She had waited so long for this, for the full joy of total intimacy. She could feel herself being pulled into a whirlpool of sensation, and she went freely, refusing to fight to keep any part of herself separate. This was right. This was just as it should be. She offered herself to his mouth, to his hands, knowing she was offering much more.

Brett sat up and unbuttoned his pajama top, throwing it to the floor. She needed his patience, and he fought the desire to end the suspense as Olivia had asked. His skin was hot to the touch; his heart pounded until there was no space between the beats; his blood poured through his veins in rushing agony. He hadn't known it was possible to need someone so much. He had never, never wanted anyone the way he wanted her.

Olivia opened her eyes and saw Brett's battle in the tense slant of his mouth and the dark, feral gleam of his eyes. She reached up and pulled him down once more to lie on top of her as her trembling hands kneaded his back. She traced the muscles that flowed under his skin with her fingertips and ran her fingernails down his spine, drinking in his groans of pleasure.

The innocence of her caresses excited him as nothing else would have. She was giving in the only way she knew how. Giving. Giving. Giving for the first time, giving to him alone. He wanted to take forever and give in the taking. Taking, giving, who knew where it began?

He was exploding with desire, his skin too stretched, too agonizingly tight, to hold him any longer. Brett wanted to feel all of Olivia, every warm satin inch of her body. He needed to feel her, to know he was feeling her in a way no one else ever had. He slid his hands between them and slipped her gown lower until there was nothing between them except the cotton of his pajama bottoms and the silk of her panties.

His hands traveled the full length of her body, and then there was nothing between them except his pajamas. And then not even those.

Olivia could feel Brett's arousal throbbing hot and hard against her legs. She tensed, sure for one crazy second that there had been some mistake. She couldn't contain him. It wasn't physically possible. Centuries of human procreation were no proof at all.

He felt the sudden tension in her body and knew its cause. Stifling a groan, he guided her hand to touch him, clasping it around him to feel his heat and his slick supersensitivity to her touch. "You can control it," he whispered thickly. "In a little while I'll be part of both of us. You'll have control, too."

"I'm sorry."

"Don't you ever apologize to me in bed." He kissed her hard to take any sting out of his words.

She sighed, reassured. His mouth found her ear, her neck, as his hand found her breasts. She explored him delicately with her fingers, learning the exact shape and feel of him until he was no longer a stranger, but the man she wanted, the man who was making love to her so sweetly she wasn't sure she was going to live through it.

Tentatively she opened her legs to invite him home. He moved away to lie beside her. "Not yet. Not quite yet." His voice was husky, each breath a torture. He was surprised that he could form words. He ran his eyes over her, the full, lush breasts, silver-white and pink in the moonlight, the tiny waist, the hips that so perfectly balanced the rest of her body, the long, slender legs. She was his. He felt humbled.

"I could lose weight," she offered.

"Olivia!" He laughed and groaned and covered her, almost simultaneously. "Not a pound. Not an ounce." He kissed her fiercely, and with a muffled cry she wrapped her legs around him and kissed him back. She could feel his hands exploring her, adoring her, and then she could feel his hand between them, readying her for their union.

She was slipping away to a place where she couldn't think at all, a place Brett was taking her where the only reality was what he was doing to her and the sound of her voice begging him for more.

Then there was more. The feel of him against her. The feel of him moving inside her. A brief moment of pain and a whispered, loving encouragement. Then nothing except an explosion of sensation and no reality at all except the feel of his body moving against hers and the knowledge that marrying him hadn't been a mistake after all.

"Merry Christmas."

Olivia turned over to stare at her new husband. Only moments ago the room had been filled with moonlight. Now it was flooded with sunshine.

"Merry Christmas, sleepyhead." Brett leaned over to kiss her. With satisfaction she saw that he wasn't dressed except for his pajama bottoms. She knew what she wanted for Christmas.

The more
you love romance . . .
the more
you'll love this offer

FREE!

*Mail this
heart today!
(See inside)*

Join us on a Silhouette® Honeymoon
and we'll give you
4 free books
A free manicure set
And a free mystery gift

IT'S A
SILHOUETTE HONEYMOON —
A SWEETHEART
OF A FREE OFFER!

HERE'S WHAT YOU GET:

1. Four New Silhouette Special Edition® Novels — FREE!

Take a Silhouette Honeymoon with your four exciting romances — yours FREE from Silhouette Books. Each of these hot-off-the-press novels brings you the passion and tenderness of today's greatest love stories . . . your free passports to bright new worlds of love and foreign adventure.

2. A compact manicure set — FREE!

You'll love your beautiful manicure set — an elegant and useful accessory to carry in your handbag. Its rich burgundy case is a perfect expression of your style and good taste — and it's yours free with this offer!

3. An Exciting Mystery Bonus — FREE!

You'll be thrilled with this surprise gift. It will be the source of many compliments, as well as a useful and attractive addition to your home.

4. Money-Saving Home Delivery!

Join the Silhouette Special Edition subscriber service and enjoy the convenience of previewing 6 new books every month delivered right to your home. Each book is yours for only $2.49 — 26¢ less per book than what you pay in stores. And there is no extra charge for postage and handling. Great savings plus total convenience add up to a sweetheart of a deal for you!

5. Free Newsletter!

You'll get our monthly newsletter, packed with news on your favorite writers, upcoming books, even recipes from your favorite authors.

6. More Surprise Gifts!

Because our home subscribers are our most valued readers, we'll be sending you additional free gifts from time to time — as a token of our appreciation.

START YOUR SILHOUETTE HONEYMOON TODAY — JUST
COMPLETE, DETACH AND MAIL YOUR FREE-OFFER CARD

Get your fabulous gifts
ABSOLUTELY FREE!

MAIL THIS CARD TODAY.

PLACE
HEART STICKER
HERE

GIVE YOUR HEART
TO SILHOUETTE

Yes! Please send me my four Silhouette Special Edition novels FREE, along with my free manicure set and free mystery gift as explained on the opposite page.

NAME _____
(PLEASE PRINT)

ADDRESS _____ APT. _____

CITY _____ STATE _____

ZIP CODE _____ 235 CIL R1WZ

Prices subject to change. Offer limited to one per household and not valid to present subscribers.

SILHOUETTE BOOKS "NO-RISK" GUARANTEE

— There's no obligation to buy — and the free books and gifts remain yours to keep.

— You pay the lowest price possible and receive books before they appear in stores.

— You may end your subscription any time — just write and let us know.

PRINTED IN U.S.A.

START YOUR
SILHOUETTE HONEYMOON TODAY.
JUST COMPLETE, DETACH AND MAIL YOUR
FREE-OFFER CARD.

If offer card below is missing, write to:
Silhouette Books, 901 Fuhrmann Blvd., P.O. Box 9013, Buffalo, N.Y. 14240-9013

BUSINESS REPLY CARD

First Class   Permit No. 717   Buffalo, NY

Postage will be paid by addressee

Silhouette Books
901 Fuhrmann Blvd.
P.O. Box 9013
Buffalo, NY 14240-9933

NO POSTAGE
NECESSARY
IF MAILED
IN THE
UNITED STATES

DETACH AND MAIL TODAY!

"Merry Christmas." She reached up to push his hair off his forehead. "What time is it?"

"Time for all good Christmas angels to get up."

"What if this little angel wants to spend the day in bed?"

"That's no angel talking. Next you'll tell me you want me to spend the day in bed with you."

"I want you to spend the day in bed with me."

"After breakfast." He smiled at her, and the smile was so warm, so satisfied, that she wanted to purr with pleasure. "I've been busy while you lay here looking desirable."

"You could have gotten me up earlier."

"I tried. You distinctly said, 'Go away!'"

"I did not!" She sat up before she realized she was naked. When she grabbed for the sheets, Brett held them away. His eyes devoured her.

"Merry Christmas," he said finally, pulling his gaze back to hers. "I believe I've just gotten my present."

"Part of it." Olivia knew her cheeks were rosy, but she made no attempt to cover herself again.

"There's more to come?"

She smiled, and the smile was as old as woman. "A lot more."

"What could it be?"

"Would you like me to show you?"

"An attorney always needs proof."

She smoothed her hand along his arm, up to his shoulder, then up his neck to his cheek. "I'm sort of new at this, but they say enthusiasm counts for a lot."

"I have a feeling they're right."

Her fingers tangled in his hair as her other hand began the same journey. She leaned over to brush her lips across his, savoring the early-morning intimacy. Then her lips parted, and she no longer savored, she ached.

"The morning after is highly underrated," Brett said with a moan as he clasped her against him.

"Will I always want you this much?" she asked, her lips traveling along his chin and down his neck. "Will this change after a hundred times or a thousand?"

Nothing in his experience could provide an answer. He could only hold her tighter and begin to resolve the question in her arms.

Breakfast was croissants, fresh fruit and coffee. Olivia ate her share happily, sure that whatever weight she gained was going to be worked off by the end of their honeymoon anyway. Brett served the simple breakfast in bed, setting it up on trays while she showered.

She felt pampered and seductively female as she sat next to him against the pillows, feeding him sections of peeled orange and slices of banana from her fingertips. He had showered and shaved while she'd slept, and with his hair still rumpled from their lovemaking, she had never seen him look more appealing.

"It really is Christmas, isn't it?" Olivia sighed, satisfied in every possible way. "Christmas has always been my favorite holiday."

"If this Christmas is any example, I think it's going to be mine, too."

Olivia didn't need to ask what his childhood Christmases had been like. Without a family of his own, she knew they must have been bleak. "Next year we'll spend it with my family," she said decisively. "Everyone should witness a LeBlanc Christmas."

"I'd like that." He covered her hand with his and brought it to his mouth for a quick kiss. "But if you're done with breakfast, it's time to witness a Terrill Christmas, Brett and Olivia style."

"I think I'm going to like this."

At Brett's insistence, she changed into jeans and a heavy sweater, then followed him into the living room. "Okay, what's on the agenda?'' she asked, pretending to roll up her sleeves.

''You don't have to do that. Yet.'' Brett pretended to whip a pad and pencil out of his pocket, like the waitress at a truck stop. ''All right, lady, what'll you have? One Christmas coming up. What d'ya need?''

Olivia pretended to think, tapping her finger on her cheek and rolling her eyes to the ceiling. ''Music. We've got to have Christmas music as our appetizer.''

''Lady, we don't have anything as plush as appetizers in a dive like this, but I can give you an order of music with your Christmas.'' With a flourish Brett opened the door of the coat closet and pulled out a portable tape player. One punch of the button and ''O Holy Night'' sounded through the little cabin.

''Incredible! What else do you have in there?'' Olivia walked toward him, but Brett stood in front of the closet and shook his head.

''Don't be pushy, lady. You'll get your Christmas in good time. What else you wanna order?''

''A tree?''

''One Christmas tree. You gotta go outside for that one, lady,'' he said, writing her request on his imaginary pad. ''Next?''

''Outside?''

''Next?'' he said louder.

''Decorations for this invisible outside tree.''

''Easy.'' Brett reached inside the closet, drew out a small box and handed it to her. ''Next?''

Olivia peeked inside. She recognized the ornaments immediately. The LeBlancs had a custom of adding one ornament each year for each person in the family. She had chosen this selection herself since the time she was old enough to go shopping with her mother, and obviously her mother had been in on this surprise. She clutched them to her.

"Next?" Brett tapped his foot.

"A wreath? Holly? Decorations for the cabin?"

He reached back into the closet and pulled out another box. "Nothing fancy, you understand. This ain't no fancy joint."

She giggled at the assortment of dime-store tinsel and plastic holly. There was a candle depicting a fat Santa stuck in a chimney and a set of plastic lights that were money-back-guaranteed to twinkle. She loved it all.

"I hate to be a glutton," she said, looking up to give him a dazzling smile. "But there are two things missing from this Christmas. Presents and Christmas dinner."

"Sorry, lady. But you gotta work for your presents. The tree's gotta go up first. Dinner's tonight, up at the plantation house. They've got guests staying there, too. And you forgot the Christmas cookies."

"Christmas cookies?"

He pulled a tin out of the closet. "Compliments of some dame name of Myriam. I think she wants a job here or sumpthin'."

"My mother made these for us?" She pried open the tin. "Oh, look. Snickerdoodles and butter cookies and ginger-bread men. How did she have time to make these?"

He shrugged. "She's a crazy dame. Said something about it bein' sacrilegious not to have Christmas cookies on Christmas day."

"Brett, I love it." She set the tin down and threw herself into his arms. "I love you."

"Bright eyes." He wrapped his arms around her and held her as tightly as he could, the charade forgotten. "I'm so glad you do."

At that moment she was sure that nothing he could have said would have been sweeter.

Brett hadn't been teasing about the tree. It was outside, all right. It was in a small grove of pines planted years ago by the far-sighted plantation owners. With dozens to choose from, Brett and Olivia found one that was small enough to be easy to drag back and large enough to hold their array of ornaments. Brett had gotten a stand from the caretakers, along with permission to cut a tree, and with Olivia's laughing supervision he installed it in the corner by the front door.

They fought over where each ornament should go, and Olivia told Brett the story behind them, marveling as she did that he never seemed to tire of hearing about her childhood and her family. The lights didn't work at first, and they adjusted and readjusted them, replacing each bulb and testing until the whole string was blinking on and off like the vacancy sign at a cheap motel.

"There now," Olivia said, hands on hips. "We're done. Where's my Christmas present?"

"*Your* Christmas present? I'm your Christmas present. Where's *my* Christmas present?" Brett came up behind her and put his arms around her waist.

"You got it this morning. Have you forgotten already?"

"That was it?"

She turned in his arms. "No exchange. No refund. Even if you don't like it, you're stuck with it."

"I guess I'll cope." Brett pulled a small package out of his shirt pocket and handed it to her. "Merry Christmas."

She pulled him over to the tree, and they sat under the twinkling lights as she unwrapped it. Inside the square box sat an emerald ring surrounded by tiny diamonds.

"We didn't have time for a real engagement. I wanted you to have a ring but there was never time to go out together and look for one. I hope you like it."

"It's beautiful. It's perfect." Olivia held out her hand and let him slip it on next to her plain gold band. "I love it."

"It suits you. The color is so vivid. Emeralds are so warm. I couldn't see you in just a diamond. Diamonds are all reflection with no warmth of their own."

Olivia was deeply touched. Obviously Brett had thought long and hard about the ring.

She had thought long and hard about his present, too. It wasn't nearly as extravagant, but she thought he'd like it anyway. "Wait here," she said, squeezing his hand.

She came back a few moments later with a large manila envelope. She held it out to him, then sat at his feet and waited.

Brett pulled a single sheet of paper from the envelope. "Crosby's Folly?"

"That's just his name for the registration papers. He's an Irish setter. His father's a champion: Crosby of County Cork. The mother is a nobody, I'm ashamed to say, although she's registered, too. Anyway, Crosby Senior took a secret liking to her despite her humble lineage, and the litter of puppies was the result of someone not watching them very carefully. That's how the puppy got his name."

"A puppy." Brett stared at the paper and wondered if Olivia understood exactly what she had just done.

She clapped her hands in excitement. "Brett, he's the most beautiful puppy I've ever seen. The breeders are friends of Cherry and Lenny's, and I got pick of the litter. He'll be ready to go home with us a week or so after we get back."

He didn't know what to say.

"Don't tell me you don't like Irish setters." When he still didn't say anything, she went on quickly. "It's okay if you don't. The breeders understand that you have final approval. If you don't like him, we can choose another kind of dog or something else. A bird or a guinea pig. Or a fern." Her voice trailed off.

Brett's smile was warmer than the Louisiana sun in August. He found his voice. "Of course I'll love him. A fern, Olivia?" He laughed softly and reached over to haul her into his lap. "It's just that dogs and I go a ways back. I wanted one as a kid and never had one. Then, when I was an adult and could buy myself one, I was working too hard to take care of it properly. It's like being offered your heart's desire and being so used to having to deny it you've almost forgotten how to say yes."

"Say yes."

"Yes. Very much yes."

"He has huge brown eyes, Brett, and this little warm nose, and a tail that's in perpetual motion. I'm going to miss Lucy and Trey terribly. I've got to have something to fuss over until I get used to being a lady of leisure."

"You can fuss over me."

She realized he was only half kidding. He was going to love that aspect of marriage: the home-cooked meals, the clean apartment, the wife waiting for him with his favorite drink in her hand. They were things she would love doing for him, too. "Fussing over you goes without saying," she assured him. "But when you're not home, I can fuss over the puppy."

"Wait a minute. Whose present is he?" he asked sternly.

"Definitely yours. But if you're smart, you'll hire me to dog sit."

"A dog nanny." He thought about it and nodded his head. "While I'm at it, is there anything else I can hire you to do?"

She smiled seductively. "Cook your meals, keep your apartment clean."

"Windows? Do you do windows?"

"Absolutely not. But after this week's training, I might be experienced enough to warm your bed at night."

"Forget a week's training. You're experienced enough right now."

She framed his face in her hands and lowered her eyelids. "Right now?" She hesitated. "So soon?"

"If not sooner."

"And does it have to be your bed?"

"What else did you have in mind?"

"Well, you seem to have a thing about firsts. And this is our first Christmas tree." She leaned forward to kiss him.

He tangled his fingers in her hair and laid her gently on the rug. "I'm all for starting a Christmas tradition."

Later, his body satiated, he lay on the rug beside Olivia and watched her sleep. He had brought a quilt from the bedroom to cover her, and she lay beneath it, her head pillowed on her folded hands. Asleep, she looked like a virginal Snow White. He, of course, knew how far from the truth that was. Already there was nothing virginal about her responses. He hadn't expected the wholehearted demonstrations of her love, the nearly immediate loss of her inhibitions. He had known she was a giver, but he hadn't dared hope that she would be this comfortable giving herself totally. He had schooled himself to patience. Now he had a large cache of it left over in case he ever needed it for something else.

It was Christmas. Carefully he reached over to touch her hair. The black strands fell across her cheek, spilling over the quilt and across his arm. In her sleep she moved closer, as if she were seeking his warmth.

It was Christmas, and Olivia had given him the best Christmas of his life. She sighed and her eyes fluttered open. "I love you," she murmured with a sleepy smile just before her eyes closed again.

Something new began to fill the empty place inside him.

Chapter Ten

"Don't worry! I grew up on roads like these!" Olivia glanced at Brett and repressed a laugh. In deference to the lack of color in his cheeks, she slowed his BMW to a more reasonable speed.

"Mario Andretti, move over." Brett watched the speedometer creep to the left. "And you seemed like such a sweet, shy little thing."

"I'm a good driver. It's just that I'm...I'm..."

"Fast?" he supplied. "A maniac? A show-off?"

She ignored him. "This car is wonderful. My Toyota strains at high speeds."

"God bless the Japanese auto industry. When we get back tomorrow I'm going to trade in this car." He peered at the speedometer again. "For a horse."

"I don't want to go back. This has been wonderful."

Olivia reached over to pat him on the knee, but Brett put her hand back on the steering wheel. "One hand won't do, bright eyes. And don't take your eyes off the road, either."

"I'll have you know I've never had an accident."

"It just takes one. See if I suggest you practice driving my car again."

She turned on to the road running in front of the plantation and stopped the car with a flourish at their cabin. "Arrive Alive. That's my motto."

"I thought it was Speed Indeed." Brett got out and came around to open Olivia's door, but she was already waiting for him.

"Let's walk down to the bayou." She held out her hand.

"If my knees will still hold me."

"It's been a perfect honeymoon."

He squeezed her fingers, and she squeezed back. In their weeks together she'd learned that Brett didn't talk about his feelings, but he still found ways to communicate at least some of them to her. He was an honest man, a man who didn't pull any punches, but he couldn't be direct about what was happening inside him if he didn't understand it. She suspected that he'd had so little practice feeling anything except pain that pain was the only emotion he could readily identify.

Somehow, none of that mattered. She loved him, and she could see the way he was responding to her love. He would open up to her someday. In the meantime she would treasure each squeeze of her hand, each spontaneous kiss, each time he looked at her as if he didn't believe she was real.

At the bayou bank Olivia sat next to Brett and put her head on his shoulder. The dark water flowed slowly in front of them, catching the glint of sunlight and reflecting it back to the winter sky. She sighed, sorry that their honeymoon was almost over, yet glad their life together was beginning. "I think we should come back here every year."

"It won't be nearly as romantic with kids."

She tried to imagine having children of her own. Somehow she couldn't. In her fantasies all children were strawberry blondes like Trey and Lucy, and they went back to their real mother at the end of the day. "I wonder what our children will look like."

"You, I hope."

"I was hoping they'd look like you."

"One of each."

"Do you want them soon?" Olivia rubbed Brett's back in wide, circular motions. It was just one of the things she'd learned he loved.

Brett thought about her question. He wanted children immediately, but he sensed a reluctance on Olivia's part to make that commitment. And as much as he wanted to start a family, he suspected she was right. They needed more time alone together first.

"Well," he said, trying to put his feelings into words, "I've wanted children a long time, but I've wanted you for a long time, too."

"Seven weeks was not a long time," she teased. "And that's if you wanted me from the moment we met."

"I've wanted you longer than that. I've wanted you since I was old enough to think about women."

She smiled her pleasure. "So you want to wait a while?"

"I'm willing. I want to spend time with you, and from what I hear, babies have a habit of making that difficult."

"I want your children. But I'm glad we're not going to rush it."

He put his arm around her waist. "Besides, we'll need a bigger place to raise them. When we get back, let's look for a house of our own."

Olivia was genuinely surprised. She had just assumed they would continue living in the apartment on Bayou St. John. She had moved most of her belongings there the week before the wedding. "A house, Brett? What kind of house? Where?"

"We have a wide choice, and there's no hurry. I'd like you to take charge of narrowing it down, if you would. There's a lot to think about: school systems, neighborhoods, security, commuting distances for me."

"Price?"

"We won't worry too much about that."

She was silent for a little while. There was so much she didn't know about the man sitting next to her. They were married, and she wasn't even sure if she should shop the sales at the local grocery store or select prime cuts from the exclusive market where Cherry made an order every week. "Maybe you'd better enlighten me about our financial status," she said at last. "So I'll know when to pinch pennies and when not to."

They were married, but they knew so little about each other. Brett realized he'd been unfair by not telling her more about himself.

"I make a good living." He named a figure that made Olivia give a low whistle in response. "But in addition to that I came into money when my mother died a couple of years ago. It's all invested, but I can liquidate anything we need for a down payment."

Olivia knew that Brett's mother was dead; he'd told her that when she'd broached the subject of inviting her to the wedding. Now she cautiously probed a little, trying to know him better. "I can't understand something. If your mother was wealthy, why were you in foster care? Why didn't she just hire someone to take care of you?"

He made the story as succinct as possible. "She wasn't always wealthy. She owned a bar, and over the years she expanded until she owned a string of them. By the time she died they were worth a considerable amount. She called them cocktail lounges so they'd be more respectable, but no matter what she called them, they were places that never closed. She was always there, and evidently she didn't have time for a child. At first she did hire people to watch out for me, but they were probably just people she'd met at the bar. One of them took to knocking me around, and a neighbor called the police. I don't even remember it, I was so young, but it was in my foster-care record. Anyway, the state stepped in, looked around a little bit and told my mother she'd have to start staying at home herself or find good-quality care."

Olivia was appalled. She was glad she would never have to look the woman who had neglected him in the face. "And did she try to work out a better situation?"

"I don't know how hard she tried. But the next person she hired drank. She passed out early one evening. I wandered outside, probably to find my mother, and ended up in the street. I was hit by a car."

Olivia drew in a sharp breath.

"That time the state stopped negotiating. When I got out of the hospital they put me in foster care, and I stayed in until I was eighteen."

"You saw your mother sometimes, didn't you?" She tried to keep her voice as even as he'd kept his, but she felt as if someone was tearing her into tiny pieces.

"Sometimes. She'd get all dressed up and come over to see me four or five times a year. She'd bring me extravagant presents that made all the other kids in the house hate me, and then she'd yell at my foster mother and tell her what a bad job she was doing. She'd always promise she was going straight to child welfare to get me back. When she left I'd be upset for weeks, afraid she'd really get custody again and afraid she wouldn't. By the time I was in my teens I knew what a lie it all was. So then I'd give away the presents and spend my time trying to calm my foster parents and persuade them to keep me so I wouldn't have to change homes again."

The story was even worse than Olivia had imagined. How could he possibly have turned into the man he was? Brett, the child, had been neglected, abused, pulled back and forth like a tiny puppet on a string, with no one able to or even allowed to rescue him. He had rescued himself. That he could pull himself out of the mire of his background and become the man she knew was more than surprising. It was a testimony to the resilience of the human spirit. It was a testimony to his exceptional strength and sensitivity. But, oh, how she ached for him.

"Did you ever tell your mother what you thought about the way she'd treated you?" she asked finally, when she could trust herself to sound calm.

He shook his head. "As an adult I just stayed as far away from her as possible. She had all the family she needed at work every day. She didn't need me, and by then I sure didn't need her. I hadn't seen her for over a year before she died."

"What about your father?"

"He was out of the picture before I was born, some patron at her bar, I guess."

Olivia compared Brett's life story to her own. He had so much to be proud of; he was well-respected professionally, and at the wedding she had seen how many people genuinely liked him. He had been given the worst of beginnings, but he had managed to thrive and grow anyway. How easy her own life had been in comparison.

His story also explained a lot about why he had married her. Brett no longer needed a mother. Even at her most insecure, Olivia didn't believe he was trying to make up for that lack in his life. But he did need and want a woman who could provide his own children with what he'd missed, and he did need and want a woman who wouldn't sacrifice her family for her own personal success.

She was that woman. Brett had chosen well. They had a lifetime together now. He would enjoy being taken care of— just as he enjoyed taking care of her—but even more, he would enjoy creating something good and strong together. So would she.

"I'm glad we're a family now," she said simply, because saying more would sound like pity, and she knew Brett wouldn't appreciate that.

His thanks for her tact was in his voice. "So am I."

She rose and held out her hand to help him up. "It's getting dark; let's go inside. This is our last night here together."

Standing, he scooped her up to carry her into the house as he had on their wedding night. Olivia clasped her arms around his neck and relaxed against him. "You know, you're not obligated to keep doing this," she said blissfully. "I can walk."

"Remember what I told you about firsts?"

"I'm never going to forget it."

"Well, I forgot to tell you that I feel the same way about lasts."

She kissed his neck. "If I recall correctly, there have been some very special in-betweens, too."

"What in the hell is that noise?" Brett sat bolt upright in bed and peered into the darkness.

"Brett, turn off the television," Olivia mumbled sleepily.

"The cabin doesn't have a television." Brett threw off the covers and swung his feet over the edge of the bed. He scrambled hastily into his jeans.

"There's a rock concert on our front porch." Olivia sat up and stretched, watching with interest as he tried to find the sleeves of his shirt. "Why?"

"You tell me. It's in French."

She giggled, no longer feigning ignorance. "I warned you." Yawning, she slid out of bed to find her robe. "You know, they're all going to be very surprised to find you fully dressed at this hour. You're supposed to show up with next to nothing on."

"All who?" He hopped on one foot as he slipped on a shoe.

"I knew you didn't take me seriously. I hope you learn your lesson."

He sat down hard on the bed and the springs protested. "This is the cherry-very?"

She giggled at his pronunciation. "*Charivari*," she corrected him. "If you're going to host one, you'd better learn to pronounce it. I was expecting it. They knew this was our last night."

"Aren't we lucky they didn't forget?" he said, his voice dripping sarcasm.

"Well, that's one way to look at it." She giggled again. Now that she was an ancient bride of one week, she didn't feel embarrassed at all. They could say what they wanted, do what they wanted, it didn't matter. "Not everyone gets one, you know. I told you the custom's just about died out. And even when it was common, they usually only did it if the bride or groom had something to be ashamed of. If she was a widow marrying a man too young or if he was a widower marrying a girl just out of school. Something like that."

"Save the lesson in Cajun culture until we get rid of them, please."

"All right." She bit her lip to stop another series of giggles and sat meekly on the bed.

Brett stopped at the door. "How in the hell *do* we get rid of them?"

"I'm not allowed to say. No lessons in Cajun culture. Remember?"

"Cute, Olivia."

"We both have to go outside and be very polite to them. You ask what they want, and they'll tell you. Then you have to give it to them. And if you're not nice, well . . ." She shrugged gracefully. "Who can say what will happen? But like I told you, they've been known to keep this up for thirty nights.''

"They can't. We're going home tomorrow."

"They can all drive."

"That's a long way."

"Did I ever tell you who taught me how to make all those hairpin turns?" Olivia knew by the look on Brett's face that he understood. "That's right," she affirmed. "My father."

Outside the noise had escalated. There were over a dozen men, and each one was banging spoons on pots as he sang or shouted at the top of his lungs.

"You wanted family," she reminded Brett as he muttered ungratefully under his breath.

He threw the door open, and the din increased. Brett and Olivia nodded and smiled, until finally her father, obviously the ringleader, lifted his hand in the air. There was instant silence.

"How nice to see you fine gentlemen," Olivia said. "I thought we weren't going to have this pleasure."

"Heh! You know better than that," Etienne said with a big grin. "You shoulda run for cover."

"Well, thank you for waiting until our honeymoon was almost over," she said politely. "Brett?"

"What can we do for you?" Brett asked, as he'd been instructed. "Anything we have is yours."

"I'll take the BMW," Richard, Olivia's youngest brother, yelled.

"No, you won't," Brett answered with the ghost of a smile. "Anything else?"

"Drinks to toast you with. That's all," Etienne said generously.

Brett looked skeptical, but Olivia patted his arm in reassurance. "There's plenty. I bought beer when I went out to replenish our groceries the other day. It's out on the back porch. I'm sure it's cold enough."

"You really knew they were coming, didn't you?"

"I told you."

Brett's back was sore from good-natured slaps, and Olivia had been kissed enough to scrape her face raw, when the men finally left. Back in their bedroom she stripped and snuggled next to Brett, her hand on his chest. "It could have been worse."

"I'd love to know how."

"Well, they're not always as kind as they were tonight."

"Mmm...." He took her hand and moved it lower. "Tell me about it."

"I'd rather not talk about that, thank you." Olivia caressed him and felt his flesh spring to life in her hands. "I thought we'd had our last earlier tonight," she teased.

"All those lewd suggestions did their job." His hands began to stroke her breasts, and her response was immediate. In a week's time she thought she'd learned an amazing amount. One of the things she'd learned was that her husband was almost insatiable, and she wasn't far behind.

He had learned the map of her body so well that he could travel there with little guidance. He knew where to kiss and when. He knew what to touch and why. He knew the scenic routes where he could linger and let pleasure build slowly. He knew the jet lanes where he could race from place to place until nothing was as important as the final destination. Tonight he charted his course for the latter.

"I guess one more last won't matter," she gasped softly, as he covered her willing body with his and made them one.

There was a distinct tinkle from under the bed.

"Did you hear something?" Brett asked, still at once.

She had, but she wasn't sure what, and she didn't care anyway. "Maybe it was just the bedsprings."

He relaxed, kissing her hungrily before he thrust again.

A series of clangs resounded through the quiet room.

Brett groaned, still immediately.

"Ignore it," she said after a groan to match his.

"I can't." Reluctantly he rolled off her. "Turn on the light, bright eyes."

She switched on the lamp with a jerk. Brett got up and knelt by the bedside. Finally he straightened.

"When you said we got off easy at the *charivari*, just what did you mean?"

"Well, sometimes they've been known to play tricks on people," she said, the truth dawning.

"Tricks like cowbells tied to bedsprings?"

"How many cowbells?"

"Remember all those trips to the bathroom? I'd say there's one for every man who passed through here."

Frustration was giving way to something else. Olivia covered her mouth, but laughter escaped anyway. Brett stood watching her with his hands across his chest. Then he was beside her, laughing too. "Here's to the cowbells," he said, pulling her beneath him once more. "Let's make them ring with joy."

Olivia tried to convince herself that going back to New Orleans was nothing more than trading one bayou for another. They left the mysterious, moss-draped grandeur of Bayou Teche early in the morning and drove up to the apartment sitting on Bayou St. John in the early afternoon.

"Home, sweet home." Brett honked in salute.

Olivia wondered how long it would be before the little apartment seemed to belong to both of them. There was plenty of room for two, but the apartment was distinctly Brett's, even though he hadn't put much of himself into it.

Surprisingly, Brett bypassed the front door altogether, grabbing her hand to drag her through the courtyard and down to the water. "I've got to check on the ducks."

She loved him most when he was this way. Open, boyish, enthusiastic. She watched as he scanned the bayou. "I don't see them."

Olivia joined him, her hand shading her eyes from the glare on the water. "Isn't that them?" She pointed to a tiny, moving spot in the far distance.

"In the middle?" Brett watched closely. "Yeah. I think you're right. I paid a kid down the street to feed them while I was gone."

"You don't think they would have found enough to eat by themselves?"

He was indignant. "I didn't want to lose their company."

"We'll have to teach Folly not to chase them or you might divorce me." Olivia linked her arm through his.

"Alienation of duck affection. I think that's in the law somewhere."

"If it's not, we'll elect you to office and you can put it there."

He smiled down at her. "Now that we've settled that, which threshold would you like me to carry you over? The front or the back?

"I know this place needs work," Brett told her as they unpacked their suitcases a little later. "Why don't you buy some furniture?"

"If we're going to be moving soon anyway, isn't that extravagant?" Olivia laid her new nightgowns in the dresser that she was using. It was surprising how little wear they'd gotten on her honeymoon.

"We can move whatever we buy. Just make sure that what you get has matching pieces we can buy later when we have more room to fill."

Selecting furniture without Brett didn't sound like any more fun to Olivia than shopping for a house without him. They had spent so much time together on their honeymoon that the reality of Brett working and her staying home just hadn't penetrated.

"Maybe we could shop for furniture one evening," she suggested. "I can call the stores and see what nights they stay open till nine."

"I trust your judgment, and I'm going to be working late for the next few weeks to catch up on what I missed during our honeymoon." Brett saw the disappointment Olivia was trying hard to hide. He put two fingers under her chin and lifted it so their eyes met. "I wish we could do everything together, but we can't. Now that I'm a married man I'm going to try and cut back on the extra work I used to take just to fill the time. An attorney puts in long hours, though. You should know that from working for the Broussards."

"I know."

"You'll find a lot to keep you busy."

"I'll be happy. Just come home when you can. I'll miss you."

"The honeymoon's over, but the marriage is really just beginning." Brett pulled Olivia close and wrapped his arms around her. "It'll take some time to adjust."

"It's going to be fine," she promised. "More than fine."

"We'll make sure it's fine," he amended. "I plan to make sure this marriage works."

"So do I." She tugged his head down for a kiss. "I won't let you down, Brett. I'll be the wife you need and want."

"You *are* the wife I want. You're the wife I intend to keep forever," he said, just before he kissed her again.

Chapter Eleven

Spring arrived on Bayou St. John, and along with the blooming of the azaleas, the aftermath of Mardi Gras and the fragrance and freshness of the newly warmed air, now a whole family of ducks appeared twice a day to accept the food religiously distributed by Brett and Olivia.

The early arrival of the ducks was one of those things Olivia could plan her morning around, just as she could plan it around Brett's goodbye kiss, Folly's scramble for the back door, the breakfast dishes and a hot cup of coffee taken at her leisure in the courtyard.

There was a rhythm to her days, a rhythm she had created out of nothing. It was a rhythm she found satisfying—most of the time. The largest part of each morning was given over to making the apartment a more attractive place to live. She bought furniture, painted walls and refinished woodwork, assuring Brett as she did that she was only practicing her skills for the house they would buy. As the apartment became more of a home, however, she found less time to go

Silhouette Romance™

Legendary Lovers Trilogy

BY DEBBIE MACOMBER....

ONCE UPON A TIME, in a land not so far away, there lived a girl, Debbie Macomber, who grew up dreaming of castles, white knights and princes on fiery steeds. Her family was an ordinary one with a mother and father and one wicked brother, who sold copies of her diary to all the boys in her junior high class.

One day, when Debbie was only nineteen, a handsome electrician drove by in a shiny black convertible. Now Debbie knew a prince when she saw one, and before long they lived in a two-bedroom cottage surrounded by a white picket fence.

As often happens when a damsel fair meets her prince charming, children followed, and soon the two-bedroom cottage became a four-bedroom castle. The kingdom flourished and prospered, and between soccer games and car pools, ballet classes and clarinet lessons, Debbie thought about love and enchantment and the magic of romance.

One day Debbie said, "What this country needs is a good fairy tale." She remembered how well her diary had sold and she dreamed again of castles, white knights and princes on fiery steeds. And so the stories of Cinderella, Beauty and the Beast, and Snow White were reborn....

Look for Debbie Macomber's *Legendary Lovers* trilogy from Silhouette Romance: *Cindy and the Prince* (January, 1988); *Some Kind of Wonderful* (March, 1988); *Almost Paradise* (May, 1988). Don't miss them!

SRT-1

Silhouette Intimate Moments

NEXT MONTH
CHECK IN TO
DODD MEMORIAL HOSPITAL!

Not feeling sick, you say? That's all right, because Dodd Memorial isn't your average hospital. At Dodd Memorial you don't need to be a patient—or even a doctor yourself!—to examine the private lives of the doctors and nurses who spend as much time healing broken hearts as they do healing broken bones.

In UNDER SUSPICION (Intimate Moments #229) intern Allison Schuyler and Chief Resident Cruz Gallego strike sparks from the moment they meet, but they end up with a lot more than love on their minds when someone starts stealing drugs—and Allison becomes the main suspect.

In May look for AFTER MIDNIGHT (Intimate Moments #237) and finish the trilogy in July with HEARTBEATS (Intimate Moments #245).

Author Lucy Hamilton is a former medical librarian whose husband is a doctor. Let her check you in to Dodd Memorial—you won't want to check out!

IM229-1

out and house hunt with their realtor. She was in no hurry to move into a larger place. There was an intimacy about sharing the cozy space with her new husband, and as far as she was concerned, the more intimacy with Brett the better.

Brett didn't really seem to mind. Olivia knew he enjoyed the bayou, and when he brought up the subject of their move, she would just point out how hard it was going to be to drain a water bed and how little space there would be for a family of ducks in the middle of the city, even if she found a house with an outdoor hot tub.

On the afternoons when she wasn't refinishing or rearranging, she visited Cherry and the children. In addition to putting the children in a preschool program for several hours each day, Cherry had decided to hire a part-time baby-sitter instead of another nanny. Olivia often picked Trey and Lucy up from school and took them to the apartment to dig in her newly emerging flower bed or to play with Folly—who also liked to dig in the newly emerging flower bed.

Late afternoons and evenings were reserved for Brett.

With the apartment taking shape, Olivia found more and more time to make up to Brett for the things he'd missed in his life. She baked bread, timing the hour it would go into the oven so that the rich yeasty smell of it filled the apartment when he walked through the door. She probed for his food preferences and learned to cook his favorites. He hated broccoli—the result of an overly conscientious foster mother when he was ten—but he loved artichokes. She stuffed them, boiled them, made them into a vegetable dip and served their hearts for salad. His favorite cookies filled the cookie jar and his favorite ice cream filled the freezer.

Olivia searched New Orleans for Oxford shirts made from the finest imported cotton; then she washed them, hung them to dry in the fresh air and meticulously ironed them so he would be both comfortable and neat. She took his suits to a dry cleaner on the other side of town because she didn't think the local one was good enough, and she drove out to

Metairie to do his banking because the interest rate on the type of account he wanted was better at a savings and loan there.

She didn't resent any of it. Each thing she did for Brett was a symbol of the love she felt for him, love that was growing at a rate she would never—not even at her most romantic—have believed. When he held her in his arms at night, whether they made love or not, she knew that whatever she had done for him that day wasn't enough. Nothing she could ever do would be enough.

Brett seemed blissfully happy. For him, married life was just an extension of their honeymoon. Olivia would catch him smiling at her sometimes for no reason at all. She would be in the middle of a sentence about something totally mundane, and she would turn to find him smiling as if she were the wittiest person in the world. She loved those times, just as she loved the nights in his arms and the mornings across from him at the breakfast table.

There were things she didn't love, however.

The silence was one of them.

Olivia had been raised in a small house with three brothers and a host of relatives who felt perfectly free to march in and out any time they chose. No one marched in and out of the Bayou St. John apartment unless it was Brett or Olivia herself. The Broussard children destroyed the silence on the occasions when they visited, but sometimes days would go by without another person setting foot inside. Even though she was training Folly not to make a nuisance of himself, Olivia actually welcomed his barking.

She didn't appreciate the many evenings she spent alone, either. So when she could plan ahead and knew that Brett wouldn't be home for dinner, Olivia would often head up to Baton Rouge to see Mary, who had managed to talk her doctors into letting her go back home.

Mary was alert. The drugs she was taking dulled her pain to a manageable level without dulling her mind. Olivia never

* * *

The problem was that she had too much time on her hands. Olivia looked around the small apartment and wondered what else she could do to make the clock tick faster. There was hardly an inch she hadn't already rearranged, cleaned or fussed over that morning. For once Folly was behaving admirably and didn't need her discipline. There was nothing to cook, because they were going out for dinner. As Brett had predicted, it was raining, so she couldn't dig in her garden, scrub the patio or check the bird feeder. Even her needlework wasn't a solution; she had run into a problem with the mother duck and had to wait to consult Cherry before finishing it.

She refused to turn on television, sure if she did that she'd become instantly addicted to soap operas. Instead she wandered into the bedroom and began trying on jeans to see which hid the largest multitude of sins. She settled on her newest pair, teaming them with a pink long-sleeved shirt and a kelly green sweater with a pink monogram. Dissatisfied with the prep-school cheerleader staring back at her in the mirror, she stripped off the shirt and sweater and belted an oversize flowered T-shirt over her jeans. The shirt slipped down over a shoulder to coquettishly reveal one plain white bra strap. It ended up on the bed next to the kelly green sweater.

She went through a demure yellow blouse with a Peter Pan collar, a tight black turtleneck and an Irish fisherman sweater over a plaid flannel hunting shirt before she settled on a scarlet silk Cossack blouse. She tucked it into her jeans, then remembered it was probably going to be raining, untucked it and put on the pink shirt and kelly green sweater again. She had wasted most of an hour.

She had too much energy. Surely other women were happy staying home. Olivia remembered her own mother. Myriam was always singing as she worked, and Myriam worked harder than anyone Olivia had ever known. But

then Myriam had had a large family to care for and a husband who was either gone for days or home for days because of the shifts he worked. Myriam had never had to try on six blouses just to kill time.

Olivia knew things would be different when she and Brett had children. Sometimes she even wondered if she should get pregnant immediately. She knew Brett wouldn't mind; in fact, she was fairly certain he had agreed to wait only because he'd felt it would be best for her.

She wanted Brett's children, but she didn't want them just to fill up her hours. She had to come to terms with her new life another way. For the first time she was beginning to understand what Mary had meant about growing.

By the time Brett arrived home, Olivia was brimming with suppressed vitality. She almost resented the time it took him to change his clothes so they could leave.

Brett thought Olivia had seldom looked more appealing. She had tied her hair back from her face with a pink ribbon that matched her shirt, and she was wearing black calfskin boots over new jeans. He loved the way the jeans tucked under her nicely rounded bottom and clung to the graceful length of her legs. He wondered how he could be so aroused when he'd kept her up until early morning making love to her.

"Do you want a drink first?" he asked, shrugging into a pullover sweater and adjusting his cuffs.

"No." Olivia realized how emphatic she'd sounded. She tried to soften it. "I'm anxious to get going. The rain kept me in most of the day."

"It should keep us in tonight." Brett looked up to see the disappointment on her face. "Hey, bright eyes, I'm not suggesting we stay home. I even bought you a surprise at lunchtime to keep you dry."

"Where is it?"

"I left it in the car."

The surprise was a huge gray man's umbrella, and Brett had bought one for himself, as well. "None of those dainty little parasols for women looked like they'd do the job," he informed her as they drove toward the restaurant. "If we're going to make a habit of walking in the rain, I thought we ought to invest wisely."

Olivia liked the sound of "make a habit of walking in the rain." There were few things she wouldn't want to make a habit of with Brett. "I love it. I almost feel like skipping dinner to try it out."

"I've never seen you skip a meal." He corrected himself. "Except on our wedding night."

"I said almost," she countered. "You promised me a hamburger."

Cozily ensconced in the nautically decorated dining room at Snug Harbor, a jazz club just outside the French Quarter, they ordered eight-ounce hamburgers and potatoes stuffed with sour cream, bacon and Cheddar cheese. They drank beer and tried to catch up on all the talking they'd missed due to Brett's hectic schedule. The band started later, and because of the rain the room wasn't crowded, so conversation was easy. They flirted and enjoyed each other's company.

Olivia was halfway through her hamburger before she realized she had run out of things to tell Brett. She had described Folly's antics in detail, told him her plans for the garden, asked his opinion about curtains for the dining room and given a verbatim report of her last conversation with Mary. There was nothing else to say, nothing that she could say, anyway. Brett wouldn't want to hear about the six blouses she had tried on or the boredom she was trying to find ways to combat.

Brett seemed to have run out of things to say, too. She had asked him about the case he was working on, but his description had been brief, as if he didn't think she'd understand or be interested even if she did. His life was so taken up by his work that there was little else she could ask him about. His past was off-limits; she knew she had heard as much about that as she ever would.

"We need a hobby. Something we can do together," she said as the waitress took her plate away with half the food untouched.

"I thought we had a hobby we both liked." Brett lifted his eyebrows lecherously, and his meaning was clear.

"Something we can do out of bed."

He was surprised by the seriousness of her voice. "What kind of hobby?"

She shrugged. "I don't know. Something we'll both like." She looked up, startled by a new train of thought. "What *do* you like, Brett?"

If he'd ever wondered whether marrying after a whirl-wind courtship might have its pitfalls, now he had his answer. They hadn't even had time to explore each other's interests. By now he knew every nook and cranny of her body, but in some ways they were still strangers.

"I'm not hard to please," he told her. "But that's not really the point, is it?"

She wasn't sure what the point was. She only knew that she was sitting across the table from her husband and they had run out of things to say to each other. Fear clawed at her. For a moment she wondered if they would spend the next fifty years of their life trying to come up with a topic of conversation.

"Hey, aren't you letting this get a little bit out of hand?" Brett reached across the table to reassure her. Her feelings were clearly written on her face. "We're just adjusting, bright eyes. There's an adjustment period in any marriage. It takes time to fine-tune a relationship, but we've got time."

Fifty years of strained silence. Olivia wondered where this sudden anxiety had come from. She didn't regret her marriage, did she? And what about Brett? Was he wondering why he had married the boring, tongue-tied woman across the table from him?

"Olivia!"

She looked up at the whip-crack tone of his voice. "You've got an interesting job," she said at last. "You're somebody, Brett. How long are you going to want to listen to me talk about curtains and paint samples and whether we should call the exterminator?"

"Forever," he said with no hesitation.

"There's got to be more," she said, shaking her head.

Since reassuring her didn't seem to help, he tried a different tack. "The problem isn't what we can and can't talk about. The problem is that you don't feel married yet."

"How do you know?"

He smiled a lopsided, endearing smile that warmed her heart a little. "Take the monogram on your sweater, for instance."

Olivia looked down at the embroidered *L* on her chest, then covered it with both hands. She knew her cheeks were quickly turning as pink as her shirt.

He laughed at her agitation. "It's all right. I'll go to court and change my name if you want to keep the sweater."

"I want to keep you, Brett."

"You will."

But for how long? Having a home and a wife who adored him was new to Brett, and he liked it. But would he wake up someday and want the stimulation of a woman he could share his thoughts with? Would he want a woman who was bringing more into their marriage than freshly baked bread?

"We're going to grow together," he told her. "And we'll find things we like to do together, too."

"Do you know what I like best?" she asked finally.

He pulled out her chair. They had made their second beer last as long as possible. "What?"

"I like just being with you like this. We nannies call it quality time when it's a parent spending time with a child."

"I'm going to find more time to spend with you this way," he promised. "Quality time. And when you finally feel married, you'll wonder what all the fuss was about."

She followed him into the rain, glad they had talked, but skeptical it would make much difference. Brett was caught up in a career that meant a lot to him. They would find things to share, but no matter how many things they found, she was still going to have a lot of hours to fill by herself.

When she finally felt married. Olivia turned her face to the raindrops and wondered just how long that was going to take.

Chapter Twelve

Brett wasn't home when the inevitable phone call came. Since the night two weeks before when he and Olivia had walked in the rain together, he'd worked late almost every evening. His weekends hadn't been free, either. The case he'd been working so hard on was winding up, and Olivia believed him when he said he'd have more free time when it ended. More time until the next big case, anyway.

She was sitting on the sofa waiting for him when he came home, but this time she wasn't asleep. All the lights were off except one, but in the dim glow Brett saw the trail of tears on her cheeks. For a moment he thought she was finally giving in to self-pity because of the way her new husband was treating her. His guilt was a bitter lump in his throat; he could hardly speak around it.

"I'm sorry." He sat beside her, tracing the path of her tears. "I promise after next week I'll be coming home like a regular husband. Every night."

"Mary died."

Brett put his arms around Olivia and pulled her head to his chest. His guilt grew. He should have been with her. "I'm so sorry."

Olivia wiped her tears with her fingertips. "She seemed to be doing so well; then she took a turn for the worse. She died on the way back to the hospital."

He smiled sadly. "Good for her."

Olivia looked up, shocked.

Brett pulled her head back to his chest and buried his face in her hair. "Listen, Mary probably planned it that way. You know she didn't want to be in a hospital, much less die in one. I think she held off death as long as she could; then she just gave in gracefully. That's why it seemed so quick."

"But I just saw her yesterday."

"That probably made it easier for her to give up fighting. You meant so much to her. She had a chance to say goodbye."

Olivia tried to remember yesterday's conversation. She had sat by Mary's bedside. They'd chatted about the school, and once again Mary had solicited her opinion about a class that wasn't going well. Olivia had taken Mary's hand and rested it on her cheek before leaving. Mary didn't like sentiment, but with great effort she had leaned over to kiss Olivia, wishing her a safe journey. Not a safe journey home, just a safe journey. Mary had said goodbye, only Olivia hadn't recognized it as the final parting.

She wrapped her arms around Brett's waist, grateful for his insight. "Mary requested there be no funeral, just a cremation. Her attorney was the one who called. She wanted a small memorial service at the school, and she wants her ashes interred there. He asked me to come into his office on Monday to discuss it. He said I'm mentioned in her will."

Brett stroked her hair. "I'll take the morning off and go with you."

There was little heart in her protest. "You don't have the time."

"I'll always have the time when you need me, bright eyes. Besides, I'm your attorney now, so I should be there. Does it surprise you that Mary put you in her will?"

"Not too much. She told me once I was the daughter she never had."

"You were both very lucky to have had that relationship."

"I'm going to miss her so much," Olivia said with a fresh burst of tears.

"Come to bed. I'll hold you, and you can cry as much as you want."

Olivia wondered what she would do without Brett's comfort. What had Mary done all those years alone?

"Mr. and Mrs. Terrill, I'm Tom Milton." The bald man in the wrinkled blue suit shook hands before escorting Brett and Olivia to chairs. He seated himself behind an oak desk buried in stacks of paper. The office was so cluttered that Olivia idly wondered how he found anything. It was surprising that someone as fastidious as Mary had chosen this man as her attorney.

"I'm glad to meet you, Mrs. Terrill, since Miss Hopkins spoke so highly of you. And I'm glad you could be here, Mr. Terrill."

At their nods, the old man went on. "I'm going to get right to the point, because I know you have a long trip back to New Orleans."

"Not the way Olivia drives," Brett said under his breath.

"Pardon me?"

"I said, the trip doesn't seem long at all with Olivia driving," Brett said with a wry smile.

"Well, I hope you're right, young man. Because Mrs. Terrill is going to be making the trip often if she accepts the conditions of Mary Hopkins's will."

Olivia drew her brows together. "What about Mary's will?"

"Miss Hopkins left you the Hopkins Academy for Nanny Development, Mrs. Terrill."

Brett sat up a little straighter.

"The academy?" The news was such a shock that Olivia couldn't digest it. Why would Mary leave her the academy? "You said on the phone I was mentioned in Mary's will. I thought she'd left me a brooch or a necklace!"

The old man unbent a little. "Miss Hopkins told me you'd have that look on your face when you found out. She told me not to tell you over the telephone. The school is yours, though. Every blade of grass, every splinter of wood. And a very healthy operating budget. Yours."

Now Olivia understood why Mary had asked her opinion so often during her last days. She had been trying to get Olivia used to the idea of running the academy herself. Olivia remembered that Mary had seemed pleased by her suggestions. Mary must have felt she was leaving her dream in capable hands.

Olivia sat up a little straighter.

"Can you tell us what the academy is worth?" Brett asked in a strangely quiet voice.

"Not in so many dimes and nickels. But the property alone is worth a fortune. Then there's the potential income in the future. I don't have to tell you how well respected an institution it is. If Mrs. Terrill were to sell it, it's safe to say she would come out with at least a million after taxes. Probably more." He paused and took out a handkerchief to wipe his brow, then his head.

"But Mrs. Terrill can't sell it," he went on when the handkerchief was back in his pocket. "At least not for a year. Miss Hopkins made a stipulation in the will that if Mrs. Terrill sells the academy before a year is up, the profit reverts to a scholarship fund for nannies. A fund, I might add, that Miss Hopkins has endowed heavily anyway, and which really needs no additional capital."

"I don't understand." Olivia shook her head slowly, trying to make sense out of Mr. Milton's speech.

"It's simple, really," he explained. "In order to inherit the academy free and clear, Mrs. Terrill, you must run it yourself for one full year from the day you formally accept this condition. At that time, if you choose, you can sell it and do what you wish with the money. Any money for operating expenses and so forth will be channeled through this office. You have only to put in a request. And, of course, you'll be paid a nice salary."

Olivia stared at Brett. He was staring back at her, but his expression was clouded. "I'd like to see the will, if I may," he said, turning to Mr. Milton.

The old man nodded and passed it over his desk. "There are provisions in there for some other people Miss Hopkins was fond of and for the scholarship fund I mentioned. She's left several small gifts of cash and distributed some of her personal belongings. As you can see, whatever isn't spoken for goes to Mrs. Terrill to dispose of as she sees fit."

"There wasn't any family at all?" Olivia asked, pulling her thoughts together as Brett scanned the will. "Mary never spoke of any, I know, but I just assumed there might have been someone."

"No one. Miss Hopkins's immediate family was killed in London during a blitz. There was a cousin or two, but they died and left no heirs. The will is valid as written. It won't be challenged, if that's what you're worried about."

Olivia smiled sadly. "I wasn't worried about that. I was worried about Mary being so alone all those years."

Mr. Milton smiled for the first time. "She had her students, and they meant the world to her. She had you."

Brett handed the document back to Mr. Milton. "Very tidy."

Mr. Milton nodded. "Thank you."

"What about the memorial service?" Olivia asked.

"I'm afraid that was just a ploy to get you in here so I could explain this without having to go into it on the telephone," Mr. Milton said sheepishly. "Miss Hopkins's idea," he added, holding up his hands in a gesture meant to forestall any criticism. "She planned her service down to the last detail. Of course, she wanted you to be there. I have a poem here she'd like you to read, and she's asked that some of her staff participate, too. It's planned for Friday."

Mr. Milton watched as Brett stood and offered his hand to Olivia. "When can I expect an answer on the conditions of the will? There will be some papers to sign."

Olivia stood and looked helplessly at Brett.

"We'll be back in touch next week," Brett said firmly. "In the meantime the school will be run by a staff council as the will provides?"

"That's right."

Olivia watched the two men discuss immediate business. She realized she was still in a state of shock. Their voices seemed to come from a long way off. She wanted to let them continue, to divorce herself from the whole affair. Still, it was now her school they were discussing. What would Mary say?

"I'll let you know my decision on Friday at the service," she interrupted, surprised that her voice was so clear when her head was so muddled. "At the latest."

Brett and Mr. Milton fell silent.

"The council will do fine for a week or two, but they've got to have some leadership. I'm not going to let this drag on indefinitely," Olivia continued.

Mr. Milton nodded approvingly. "That's just as Miss Hopkins would have wanted it."

"I know." She smiled weakly and turned to find her way out of the office.

Outside in the parking lot she let Brett seat her on the passenger's side of the car. For once she was in no mood to

drive. They were both silent until they'd left the Baton Rouge city limits far behind.

"That's some of the slickest blackmail I've ever seen," Brett said finally. "With some of the highest stakes."

"I just can't understand it." Olivia had been deep in thought, staring at the passing marshy scenery. Now she turned to look at Brett. "Why would Mary leave me the school in the first place, much less insist I run it?"

"It's perfectly obvious."

Olivia was surprised by Brett's tone. He sounded distinctly angry. "It's not obvious to me."

"Shall I make it clear to you? Miss Mary Hopkins wanted to break up your marriage."

Olivia was shocked for the second time that day.

"We both know Mary didn't want you to marry me," he went on. "You've told me that yourself. Now she's trying to change your mind from the grave. If you accept, you'll be in Baton Rouge. I'll be in New Orleans. She knew the strain that would cause."

"Don't you think you're overreacting a little?" Olivia said, putting her hand on his arm. "Mary didn't want me to marry anyone, but she liked you. Maybe she just left me the academy because she thought I'd do a good job of running it."

"What do you know about running a school?"

The disdain in his voice cut Olivia to the quick. She dropped her hand in her lap and turned back to the window.

"I don't mean to insult you," Brett went on. "What I mean is that you're young. You don't have any business experience at all."

"I was an executive secretary before I attended the academy," Olivia reminded him. "And while I attended I worked closely with Mary. I'm sure that had an effect on her decision."

"You're sweet and trusting and remarkably innocent. You're not nearly as aggressive as you'd have to be."

"It's a good thing I'm not aggressive," she said with a spark of anger. "I seem to be married to a man who's aggressive enough for both of us."

Brett took a deep breath and tried to calm down. He was angry at Mary's manipulations, but under his anger he knew there was a deeply buried fear. He could feel it gnawing away, trying to devour everything in its path until it reached the surface.

"Look, Olivia, I'm not trying to hurt you. It's just that I'm perfectly capable of supporting us both, and this first year of our marriage is important. I don't want us to spend it apart."

"We are spending it apart."

His attempt at control shattered. "I wondered how long it would take you to bring that up!"

Olivia couldn't understand Brett's anger. She'd just been given a huge gift, not the least of which was Mary's confidence that Olivia could continue Mary's dream and continue it well. Brett was acting as if Mary had not only made an error but had attacked him personally.

"Brett, you're gone every night," Olivia said evenly. "I know you're trying to change that, but even when things smooth out a little bit, you're still going to be away a lot of the time. I love being married to you." She tried for a touch of humor. "I love cooking your meals and washing your shirts and housebreaking your dog. But sometimes I've wished I had more to do, more to talk about when I do see you."

"You'll have more to do when we have children."

She faced him again. "I'm not ready to have children. I'm not going to have them just to fill up my empty hours."

"It's funny you've never mentioned any of this before."

She touched his arm once more, trying to soften her words. "You're not home often, Brett. And when you are

home, I don't want to waste our time complaining. I haven't been looking for a job. I've been trying to find ways to spend my time creatively, but it's been lonely.''

Brett's anger was diluted momentarily. "I'm sorry you've been lonely," he said contritely. "You know I'm trying to lighten my work load."

"It's not your job to keep me entertained. Of course I want to spend more time with you, and I hope we will. But I think I need a life of my own, interests of my own. You shouldn't have to worry about me."

Brett thought about Meg Sherwood. He had thought he understood Meg's need for an identity separate from Drew's. Somehow that was fine for Meg, but not for Olivia. Olivia was his wife.

"You sound like you've already decided," he said coldly.

"Why are we fighting?"

They were fighting because he was afraid he was going to lose her to the academy. Brett knew it just as surely as he knew his own name. Despite what he'd told her, he knew just how competent Olivia was at everything she put her hand to. She wasn't a perfectionist, but she prided herself on doing everything well. Whatever she didn't know about administering the school, she would learn quickly. He had taunted her about not being aggressive enough, but it was precisely her sweetness that would make her a successful leader. People would follow Olivia because they believed in her, not because she was cracking a whip. Besides, he had seen her in action with the Broussard children. She was all gentleness and mother love, but when she had to be firm, she could be. Mary had chosen well, damn her.

"Brett," Olivia repeated, "why are we fighting? I need your help and support."

"My help and support to make your decision? Or my help and support to help you live with it now that it's made?"

Olivia sat in silence for a few minutes, watching Brett drive. Nothing hurt worse than knowing that he didn't be-

lieve she could be a success. He wanted her at home—even though he was seldom there himself—because home was the only place he thought she was fit to be. She had never imagined herself doing such a difficult, important job; she had wanted nothing more than to marry and raise children. But now that she was faced with this incredible opportunity, she wanted to believe in herself. She wanted to believe that Mary had been right. Knowing Brett didn't believe in her destroyed what little self-confidence she had.

"I don't know what to do," she said at last. "I don't feel qualified, but how can I turn down an opportunity like this? It's just for a year, Brett. Then I can sell everything."

"The money means that much to you? Even with what I make?"

She couldn't believe he was almost sneering at a million dollars. This was a Brett she didn't know; she had never seen him so coldly hostile. She decided to be honest with him, even if it was painful.

"It's not just the money. It's the fact that Mary wanted this for me. Can you understand that? She had faith in my abilities. No one else in my life ever thought this highly of my potential. I made good grades in school, but no one there paid any attention to my academic possibilities. I was too shy to push myself, so I never ran for student council or tried out for the debating team. I was just Olivia LeBlanc, good student, and I was easy to lose in the crowd. When it was time for me to think about college, I didn't believe I'd be able to win any scholarships, so I didn't try. My parents could have sent me, but as much as they loved me, they didn't see the point, since they figured I'd just get married anyway. Mary was the only person I've ever known who saw more in me. Mary believed I could run the academy, and I want to prove her belief in me wasn't wrong."

"Mary's dead."

Her eyes filled with tears. "I know."

Brett was ashamed of his own cruelty. "I'm sorry," he said shortly. "Let's finish this later, after you've had time to put it all in perspective."

For a moment Olivia wondered if there was more to Brett's protests than anger at Mary's scheming and lack of faith in Olivia's ability to handle such a difficult job. Was he truly worried this would affect their marriage? That he might lose her?

"Whatever I decide," she said, probing a little, "it won't change our relationship. You'll always come first with me, no matter what else I choose to do."

He didn't nod; he didn't smile; he didn't speak. He just continued driving until they reached the house on Bayou St. John. He dropped her off without so much as a kiss on the cheek.

Olivia suffered Folly's ecstatic greeting with stoic resolve. She didn't want to be home alone; she wanted Brett with her. They needed to talk. She couldn't understand his attitude. The will called for her to be headmistress of the academy for one year. Surely one year couldn't make this much of a difference to Brett. They weren't going to start their family right away, anyway. With careful planning she could usually be home before he walked in the door, even with an hour-and-a-half commute.

Olivia forced herself to do her daily chores and begin preparations for the evening meal. She was exhausted by six, not because of what she'd done but because of the battle raging inside her. When she heard Brett's key turn in the front-door lock, she summoned all her available energy to greet him.

"You're home early." She went to him for a kiss.

The kiss was perfunctory. "What's for dinner?"

"Oyster and artichoke soup, baked chicken, salad," she recited. "Strawberry shortcake for dessert. It'll be ready soon."

Brett saw the pleading in her eyes, and he listened carefully to the menu. He knew he had lost. "So you've decided to run the academy," he said, turning to take off his jacket and hang it in the closet.

"How did you know?"

"You're serving guilt with the baked chicken."

"I didn't think of it that way. I thought I was just making your favorite dinner." Olivia had prepared herself for a difficult evening. She hadn't expected it to begin so soon.

"And were you going to wear my favorite nightgown when you broke the news to me? You're not above using feminine wiles, are you, Olivia?"

His anger was irrational, and Olivia knew it. It still hurt. "Would you rather I'd served cold beans and worn a flannel robe when I told you? I don't want this to hurt either of us, Brett. I made your favorite dinner because I wanted to show you how much I love you. My decision about the academy has nothing to do with my feelings for you."

"True. My feelings weren't considered at all."

She put her arms around his waist when he tried to move around her. "You know that's not what I meant. Of course I've thought about how this will affect you. It's just that I can't see what the problem is. Even if I fail as headmistress, the school isn't going to be ruined. In a year's time it'll be clear whether I'm capable of doing the job or not. If I'm not, we can sell it. If I am . . ."

"If you are?" He unwrapped her arms and pushed her away so he could look her in the eye. "What then?"

She was as surprised by the "if I am" as he was. What on earth had she been going to say? If she were capable of running the school, was she unconsciously considering keeping it? She hadn't even had time to think that far ahead. "If I am," she said lamely, "then I'll be very proud of my accomplishments. I hope you'll be proud of me, too."

"I'm proud of you now. I don't need proof you're smart or proof you're capable."

She tried to smile, but she felt like crying. "That's the first nice thing you've said to me since we came out of Milton's office."

"I don't feel nice. I married a woman who wanted to stay home and raise my children. All of a sudden I'm married to a career woman."

"You're married to *me*. If you wanted domestic help, you could have hired a maid or a nanny." She blinked back the tears that had been threatening all afternoon. "Or maybe that's why you married me. I was a terrific compromise, wasn't I? Half nanny, half lover. The perfect wife."

Brett dropped his hands. "I married you because we suited each other's needs. I thought we could build a relationship that was good for both of us."

"And now you're not so sure?"

"That's right." He didn't seem to be able to stop the next comment, even though he knew how it would wound. "I don't want another woman like my mother or Kate Parsons in my life."

She was shocked that he would throw his mother's and Kate's failures at her as if they were her own. She wanted to hurt him the same way. "I'm not so sure you want any woman in your life! Maybe you need some kind of domestic robot that you can program to do what you want. Someone without feelings!"

Brett turned back to the closet and got his jacket out again, shrugging it on as he opened the front door. "I'm going for a walk."

"Dinner comes out of the oven in fifteen minutes. If you're not here then, I'll feed your share to Folly!"

Her answer was the slam of the front door.

Olivia sat down on the hallway floor and covered her face with her hands, rocking back and forth and sobbing out her misery. It was only minutes later, when she felt the wet, warm wash of Folly's tongue between her fingers, that her

tears began to subside. She put her arms around the puppy's silky neck and held on for dear life.

The frozen statues of dog and mistress were the first thing Brett saw when he opened the front door quietly, in penance for slamming it earlier. He saw the remnants of Olivia's misery, and he was filled with shame. When had he last felt that enraged? Brett Terrill didn't slam doors; he didn't let anyone know if he was angry. Brett Terrill viewed both sides of an issue, carefully collected whatever evidence was available, then turned it to his own benefit. That's what any good attorney did.

The problem was, he wasn't acting like an attorney. He was acting like a husband. He had wanted to be a husband, but he had never expected the role to become so ingrained that it took over his life. Husbands demanded; husbands presumed; husbands stormed out of the house over irrational fears they didn't fully understand. And how much more irrational could one person be than to ask another to give up a small fortune? Olivia was right to want to protect what was hers. They had been married for only a matter of months, and he was already acting as if he owned her.

Olivia wiped her eyes and loosened her grip on Folly's fur when the kitchen timer finally buzzed. "Folly," she said with resignation, "I sure hope you like baked chicken."

The front door closed with a soft thump, and she heard Brett's footsteps. "You'll never know."

Olivia felt strong hands on her shoulders; then she felt Brett kneeling behind her. She leaned against him as his arms came around her.

"I'm sorry, bright eyes." Brett's arms tightened, and his cheek nuzzled hers. "I've been a real bastard, haven't I?"

She turned and threw her arms around his neck.

Brett held her and felt the heavy weight inside him lift. "A year," he said as he rocked her slowly back and forth. "Just a year."

"Just a year," she promised. "No more than that, Brett. Just let me prove I can do it."

"Just don't forget you're my wife."

How could she forget? And how could she make him believe it? Olivia clasped him fiercely and silently vowed that nothing, no part of their marriage, would change as a result of her new position. She would still be the woman he'd married, the wife he wanted. She loved him too much to give him less.

Chapter Thirteen

The alarm watch beeped twice. In a motion that was now thoroughly ingrained, Olivia shut it off before it could beep again and rolled over to sit on the side of the bed. Every weekday morning started the same way and had for six weeks. She no longer had to think about what to do next. She got up, careful not to wake Brett, gathered the clothes she had laid out the night before and went into the bathroom to shower and dress.

If the morning routine was totally familiar now, the body she soaped was not. In six weeks' time she had lost five pounds. There was no reason to believe her weight was going to stabilize, either. She was eating less, due to her hectic schedule. There was no time for snacking, no time to bake luscious desserts. She could buy Brett his favorites at Lawrence's Bakery and not buy portions for herself. She fully expected to lose another ten pounds so she would have to worry about being too thin. It would be a welcome change.

The hair she washed seemed unfamiliar, too. It was shorter now, falling just below her shoulders and tapering toward her face at the sides. The missing six inches took minutes off her preparation time in the morning, as well as adding a new sophistication to her appearance. Even Brett, who fought every change she made, grudgingly admitted he liked it.

As soon as she was out of the shower, she dried her hair and dressed in one of the new summer suits she had bought the week before. March had begun with an unusual cold spell, but now the weather was turning warm. She had shopped carefully for clothes that would be comfortable but professional, settling on colorful, lightweight suits that flattered her changing figure and vivid coloring. Sometimes, when she was all ready for work, the woman staring back at her in the mirror seemed completely unfamiliar.

She was becoming increasingly used to the shadows under her eyes, however. She was tired all the time. In order to spend three to four hours a day commuting, eight hours at the academy and all the rest of her time maintaining her roles as wife and housekeeper, she had been forced to drop something.

That something had been sleep. She was never in bed—not to sleep, anyway—before midnight, and she was never out of bed any later than five. In the two hours between rising and heading up to Baton Rouge she dressed, cleaned the apartment, took Folly for a walk so he would behave on the long commute and made what preparations she could for the night's dinner. Then she woke Brett up, and while he showered, she fixed breakfast—a big one for him, a cup of coffee and a piece of toast for herself.

By the time he came to the table she was sitting down, seemingly unruffled, reading the newspaper and drinking her coffee as she waited for him to join her. To her knowledge he had no idea of the chaos that reigned while he slept blissfully on each morning. That was just the way she

wanted it. She was determined to prove to him that nothing important had changed.

This morning was no different. The apartment was straightened and Folly had run off his excess energy and most of hers before she went back in the bedroom to kiss Brett awake. He was sprawled out, covering the queen-size water bed with most of his body. He was naked, and she wanted to run her hands over him and demand a repeat performance of last night's activity, but there wasn't time. Still, if the mornings were too busy for lovemaking, the nights were not. One thing that seemed in no danger from the hectic pace of their lives was the quality of their love life.

"Wake up." Olivia chanted the words as she knelt beside Brett and bounced gently to rock the bed. She rubbed his back and kissed his neck. "Wake up."

He turned over and pulled her down on top of him, raising his hands after she was settled to mess her carefully brushed hair. "Good morning." He brought her face to his for a long kiss. "Hey, I remember you from last night. Weren't you the lady who..."

"Shh." She kissed him again, then kissed his cheeks, his forehead, his chin, before she found his mouth once more.

"That was you all right." He resisted when she tried to pull away. "Stay here a minute and cuddle," he demanded. "I miss waking up with you next to me."

"We'll both be late."

"No, we won't."

She snuggled closer, pleased that he'd admitted missing her. With her eyes drooping shut, she sighed. She'd make up these minutes somehow.

Brett felt Olivia relax, and he settled her more comfortably against him. He wondered if he would ever get tired of having her so close. For two people whose marriage had been largely practical, they were reaping benefits he hadn't expected. The first flush of physical attraction should have ended by now, but it had only increased. As soon as Olivia

sold the academy, their relationship would be just about perfect.

He stroked her hair away from her ear, nipping it softly with his teeth. As much as he hated to admit it, they both had to get moving. "What do you have planned for today, bright eyes? Is it going to be a busy day?"

She twisted her head as if to avoid his delicate torture, but she was silent.

"Olivia?"

His answer was another sigh. She was asleep. Brett held her tightly and wondered how tired a person had to be to succumb to the sandman in three seconds flat.

"Olivia?" he said a little louder.

She stirred, and he felt the utter relaxation of her body change by slow degrees. Finally she sat up and moved away to straighten her clothes.

Brett decided not to comment on the obvious. In fact, he didn't even know what he could say to someone who allowed herself to get so exhausted, or, for that matter, what he could say about himself for letting it happen. He only knew it was going to give him something to think about for the rest of the day.

He forced himself to smile as if nothing had happened. "You look pretty this morning. I like that suit."

"Do you?" Sleepily she modeled it for him, pulling back the fuchsia jacket to show him her lacy white blouse.

"Very nice. Now show me what's beneath it."

"I'll show you tonight," she promised. Had she really fallen asleep? Olivia couldn't believe she had let her guard down so completely. Did Brett know? She forced herself to smile as if nothing had happened. "Do you want pancakes for breakfast? The grill is hot. It won't take long."

"That sounds great," he said doubtfully, "but I don't want you going to a lot of trouble."

"Nothing I do for you is trouble." She blew him a kiss before heading to the kitchen to mix the pancake batter.

He appeared at the table at the same time the last of the pancakes came off the grill. She brought them to him, along with orange juice and freshly cooked bacon. "The coffee'll be ready in a minute."

"Where's yours?"

She looked at her plate. There was nothing on it. "I'll take one, Brett, and that's it."

"You're going to waste away to nothing."

"The highest ambition a woman can attain."

"I liked you . . ."

"Fatter?" she supplied. "Rounder, plumper?"

"Lusher."

"Admit it. You're not too unhappy with the five pounds I lost." She spread a wafer-thin slice of butter on her pancake and ate it with no syrup.

"There was more of you to love."

She was surprised by his joke. The word "love" wasn't normally in his vocabulary. It gave her a warm glow even though she knew he was just mouthing a cliché.

"We've been married three months today," she said, reaching across the table to take his hand.

He toasted her with his orange juice. "To three more."

She laughed. "I married such a romantic."

"Let's go out to dinner tonight to celebrate."

The idea was heavenly. He had suggested it before, but she had been so set on showing him that she could manage everything, she had always found reasons to refuse. This time she didn't have the energy to be a martyr. "I'd love it. Where shall we go?"

"Good for you."

"What do you mean, good for me?" She was surprised by the concern in his voice.

"You're going to let yourself relax. I'm glad."

She looked down at their hands, still clasped together. "I relax. Look at me now. I'm the picture of relaxation."

"You relax in two-minute stretches, just like you take two-minute naps." He brought her hand to his lips for a kiss before he released it. "Let's go somewhere decadent and expensive." He watched her face light up. "My choice. I'll make the arrangements."

"I'd like that." She wondered if her eyes were saying the things her lips never said: how much she wanted their life together to be perfect, how much she wanted him to love her the way she loved him.

Brett smiled at her. "You'd better go. You'll be late if you don't leave now, even the way you drive."

"I can be late. Who's going to have the nerve to complain?"

He laughed at the new jaunty Olivia. "I'll complain, because you'll stay late to make up for every second you missed."

She stood. "We've been married too long. You know me too well."

"Never."

She met his eyes and was surprised to see how serious they were. She circled the table and gave him a kiss that said everything she couldn't find the words for.

"So to finalize, we're suffering from an increase in competition for students from less expensive, shorter-term programs while at the same time we're getting twice as many requests for our graduates." Olivia sat down at her seat at the head of the table and looked out over the faces of the men and women who had recently been her teachers and were now her staff. She still had trouble believing that any of them could take her seriously, but the truth was indisputable. In her six weeks as headmistress she had garnered their support and was making headway on their devotion.

"Over three dozen new nanny-training centers," Joe Riskoff, psychology instructor, said, shaking his head. "To

think that once upon a time the Hopkins Academy almost had the American market cornered."

"It's a good trend," Olivia reminded them. "None of us would want it to be any different. If these centers are good, and from reports I receive, most of them are excellent, then the quality of individual child care is going up. The only thing we have to worry about is maintaining our share of the students. Let's face it, we're training nannies for the very wealthy here. Our graduates train twice as long as most of the other schools, and pay twice as much tuition. Their reward is that they get twice as much in salary and benefits when they graduate, but for some of our potential students, that reward is too far in the future to matter."

"I'm not sure I like the thought that we're only catering to the elite," Carol Darwin, pediatric nurse and instructor in child health and safety, said thoughtfully.

"Rich children need good child care, too," the staff's part-time nutritionist pointed out. "Our nannies are trained to cope with the problems of the wealthy. And if our nannies weren't so highly trained, they wouldn't be hired and there'd be a gap no one else is as equipped to fill as we are."

"I've been wondering if we could do both," Olivia said when the discussion had died down a little. "What if we instituted a one-year program as well as a two-year? The second year would be a sort of graduate school for those who wanted to continue. The two-year graduates would still wear the official uniform, and employers would know they were getting the most qualified nannies available in the United States. The one-year graduate would have a different uniform and a different diploma. We would encourage her to come back for more training after she'd had a chance to earn the additional tuition, but if she didn't, we'd know that we had still educated a top-notch nanny."

The idea got the attention Olivia had known it would. Everyone was interested in increasing enrollment in the school, but no one was interested in lowering standards. She

listened to opinions being tossed back and forth. When the meeting ended, she stood at the door to say goodbye and shake hands. There would be a number of meetings before any decisions were reached, but at least the process had begun.

"Are you done for the day?"

Olivia nodded to Loretta, the young redhead who was now the academy's administrative secretary. Mary's secretary, Sara, had retired immediately after Mary's death. On top of everything else, Olivia had been forced to interview two dozen prospects before hiring Loretta. Luckily, she was proving to be an excellent choice. "I think I'm done."

"You look beat." Loretta straightened chairs and emptied ashtrays with brisk efficiency. When she had finished she bent over to pet Folly, who was asleep under a chair. "Your husband called while you were in your meeting. I told him I'd put him through, but he said not to bother." Her eyes were sparkling as she finished. "I'm supposed to tell you to meet him at the Bellemont, room 131. He bribed me to take Folly for the night."

Olivia was almost too tired to think. She sagged against the door frame and shut her eyes. It was five-fifteen and she had been going nonstop for twelve hours. How was she going to make the drive to New Orleans, much less dress to go out to a fancy restaurant? "The Bellemont? I wonder where that is."

"Are you kidding? It's the big hotel over on Airline Highway."

"Hotel?" Olivia opened her eyes.

"Room 131. Do you want me to drive you? I'm not sure I trust you behind a steering wheel right now. Or ever," she added matter-of-factly.

"You'll never forgive me for making you shop for office supplies with me yesterday, will you?"

"Oh, I forgive you for making me shop. I just won't forgive you for driving me to the store."

"Well, you can't drive me all the way to New Orleans or Metairie or wherever this place is. I'll make it."

Loretta giggled. "You really are tired. The Bellemont is on Airline Highway here, in Baton Rouge, and your husband is waiting for you. Personally, I think it's the most romantic thing I've ever heard of in my life."

Brett lit dime-store votive candles that he'd bought at a local shopping center while he waited for Olivia. The air was quickly filled with the scent of vanilla, and shadows flickered against the wall in ever-changing patterns. Champagne was chilling in a silver bucket; room service was set to deliver the first course of a lavish dinner at eight o'clock. He wondered if he had forgotten anything.

Music. He flicked on the radio and hunted for a station playing classical music, smiling when he found one. Apparently his mood-setting maneuvers had been just in time, because the Cleveland Symphony Orchestra's percussion section was now getting help from someone knocking on the hotel-room door.

"Yes?" Brett leaned against the door frame and leisurely examined the pretty brunette in the fuchsia suit. Nothing about her was as pretty as her smile, however. Her smile looked like a million dollars. Any doubts he'd had about arranging this surprise disappeared. "May I help you?"

Olivia lifted her eyebrows. Brett was dressed in a terrycloth robe, startlingly white against his tan. The robe was open down to his waist, where it was belted loosely. She had to resist the urge to see how much effort it would take to untie it. Instead she played along with his game. "I don't know if you can help. Were you expecting me?"

"I was expecting someone." He stretched out his hand and fingered the collar of her suit. "Nice material. What's under it?"

"How badly do you want to know?" She lifted her hair and held it off her neck in a provocative pose, pouting as she did.

"I don't know. What'll it be worth to me?"

"You couldn't pay what it'll be worth."

"Sounds tempting."

"Shall we discuss it inside?"

He stepped back, but not far enough for her to avoid him as she entered the room. Not that she minded. With studied care she swished her skirt against his legs and drew one fingertip along the bare skin of his chest as she passed. "Nice place you've got here."

"Do you think so? It's a little small. I was thinking about adding a house to it."

She nodded, trying not to smile. "You've got taste."

"Apparently I do." He rested his hands on her shoulders and ran his thumbs under the collar of her jacket. "Why don't you make yourself comfortable?"

"Oh, I'm depending on you to do that." She arched her neck like a cat so he could caress it, shivering when he lifted her hair and explored the warm hollow of her nape with his tongue. When her hair tumbled back to her shoulders she leaned against him and relaxed her arms to let him slip off her jacket. "I see you've got champagne. Not everyone buys me champagne."

"I should hope not. I'm not like everyone."

With provocative grace she faced him and fingered the lapels of his robe. "You'll have to prove that, won't you?"

"What kind of proof did you have in mind?"

Her hands glided down the robe to the loosely tied sash. She wound the fabric through her fingers for a moment, then pretended to think better of it. Instead she turned away and wandered to the bucket of champagne to read the label. "Dom Perignon. My favorite."

"I drank it at my wedding."

Olivia spun around, wide-eyed. "Oh? Are you married? Too bad. I'll bet your wife doesn't understand you."

"Actually, she understands me very well."

"Does she? How unusual." She let a smile blossom slowly. "Then why are you here?" She reached for the top button of her blouse and undid it, moving down to the next one.

"Because I understand her, too."

"Even more unusual." She undid the third button and then the fourth. With the fifth the blouse came apart and she slipped it off, revealing a white satin camisole. "And just what is it you understand about your wife?"

Brett moved subtly closer. "I understand that she needs an evening like this, even if she refuses to admit she's completely exhausted."

Olivia unbuttoned her skirt and let it fall to the ground. Then she swept her slip over her hips. From the expression on Brett's face, she knew making the effort to wear stockings with a black-lace garter had been worth it. "If this evening was so important for your wife," she said sweetly, "why isn't she here?"

His eyes were gleaming. "You are my wife."

She reached down to unclip her stockings. They glided down her legs to pool at her ankles. "Are you sure? You hardly look familiar."

He untied the belt of his robe and let it drop to his feet.

Olivia examined his naked body leisurely from the top of his head to the tip of his toes. Finally she nodded. "What a lovely surprise. It is you."

"Come here, Olivia."

She backed away a little and stuck out her lower lip. "Make me."

"Is that what you really want?" He took a step in her direction.

"Oh, I may be your wife, but I'm not easy."

"No?" He took another step.

"No." She edged toward the king-size bed in the middle of the room, but once she felt it pressing against the back of her legs she realized her mistake.

Brett had realized it before she did. His hands settled on her shoulders before she could move away. He smoothed his fingers up her neck to tangle them in her hair. "I'd say you were pretty easy."

"I'll fight to the death."

"Which death is that? The little death, as the French call it?"

She tried not to smile, but she couldn't help herself. "You take a lot for granted, don't you?"

"I base all my calculations on experience." He brushed his mouth across hers, then again. "Three months of experience."

"Only three months? Poor man." She slid her hand under his chin and along his jawline. "You've obviously been deprived."

"I'll take three months with this particular woman to a lifetime with anyone else."

Olivia brought his head back down to hers. "Maybe I won't fight, after all."

"See what a little sweet talk can do?"

"It's what your hands can do," she corrected him. Olivia lifted her arms over her head as Brett pulled off the camisole. She felt him unhook her bra. Her garter belt and bikini pants were the last to go.

"My hands are going to be doing a whole lot more."

"Not just your hands." Olivia put her arms around Brett's waist and began to explore his chest with her mouth, following the defined muscles with her tongue, flicking it back and forth over each tiny nipple until she felt him shudder against her. She filled her hands with his flesh, kneading and caressing as she kissed him. The teasing game had excited her. Normally content to let Brett take the lead, tonight she felt bold.

"What you've learned in three months!" He pushed her to the bed, lying beside her to cover her body with kisses as she had covered his. He could feel the rapid beat of her heart against his mouth; he could taste the salt and honey flavor of her skin, smell the fragrance of spring. He drew one rose-tipped nipple into his mouth and heard her soft cry. His hands slipped lower, and he knew she would arch to meet them.

He had known almost from the beginning that he'd wanted Olivia for his wife. But even in his dreams, he hadn't imagined she would be so responsive, so giving. He kissed her, and she burned; he caressed her, and she melted. He filled her emptiness, and she was rippling velvet around him. When their lovemaking ended, along with the deepest possible pleasure he felt regret at the separation to come.

"Oh, Brett, what are you doing to me?" The charade had ended. Olivia felt a torrent of sensation rush through her. Shouldn't she want him less now? After endless nights of passion, after months of sensual explorations that had taught her the powers of her body and his, shouldn't she be satisfied? Shouldn't this be slower, gentler?

"I'm making love to you."

Making love. Creating love? Was that what was happening each time their bodies joined? Creating love from the good feelings between them? If so, let it begin.

Her feelings built at lightning speed. Making love. He had cared enough about her to arrange this surprise. He cared. Forming love, building love, love evolving. She arched higher to meet the demands of his mouth. Already she could feel the greedy demands of her body as all feeling focused and centered where she most needed his touch.

His mouth trailed lower, to her sensitive navel, then lower still.

At the first touch of his tongue, she knew she was lost.

She twisted to evade him. Her body was rigid with the effort to control her response. "Brett. Brett." Olivia begged

him to come to her. It was going too fast. It had built from the moment she had discovered his surprise, rocketed from the moment she had seen him standing in the hotel doorway. Now his touch was sending her spinning out of control. "Now. Oh, please, now."

She pulled him to her, but he was in no hurry. He wanted to savor her. "Not yet."

She whimpered in protest and twisted to bring him inside her anyway, but he didn't comply. He wanted it slow; he wanted it to last forever. He lay back and brought her on top of him.

It was all Olivia needed. With her gaze locked to his, she triumphantly sheathed him inside her. Nothing more was needed. She moaned and fell against him, shudders of ecstasy claiming her. Brett held her until she was spent, stroking her hair and soothing her. Then he turned over and drew her under him. "Look at me."

She could hardly open her eyes, but his voice compelled her. Brett could read satisfaction and just a hint of shyness in them. He laughed as he began to move against her. "God, bright eyes. You've learned to take what you want, haven't you?"

She shut her eyes, and he kissed her eyelids. He moved faster, rapidly losing control as she matched his pace. He had married a shy, young virgin, and he'd thought he could never want anyone more. But the woman in his bed now was the most desirable woman he'd ever known. She wrapped her legs around him; he wrapped his arms around her. When he filled her completely, he knew a pleasure so intense it seemed impossible to survive it.

Later Brett folded back the covers, gently moved Olivia between the sheets and tucked a pillow under her head. She had fallen asleep immediately after their lovemaking. There would be time to wake her when their dinner arrived. For now he just lay next to her and watched her sleep.

She was lovelier than ever, but the violet shadows under her eyes owed nothing to cosmetics and everything to the frantic pace of her life. One night in a hotel room in Baton Rouge wasn't going to make enough of a difference to erase them. She was committed to staying at Mary Hopkins for a year; he was committed to his job. There had to be something they could do to ease her load.

Much later Olivia turned over and her eyes fluttered open. She lifted a hand to stroke Brett's cheek. "I didn't dream this, did I? What made you think of it?" she asked.

"You're exhausted. I started thinking about that commute to New Orleans. I just couldn't let you do it tonight."

"I could have managed."

"Just like you've managed everything else? You probably could have." He pulled her into the crook of his arm. "But why should you? We can't do anything about the traveling, I'm afraid, but I think I may have come up with something we can do to make things easier. When I go home tomorrow I'm going to find a housekeeper. At least that way you can get an extra couple of hours of sleep every day."

She opened her mouth to tell him that no housekeeper was going to set foot in her house, but he put his finger on her lips and held it there.

"You can't do everything. We'll get someone part-time. Someone who'll start dinner a couple of nights, do the shopping, clean the apartment. The rest of the time we'll eat out or have frozen dinners."

"No frozen dinners," she mumbled past the barrier of his finger.

"I sort of miss the ones with the greasy chicken and the dried-up peas."

She kissed his finger, and he removed it. "I want to be your wife. I don't want someone else filling in."

"You are my wife. We'll get through the next year, but I'm not going to let you wear yourself out. I want you to save your energy for the important things. Like this."

She knew he was right. "Thank you," she said, a catch in her voice. "Thank you for caring so much about me."

He held her tight and wondered if he was beginning to care more about her than he had admitted even to himself.

Chapter Fourteen

Brett braked the BMW and waited while a neighborhood child retrieved a bright orange soccer ball that had rolled into the street. If he'd had any doubt that summer was on its way, the activity on Bancroft Drive would have put his mind to rest. In addition to the young boys in iridescent surfer shorts and T-shirts playing sidewalk soccer, he'd seen one neighbor washing his car and another mowing his lawn. Both chores would probably be passed on to hired help in a month or two, when the heat and humidity got so fierce that every breath the men drew would be as wet as the sweat dripping down their faces. In the meantime the men enjoyed themselves.

In his own yard the summer-is-coming fragrance of magnolia blossoms and Confederate jasmine blended with a tantalizing aroma wafting out of his kitchen window. Brett stood just outside the entrance to the Bayou St. John apartment and wondered what Mrs. Minn was cooking tonight. Whatever it was, she had apparently taken a crash

course in gourmet cookery. Mrs. Minn could broil a steak or roast a chicken, but in the five weeks that she'd been their housekeeper, he'd learned that if a recipe called for mixing more than two ingredients, she would ruin it.

Actually, it wasn't Mrs. Minn's night to be here. It was a Friday, and that usually meant pizza, delivered after Olivia got home from Baton Rouge. That meant six-thirty at the earliest, and usually more like seven if the traffic was bad. Brett inserted his key in the lock and turned the knob. "Mrs. Minn?"

"You weren't supposed to come home this early!" Olivia appeared in the kitchen doorway and blew him a kiss. Then she disappeared.

Brett checked his watch. No, he hadn't made a mistake. It was only five-fifteen, and besides, her car hadn't been in the driveway. "What are you doing home?" he called.

"You'll have to come in the kitchen. If I leave this right now it's going to burn."

He followed the unmistakable smell of seafood. "You're not supposed to be home for at least another hour."

"I could leave," she teased, flashing him a big smile.

"Don't you dare." Brett came up behind her and put his arms around her waist to watch with interest as she stirred a thick sauce.

"Actually, you're home early, too," she said, leaning back into his arms. "You spoiled my surprise."

"I'm surprised."

"Not as much as you would have been if you'd come home when I expected. I was going to greet you in Saran Wrap."

"Saran Wrap?" His arms tightened.

Olivia lowered the flame under her pan and wiggled around to face him. She rested her arms on his shoulders. "Loretta read a book that says if you want to keep your husband interested, you should greet him at the door every

night in costume. The author suggests Saran Wrap as an all-time favorite.''

"Buy the book." He found her lips for a leisurely kiss.

"I will. As soon as they write one to match it."

"To match it?"

"One for men." She tweaked his nose and turned back to the sauce.

Brett's laugh was husky. "Now tell me why you're home."

"To surprise you."

"Really?"

"Really. I left about two. I figured that everything I had to do I could do here just as well as in my office."

"I didn't see your car."

"I parked it down the block. I even left Folly with Loretta so his barking wouldn't alert you. See what you spoiled?"

"I didn't spoil dinner, did I?" Brett took the spoon out of Olivia's hand and tasted what was obviously a master-piece. "Magnificent. What is it?"

"Crawfish *étouffée*. There's a salad in the refrigerator, and I've got a loaf of French bread so fresh it's still warm from the baker's oven."

"Is this another anniversary?"

"No."

"Did you do something you feel guilty about?"

"No!" She grabbed the spoon out of his hand as he attempted another taste.

"Then why?"

"Because I love you."

Brett became absolutely still behind her; then she felt his hands rest lightly on her shoulders. "What did I ever do to deserve you, bright eyes?"

"It must have been something wonderful," she said loftily.

"Whatever it was, I'm glad I did it."

"Would you do something else, then?"

"Why do I have the feeling I'm being led into a trap?"

"Will you finish stirring this? You can turn it off when the timer buzzes. No tasting allowed."

"Where are you going to be?"

"Changing."

"Into Saran Wrap?" he asked, a wicked gleam in his eyes.

"You'll see." Olivia left him with a kiss on his cheek and a spoon in his hand. In their bedroom she peeled off her jeans and T-shirt and took her newest purchase out of the closet. Zipped and buttoned, she smoothed it over her hips. It might not be transparent, but she thought Brett was going to approve anyway. Brett's approval was as important to her as the air she breathed or the food she ate. If she couldn't have his love, she would have that, even if it cost her the price of the new jumpsuit and an afternoon at the academy.

Some days she wondered if she should give up more for him. She and Brett were apart much too often. No matter how she was blossoming with her new responsibilities, no matter how much she loved her work, she still felt guilty that she had taken it on without Brett's full support. He had married a woman who seemed to be the fulfillment of his dreams, and now he woke up each morning next to a career woman who had to juggle her schedule to spend time with him.

But some days she wondered if things would be different at all if she had turned down the terms of Mary's will. Would her constant presence at home really change anything? Would it change anything after February, when she reluctantly gave up the academy and her position there? She had come to the conclusion that no matter how many times they made love or talked or shared their daily lives, she still loved Brett from afar. He was always an arm's length from her; he was isolated in the most primal of ways.

More than anything, Olivia wanted to change that. She wanted to touch him and know he had really been touched, but she didn't know if changing Brett was possible, even if she was at his beck and call twenty-four hours a day. For now there was nothing she could do other than lavish affection on him every chance she got and hope someday it would bring him closer.

"I turned the crawfish off, and the rice looks like it's ready..." Brett stopped in the doorway and gave a high-pitched wolf whistle. "Look at you."

"You're doing enough looking for us both." Olivia slipped her second onyx earring in place before her arms fell to her sides. "Do you like it?"

Like it? Brett wondered if Olivia had any idea what the sight of her in the clinging, plunging black jumpsuit was doing to his blood pressure. He wondered if Delilah had ever asked Samson the same question. "You're not planning to wear that for anyone but me, are you?"

"The mailman, the meter reader, the milkman..."

"No one delivers milk in New Orleans."

"Darn." She snapped her fingers.

"You're gorgeous."

She practiced her slinkiest walk until she was just in front of him. "Guess what?"

"What?"

She turned around and exposed a completely bare back. "The best was yet to come."

"You're going to catch cold."

"The look on your face is worth it."

"How do you know what the look on my face is?"

"We've been married almost five months." She peeked over her shoulder. "I was right, too."

"How long will the *étouffée* keep?"

She stuck out her tongue. "Not long enough."

"Next time you wear that, we're ordering pizza."

"It's a size seven!" She spun around, her pose forgotten, and clapped her hands. "The last time I wore a size seven I wasn't much older than seven. I've lost fifteen pounds!"

Brett had seen the weight coming off, but he hadn't realized how much it had meant to her. Her figure was proportionally the same, but somehow tauter, firmer. She was still far too womanly to be a fashion model, but without the extra pounds, the symmetry of her body was breathtaking. It was a body any man would want to lose himself in forever.

The weight loss also had a maturing effect on her face. Her perfect milk-and-roses complexion stretched more sharply over her cheekbones. Her eyes seemed larger, her mouth more sensual, less childlike. Framed by her gleaming, beautifully cut hair, the face was one no man would easily forget.

"How did you do it?" He brushed his fingertips along one nearly bare shoulder. "I know you've cut down on what you eat, and I know how hard you're working, but how did you lose those pounds in all the right places?"

"I might explain someday if you're good." She slipped her arm through his. "Now I'm starving, and I want to hear about your day."

Brett reflected on the way this part of their marriage had changed over the months. Marriage to Olivia was different from what he had wanted or expected. Most nights he came home to a crotchety housekeeper, not to the woman he'd pledged to have and to hold till death parted them. He resented the hours they spent away from each other, hours that cheated him out of the love she gave so freely. But when he could rise above his resentment, he could see how much more they had to share than they had in the beginning.

Had he ever doubted that she would understand his work? Olivia had the kind of mind that grasped the most essential concepts without needing to understand all the tiny details. He had come to welcome her input on his cases, even to the

point of being pleasantly surprised that she sometimes saw new angles that he hadn't touched on himself. Now he was no longer just eager to touch her, to drink in her sweetness; he was eager to talk to her, to share his day with her.

He'd expected marriage to level out, to become the humdrum institution the comic strips and situation comedies insisted it was, but it hadn't. Instead, the hurried passion of their early marriage had mellowed like fine wine. They still made love often, but they were so attuned to each other's bodies that sometimes he was sure their heartbeats were synchronized.

Because of her job their marriage wasn't what he'd expected it to be. But at moments like these he had to admit that different might not mean worse.

In the kitchen they dished up a plate apiece and took it out to the courtyard to eat. Mrs. Minn wasn't a terrific cook, but she did have a green thumb. She had taken Olivia's sadly neglected flower bed and turned it into something wonderful. Even the Mexican pots that had stood empty so long were filled with cascading annuals. The courtyard was fulfilling its promise.

Brett drank in the freshness of the early evening, the sweet fragrances of springtime, the sounds of laughter from across the bayou. He wanted to hold on to the moment, because moments when he felt this in tune with the world were rare. He touched Olivia's hand.

"Put a courtyard like this one on your list."

Olivia swallowed a mouthful of crisp lettuce. "What list?"

"The list of things we want in a house."

Olivia took another bite of salad without commenting.

Brett didn't want to let the subject drop. "I called the realtor myself yesterday. She says she's got a new group of houses for us to see. We could go tomorrow if you like." He settled back and watched Olivia over his wineglass.

"Not tomorrow. I've got a million things to do. Banking, laundry, shopping."

The feeling of being in tune began to vanish. "You don't want a house, do you?"

She looked directly into his eyes. "I want a fight even less."

"We're not going to fight."

Olivia pushed the *étouffée* around her plate, trying to think of a way to explain her feelings. "It's just one thing too many," she said finally. "Moving into a house is a big job."

"We could time it for the summer, August maybe, when classes at the Hopkins Academy have ended. You'll have a few weeks off then, won't you?"

"Not as many as you'd think. We may be making a big change at the school next year. I'm going to be in the thick of it by August."

Brett continued to watch her. "Do you think it's wise to make any kind of change? Shouldn't that be for the new owner to decide? I'd think you'd want to just put everything on hold until you can sell out."

"We *are* going to fight." Olivia put her fork down and folded her hands. "We always fight when we talk about the future."

"Is that why you hardly ever bring it up?"

"That's why."

Brett realized they were moving beyond their usual boundaries. They could talk forever about the day-to-day routine of their lives, but Olivia was right, the future seemed to be off-limits. "Do you know why we fight about it?" he asked.

"Our view of it's different, I guess."

"Maybe we should bring our differences out in the open," he said with little enthusiasm.

"I don't know if we can. I don't know if I can express what I see happening."

"Go ahead and try."

Olivia took a sip of wine, then rolled her glass back and forth between her palms as she thought about how to begin. "Well, what it comes down to, I guess, is the way we look at our marriage. I think you see it in terms of what it can be, and I see it in terms of what it is."

"Go on."

She set the glass down and leaned forward earnestly, propping her elbows on the table and her head on her hands. "I'm so happy, Brett. I love our life. Sure, sometimes I wish we could just be together more; I wish neither of us had jobs, that we could spend hours together choosing a house, painting walls, putting up wallpaper. But we can't do that now, and I don't mind waiting. Isn't it enough that we have each other? That we have moments like these? We don't have to have it all right away, do we?"

"I don't know how you manage to make buying a house sound like something decadent. I want us to have a house, Olivia, not an orgy with our neighbors."

"There's nothing wrong with buying a house. It's just that I can't do one thing more than I'm doing."

"But by next February you're going to have a lot of time on your hands."

Olivia wondered if his statement had really been meant as a question. Did Brett sense her growing reluctance to cut her ties with the Hopkins Academy? She wanted to put his mind at rest, but she couldn't, because her own was in turmoil. "Not necessarily," she hedged. "It will take some time to sell the academy. You know that."

"Especially if you start making major changes." Brett finished the rest of his wine in one long swallow. He wished he'd brought the bottle out to the courtyard so he could pour himself another glass.

Olivia saw the change in Brett's posture. She felt the loss of his relaxed smile. She always avoided the subject of plans for the academy because she knew Brett saw them as a be-

trayal. Perhaps if she could explain her plans now, he might understand that they weren't a betrayal of him but a natural outgrowth of her own developing leadership style. Maybe he would begin to understand what being headmistress meant to her.

She took a deep breath. "Can I tell you what I'm thinking about? I've been wanting to, but I've been afraid you wouldn't understand."

In spite of himself, despite his anger, he felt reluctant admiration. Olivia wasn't ordinarily manipulative, but neither was she so guileless that she couldn't see a good approach to solving a problem. She was trying to enlist his support by soliciting his opinion. Damn her, it was probably going to work.

Olivia read his feelings correctly. She also saw his effort to control them. Reaching across the table she took his hand. "We're lovers, not enemies. I need you beside me."

He gave up the fight. "Tell me what you're planning."

"You know enough about the academy to know that the program is a two-year one."

Brett realized that was about all he knew. He had purposely divorced himself from the school that was taking his wife out of their home and away from him. Against his will he understood how unfair he had been. Until it was sold the academy was a large part of Olivia's life. She deserved a husband who understood that and listened to her with as much enthusiasm as she listened to him.

"From what I know, it's the best nanny school in the country," he said, trying to put his prejudices behind him.

"The oldest," she corrected, "and the most thorough. We hope we're also the best. Anyway, our program lasts two years, and it's expensive. That's why I didn't go into it until I..." She stumbled, unsure how to explain the way she had come up with her tuition. "Well, until I had a chance to borrow the money interest free. There are a lot of women like me, women who would prefer being nannies to being

secretaries or beauty consultants or day-care aids. Unfortunately, they can't come to the Hopkins Academy because the tuition is so high. So, to make a long story short, we need to develop a program that's more affordable, an intensive program that can be built upon later if a nanny wants more training.''

"Can you do that without sacrificing quality?"

"I think we can. We're all working on course development right now. We'd continue the two-year program. There's a lot of demand for those graduates, and that's not going to change. But because of the addition of a one-year program, we're having to overhaul all our classes. Now we have to teach everything that's absolutely mandatory in the first year. The second year has to be an in-depth exploration of what was covered first."

"Give me an example." Brett realized she'd hooked him. He was interested.

Olivia was delighted to. She was delighted that he was still holding her hand and talking to her. She couldn't believe how good it felt to be able to share her thoughts this way.

"Well, take child health and safety, for instance. When our nannies come out of school after two years, they're just one step away from being pediatric nurses. They know the signs and symptoms of every childhood illness; they can do C.P.R. and all advanced first aid techniques; they can use stethoscopes and just about anything else a doctor carries in his little black bag. They can total the vitamins and minerals, protein and carbohydrates, in a child's diet quicker than Casey Stengel could total the hits in a baseball game."

Brett smiled, and Olivia felt it grow inside her. "How do you know anything about Casey Stengel?"

"I've been reading up on baseball," she said shyly. "You said it was one of your passions."

"Just one," he said with an even warmer smile. "But go on."

"Well, the way we've taught these things in the past was to take two months on this subject, two months on that. Now we have to redivide the training. We'll teach C.P.R. to everyone the first year, but maybe only the second-year graduates will be trained to use diagnostic equipment."

"So it's a process of deciding what's essential and how you're going to approach it?"

"Exactly. And it's tricky, because if we choose incorrectly and endanger a child's safety or happiness, then we've failed."

Brett had never realized just how strongly Olivia felt about what she was doing. He had believed she saw her participation at the Hopkins Academy as an investment in their future and as a chance to prove her abilities. He hadn't realized how much she believed in the training the academy provided. He forced down the fear that her enthusiasm would make it impossible for her to sever her ties when the time came. She had promised she would only stay for a year. He had no right to doubt her.

"Is there more to establishing the one-year program than just being able to appeal to additional students?"

Olivia was thrilled that he understood more than she had said out loud. They really could communicate. "There is. You've caught me, haven't you?"

"You want to turn out more nannies because you believe it's such a good alternative to day care. You want to broaden the definition of who can afford one and—" he made a stab in the dark, certain he was going to find his mark "—you hope that if you can get more women to go through the program, you'll upgrade parenting skills, because most of these women are going to be parents someday themselves."

"Women and men," she said triumphantly. "I just approved an application for a young man for September. He's an ex-Marine, and his references are impeccable. But yes, you're right about all of it. I know day care is essential, and I know that nannies are only a tiny part of the solution to

the problem of quality child care. I want to broaden the base so more people, students and parents, can benefit. The more people who are trained to raise children correctly and do, in whatever capacity, the better the world is going to be."

"All the way from cleaning baby bottles to saving the world."

Olivia mirrored the smile on Brett's face. His teasing had been gentle. She knew he understood her excitement. "Well, maybe it sounds a little grandiose, but I do believe that taking care of children properly makes a lot of difference."

"I'd be the first person to agree with that."

She squeezed his hand and thought about how much difference a loving "parent" would have made in his childhood. "I thought you might understand."

"So what other changes are in the works?"

"You're not bored silly?"

Surprisingly, he wasn't. "Not at all."

"Well, we've added something brand-new to our curriculum. Next year it'll be for both first- and second-year students. I call it the ego-expanding part of our training. The academy's always paid attention to teaching nannies how to take care of children, but we've never paid attention to those nannies themselves. Not beyond checking their references and approving their psychological testing before we admit them, anyway. Now we're concentrating on the people inside the uniform."

"How?"

"We're teaching diet and hairstyles, bringing in an image consultant, even having an aerobics class every day. Then, when everyone is feeling prettier..."

"Even your Marine?" he interrupted.

"Even our Marine, when he gets here. When everyone is feeling prettier, we're going to teach them a bit more about themselves, do some assertiveness training. We want them to leave the school feeling confident of their abilities and the impression they're going to make."

Had he ever wondered why Mary had chosen Olivia to run the school after her death? The answer was so clear that he couldn't believe he'd been blind to it for so long. Mary had chosen Olivia because she was the right person for the job. Olivia was the perfect person to provide the transition between Mary and whoever eventually took over. Not only was Olivia providing excellent leadership now, she would choose her successor well, considering ideology and commitment as much as her own financial gain.

He wanted Olivia home; he wanted her beside him all the way, but how could he deny her his support when it obviously meant so much to her? She was glowing just because he had taken the time to understand her, to listen to her talk about something that was important to her. In the past few minutes something vital had happened between them. As far as he was concerned no word had been invented for it, but it had to do with caring and giving and putting his own needs second to hers for a change. It felt good.

"It all sounds great," he said, trying to put all his unfamiliar feelings into his voice. "Does your size seven have anything to do with this ego-expanding class?"

She examined a speck of dirt on the table. Brett could see through her as easily as through the Saran Wrap she'd teased him about earlier. "We started the aerobics class in March. I felt it was my duty to participate. See how well it works?"

He stood and held out his hand. "It could backfire, you know."

"How?" She rose and put her hand in his. She felt closer to him than she ever had. She had never loved him more.

"If your nannies are as pretty as you are, they may run off and get married before they even work a day."

"Think of what wonderful mothers they'll be."

Brett had never wanted to make love to her more. He wanted to hold her, to share her body as he had just shared her mind. But he also wanted to hold on to her, to hold her

down, to hold her back. He wanted to remind her of her commitment to him. He started toward the house, but Olivia stood her ground. "You haven't told me anything about your day. I've done all the talking."

"I'm going to tell you all about it a little later."

"We haven't had dessert."

"We're about to have my specialty."

"And what about the pecan pie?"

"We'll have it later."

"How much later?"

Brett dropped her hand and folded his hands over his chest. Olivia didn't want to be led. It was strange how quickly things could change in a marriage. "You tell me."

"Much later," she said decisively.

"Are you going to teach that assertiveness-training course yourself?"

"I just might," she said, slipping her arms through his. "Right now I feel like I could do just about anything."

Brett stared at the dark water of the bayou and held her as tightly as he could.

Chapter Fifteen

The changing seasons weren't as noticeable in New Orleans as they would have been farther north, but by June Olivia recognized the signs that summer had definitely arrived. Magnolia blossoms no longer perfumed the air; the baby ducklings had real feathers now; more often than not Folly lay in the shade of the tiny tree in the courtyard, his long tongue lolling as he panted from the heat. And, most of all, Brett was more impatient about buying a house.

June had also brought with it an invitation to the annual Bar Association dinner. That morning Olivia stood outside a familiar Garden District house and hoped that Cherry would be at home.

Ringing the doorbell of the Broussard house felt strange. As she did, Olivia remembered all the other times when she had balanced Lucy on her hip while she unlocked the door with one hand and tried to keep Trey from shinnying too far up the front-porch pillar with the other. She no longer had a key; she was no longer a part of their daily lives. She was

Olivia: friend, wife of Lenny's colleague, ex-beloved nanny. If all the nannies who were now training at the Hopkins Academy came away from their first position with as many happy memories as she had, then the school would be a success in the ways that counted most.

"Olivia?" Cherry opened the door and embraced her warmly. "What brings you here? I thought you'd be up in Baton Rouge today."

"I played hooky." Olivia clutched her shopping bag and followed Cherry inside. "I'm only going to stay a moment, because I know how busy you always are. I just needed your advice on something."

"Don't be silly. Stay for lunch." Cherry lowered her voice to a conspiratorial whisper. "The children are all gone for the afternoon. I'm in the house alone. I'd love to talk to a grown-up."

"And I'd love to talk to a friend."

"Then come in and help me make lunch. You won't even have to cut the sandwiches into little stars. Do you know Trey still makes me do that for him or he refuses to eat? You spoiled him rotten."

"Little stars now, caviar and pressed duck when he's thirty."

Cherry chuckled as they negotiated the maze of rooms leading into the kitchen, the most modern room in the house. Gleaming stainless steel and gray quarry tile set off the salmon walls and oak woodwork. Olivia settled herself on a stool at the free-standing butcher-block island and waited for Cherry to supply her with sandwich fillings. She started by slicing tomatoes.

"What did you need my advice about?" Cherry set a head of lettuce and a block of cheese next to the tomatoes.

"A dress I bought for the Bar Association dinner to-night." Olivia looked up and grimaced. "I've been buying my own clothes for years. I know what looks good on me and what doesn't. Then I went into this shop over on St.

Charles and I was paralyzed. I kept thinking how important the dinner was and how great I wanted to look, and suddenly I couldn't make a decision.''

"Evidently you did if you bought something."

"Do you know how I decided?" Olivia was embarrassed to confess, but she knew Cherry would love the story. "I just took everything they had in my size and tried it on. Then I put the four dresses that fit in a pile, shut my eyes, shuffled them up and picked one."

Cherry broke into laughter.

"I think it was my least favorite, too," Olivia finished. "But by then I was too confused to care."

Cherry's laughter trailed her to the refrigerator. "Ham or roast beast?"

Olivia smiled at Trey's name for his favorite luncheon meat. "Roast beast if the Grinch carved it.''

"The deli man carved it."

"Just as good."

Cherry set the roast beef next to Olivia and began to cover slices of French bread with mayonnaise. "If the dress is awful, I'll go with you to take it back. You can try on the others and I'll tell you what to buy. I love spending other people's money."

"That would be terrific."

"So why is this dress so important?" Cherry handed Olivia a piece of French bread and took one for herself. They finished making their sandwiches.

"I just want to look nice.''

"Nice? You said 'great' before. Which is it?"

"Great," Olivia amended.

Cherry continued to probe. "And why great for this dinner? I can tell you right now it's going to be one of the more boring things you've done this week, maybe this year."

"I haven't met a lot of Brett's colleagues. I just want to make a good impression. Here, you sit down and let me get the tea."

Olivia went to the freezer to fill glasses with ice while Cherry sliced a lemon from a copper bowl on the island. "I can't imagine you making any other kind of impression," Cherry complimented her. "You don't need the perfect dress for that."

Olivia decided to be honest. Cherry would understand. "Brett has one colleague I'd like to outshine tonight."

"I wondered if Kate Parsons had anything to do with it."

Olivia was glad she didn't have to explain any further. "Am I being silly?"

"That depends. If you think you have to show Brett that you're as beautiful as Kate, then you can forget it. That man's got eyes for you alone. His life could depend on knowing what Kate wears tonight and I'll bet he wouldn't be able to remember. But if you're doing it for yourself, to prove something to you and no one else, then it's not silly. It's female. It's human." She tossed and caught the leftover lemon for emphasis. "It's wonderful!"

"Kate was so awful at the wedding." Olivia had never mentioned Kate to anyone before. She was glad to be able to talk to Cherry about her. "She came up to me, and in five or six sentences she tore me to shreds. And so politely, too. I felt like I was six years old and about that attractive."

"What would it take to make you feel that way again?" Cherry watched as Olivia set tea in front of her and settled on her stool again.

"Going back to the store on St. Charles to exchange my dress." Both women laughed, but when they sobered, Olivia continued. "Really? I don't think anything could make me feel that way again. Not anything or anyone. You know, when I married Brett, I felt like Cinderella. I was sure there was a fairy godmother out there somewhere making it all happen. I mean, why else would Prince Charming want me?"

"And now?"

"Well, now I know why he wanted me. I'm pretty wonderful."

"I'd cheer if my mouth wasn't full."

Olivia could feel color rising to her cheeks. Complimenting herself was hard, but it was a step in the right direction. In twenty-four years she had hardly ever considered what she had to offer anyone. Since she'd become the headmistress of the Hopkins Academy, she'd been forced to evaluate her abilities and attributes every day. She was truly pleased with what she'd found.

"I never thought much about it before, but I like myself," she said, trying out the words. "I really do, and it feels so good."

"And you've got a husband who's crazy about you. You've got the world by the tail. You can go to that dinner tonight and not have to feel like you're in Kate's shadow."

"I wonder if Brett loved her?" Olivia said, facing Cherry. "He says he was the one who left, but I also know he wanted to marry her."

"Even if he did, what difference does it make?" Cherry was obviously puzzled. "He doesn't love her anymore. He loves you."

That was precisely the point. Brett didn't love her, but Olivia couldn't admit it to Cherry. Her pride wouldn't let her. "I guess every wife wonders about the women in her husband's past."

"I didn't know either of them well enough to make a guess about their relationship," Cherry said finally. "I do know I always felt that Brett was so remote, so..." She tried to think of a way to phrase it. "So untouchable. He doesn't seem that way anymore. You've helped him open up. Kate was so remote herself that she never could have done that for him."

Olivia knew there was a difference between being good for someone and being loved by that someone. She loved Brett. She loved him more each day, even as she discovered things

about him that were less than perfect. She had fallen in love with a knight in shining armor, but it was the real Brett Terrill that she loved now. She could forgive him for his faults because she knew his strengths. She could even forgive him for not loving her in return. She just wasn't sure she could forgive him for loving Kate Parsons, even if the love had ended months before Olivia and Brett had met.

"I guess I'll never know." Olivia took the last bite of her sandwich. "Maybe it's just as well."

The dress went back to the shop on St. Charles, and with Cherry's help, Olivia found a better one. She wouldn't have chosen it herself, but when it was on and she saw what it did for her, she knew asking Cherry for help had been the right thing to do.

At home she washed her hair and dried it so that the sides curled softly around her face. She rarely bothered much with makeup, but today she bothered until the face staring back at her was subtly altered to emphasize her eyes and rose-tinted complexion.

She was dressed and Brett's tuxedo was carefully laid out on the bed when he arrived home from work. He took one look at her and showed his appreciation with a long, low wolf whistle.

"Gorgeous."

"Do you think so?" She remembered the night she had modeled the daring jumpsuit for him. She turned slowly so he could get the total effect. The dress was a long-sleeved white crepe de chine draped in diagonal pleats from the shoulders to her slender waist, where it was clasped with a sunburst of rhinestones and seed pearls. The skirt draped gracefully to the floor, but it parted at one side as she moved, revealing just a glimpse of leg.

She wouldn't have chosen white for herself; looking like an innocent debutante wasn't her plan for the evening. But Cherry had made her try on the dress, and once it was softly

molded to her body, there was nothing innocent about it. With pearl earrings and no other adornment, it was stunning.

Brett tried to remember what Olivia had looked like when he'd first met her. Was this the same woman who'd been dressed in a green sweatshirt and wet jeans? How could she have changed so much in a matter of months? Where was his endearingly shy young bride?

He covered what bordered on dismay with a forced laugh. "You should have let me know what you were going to wear. I could have hired a bodyguard."

"Is it too revealing? I can change."

The strange thing was that the dress wasn't revealing at all, not like the jumpsuit that she wore exclusively for him. It was just that the dress pointed up so well who she had become: Olivia LeBlanc Terrill, woman superlative.

He had the undeniable feeling that he was going to lose her.

"The dress is fine. You couldn't be more beautiful." Brett turned away and began to strip off his clothes.

"I'm glad you like it. I'm a little nervous about tonight. I met some of your friends at the wedding, but I haven't seen them since." Olivia put her arms around Brett's waist and rubbed her cheek along his bare back. "You won't leave me alone, will you?"

"I can guarantee you're not going to be alone. If I even step away from your side, three men will take my place."

"I don't want three other men. I want you." She tightened her arms around him momentarily, then stepped away to let him finish undressing. "Why don't I make us a drink while you get ready?"

Olivia mixed wine spritzers in the kitchen, humming to herself as she added ice cubes. The look on Brett's face when he'd seen her was enough to let her know he'd been impressed. She wondered when his opinion would cease to matter so much to her. She hoped it never did.

It was her turn to be impressed when he came out for help with his cuff links. Brett looked wonderful in the stark black and white. His hair seemed darker, his eyes bluer. The pleated fabric of his shirt emphasized his broad shoulders and narrow waist. It reinforced the power of his presence. He was aloofly elegant, and very, very desirable because of it.

What woman wouldn't want him? Her eyes widened as she remembered Kate's comment at the wedding. Yes, Brett looked wonderful in a tuxedo. For a moment Olivia toyed with the idea of trying to convince him not to go tonight. She suffered a moment of pure, unadulterated jealousy for what he and Kate had once shared. It was quickly replaced by fear.

Did what she and Brett have together stand a chance if she wanted to continue with her job after her year was up? She had no illusions about why Brett had married her. She had been the perfect choice for his wife: sweet, docile, domestic. She had been his dream of the woman he wanted to share his life and his home with. There was little left of that dream. True, they had so much to talk about now that there were never any awkward silences between them. Their love-making was still unbelievably satisfying to them both, but wouldn't that fade? What would happen when Brett woke up one morning and demanded that she become the woman he had married? Could she do it? *Would she do it?* And if she didn't, would Kate or someone like the woman Olivia had once been suit him better?

"If you can't get the cuff, I'll try again."

Olivia realized she had been standing with Brett's cuff link in her hand for a full minute, staring at it as if it held the secrets of the universe.

She looked up at him and wondered if he had any idea how she was feeling. "I'm sorry. I can do it. I was just thinking."

"About what?"

She gathered his cuffs together and poked the engraved gold link through them. "I don't know." She changed the subject, focusing on the cuff links as an escape. "These are lovely. Where did you get them?"

Brett hesitated too long, and Olivia looked up. He was obviously uncomfortable. "Kate?" she asked softly.

He nodded. "I hadn't even thought of it until you asked."

"She has excellent taste." Olivia began on the second cuff and tried to hide her distress.

Brett silently cursed his carelessness. Kate was so far out of his life that he hadn't given the cuff links any consideration. For the first time he realized that Kate would be at the dinner tonight. Suddenly he understood Olivia's dress just a little better. He felt a rush of warmth. He wouldn't have caused Olivia's insecurity for the world, but knowing she was worried—even jealous, perhaps—was nice. No, more than nice. It was . . . well, what was the word for relief and pleasure and just a bit of conceit mixed together?

"Kate had excellent taste," he said, smiling slightly. He stroked the soft skin under Olivia's chin and lifted her head so that their eyes met. "Her taste was excellent, but she would never have thought of giving me the puppy I always wanted. She would never have come home early to make me dinner, or buy a dress just because she wanted to impress me." He smiled more as her cheeks pinkened. "She was never you, Olivia."

Olivia knew her heart was in her eyes. "Did you love her, Brett?"

He shook his head, and his face grew serious. He wondered what it had cost her to ask. "No. I didn't love her. And I don't miss her, and I don't want her. Right now I'm with the only woman in the world that I want, and that's how I want it to stay."

She rested her cheek on the pleated front of his shirt and soaked in the warmth of his body next to hers. "Thank you."

"What am I going to do with you, bright eyes? One minute you're so gorgeous, so confident, that I feel like you
don't need me at all; the next minute you're a mass of insecurities. Sometimes I'm not sure I know you anymore."
He held her against him, surprised that he'd said the words
out loud.

Olivia was surprised, too. Brett never talked about his
feelings. "Maybe we still have a lot to learn." Her arms
tightened around him. "Maybe that's one of the wonderful
things about marriage. We can keep learning about each
other, enjoying what we discover."

Brett wasn't sure he wanted to discover anything else
about Olivia. The discovery that she'd been left an estate
worth a small fortune had been hard enough to take. The
discovery that she wanted to run the academy herself and
was, in fact, an excellent administrator had been even
harder.

He wasn't sure he wanted her to discover anything more
about him, either. Because someday she just might figure
out how much he needed her. And he didn't want anyone to
have that much power over him.

"We'd better go," he said finally. "I want to show you
off."

"I'm ready." She gave him one last hug. "Now I'm even
looking forward to it."

The drive took fifteen minutes. The Bar Association dinner was always held at the same French Quarter hotel.
Crystal chandeliers and plush burgundy carpet set off the
mahogany wainscoting and white and gold flocked wallpaper in the lobby. Olivia expected to hear a ragtime pianist
tickle the ivories as a corpulent madam glided down the
stairs to officially begin the night's festivities, but Brett reminded her that Storyville, New Orleans's long-gone red-
light district, had been in another part of town.

The lounge where a small jazz ensemble was entertaining
was filled to overflowing when they arrived. The men were

a sea of black and white, while the women were islands of brilliant colors. Brett introduced Olivia to his colleagues and their spouses against the wail of a saxophone and the bleat of a trombone. She made careful note of names, exchanging greetings and small talk as they threaded their way across the floor toward the bar.

"Just club soda," she told Brett as she scanned the crowd for familiar faces. The floor was so crowded that they hadn't seen anyone from his firm yet. He nodded and pushed his way through the masses of people around the bar to order for both of them while Olivia stood off to the side.

She spotted the Broussards and Sherwoods talking together not far away, and when Brett turned in her direction, she signaled him to meet her there. The ensemble was taking a break, and conversation and laughter buzzed loudly through the room as she went to join them.

"You look wonderful!" Cherry leaned over to kiss her cheek in greeting, and the others followed suit. "I knew the dress would be perfect."

Olivia told the Sherwoods and Lenny Broussard an abbreviated version of the story of her afternoon. Meg, who with her no-nonsense cropped brown hair and basic black dress looked as if she'd never worried about her appearance, nodded in sympathy. "I remember the first time I went anywhere important as Drew's wife. He was fresh out of law school, and we were fresh out of money. I couldn't afford a new dress, so I bought material to make one. Halfway through the predinner drinks I realized I'd forgotten to take out some very important pins."

"I still needle her about that every chance I get," Drew said smugly.

"Don't pin your hopes on doing it again," Meg shot back. "We all know you can be a real sew-and-sew."

"They do that often," Cherry informed Olivia when everyone's groans had died.

"Is it a contest to see who can think of the worst or the most puns?" Olivia asked, smiling at both the Sherwoods. They were an interesting couple. From what she could tell they both went their separate ways, but they still seemed madly in love. She suspected there was one place where they were very much together.

"Any puns will do." Drew put his arm around Meg's waist. "But there's no contest. Meg just can't keep up."

"Meg probably has better things to do with her time." Brett arrived and handed Olivia her drink.

"Meg has more things to do with her time than any woman I know, except Olivia," Cherry added.

"How about you? Six children and Lenny would keep any woman running," Olivia reminded her.

"All three of you are victims of the Superwoman complex," Drew said after the women had compared their schedules, agreeing finally that each one of them had too much to do. "Whatever happened to the little woman who sat in front of the fire knitting calmly while a cat chased her ball of yarn?"

"She never existed," Meg told him firmly. "That image was created by some man who wanted to believe he was superior. The sad thing is that the image still exists. Men still want to believe that the work women do is less important than theirs."

Cherry chimed in. "If the lady in that fantasy was knitting, it was because somebody in her family had to have mittens and she was the only one who could make them. Chances are she was stirring the soup kettle, rocking a cradle and singing to a fretting toddler at the same time. If she even had a cat, it was only to help her keep her cabin free of mice."

"And where was her husband all this time?" Lenny asked with a smile that said he knew he was goading them both. "Out in the barn playing pinochle?"

Olivia answered before anyone else could. "No, he was farming and hunting game and greasing wagon wheels and building a new room on the cabin for the children. But don't you see the point? Each of them had a job to do. In some ways it was fairer than it is today. They knew how valuable they both were. They knew how hard they both worked. Neither of them had any illusions about whose job was harder. I remember when my grand-mère died. Not only was my grand-père sick with grief, he was lost. He had depended on her for so many things, and suddenly she wasn't there anymore. And I'll bet before she died, she never once worried whether she was really contributing."

Meg applauded. "I couldn't have said it better."

"Times have changed," Lenny pointed out. "Now women have more leisure."

"Some do," Olivia admitted. "But most don't, not even in our affluent society. A lot of women work because they have to support their families or because they have exciting, fulfilling jobs they don't want to leave. But you know, I think a lot of women work just because they want to feel as useful as my grand-mère did. They want to contribute everything they can, both to their families and the world. The Superwoman complex isn't anything new; it's just that now we've given it a name."

Brett listened to the debate. He was proud of Olivia for being able to articulate her beliefs so well, but at the same time he wondered just how what she was saying fit their lives.

The crowd began to move into the banquet hall for speeches and dinner. Brett took Olivia's arm, but Meg took her other one. "There's someone you've got to meet," she insisted. "She'll probably leave right after the dinner, so if you don't meet her now, you won't have a chance. We'll have the men save us places."

"Go ahead." Brett watched Olivia and Meg wend their way through the crowd.

"Afraid Meg's going to corrupt her?" Drew asked with a grin.

"I doubt there's anything Meg can say to her she hasn't thought of herself," Brett answered dryly.

Olivia met Meg's friend and chatted for a moment; then she was introduced to several other women, all of whom had obvious respect and affection for Meg. Olivia realized one of the things she had cheated herself out of by working so hard was the company of other women, women who were growing and learning just as she was. She vowed silently to make sure that changed.

The last woman she spoke to wasn't a stranger. The woman was Kate Parsons.

"Hello, Olivia." Kate stood between Olivia and the door into the banquet room, as if she were purposely forcing a confrontation.

Olivia smiled. "Hello, Kate. What a lovely dress." She admired the intricate beadwork on the black and silver gown. Kate looked sexy and coolly unapproachable at the same time. With her natural beauty, it was a combination guaranteed to drive a man wild.

Kate's answering smile was colder than the blast of air-conditioning from the vent overhead. "You remember me? I'm surprised. You must have met so many people at the wedding."

"You weren't just anybody."

Kate lifted one eyebrow in surprise.

Olivia realized her honesty had caught the other woman off guard. Catching Kate off guard was obviously the key to dealing with her. Olivia turned a little to include Meg. "Do you know Meg Sherwood?"

"We've met," Meg said with no enthusiasm. "We'd better find our seats, Olivia, or somebody might grab them."

Kate ignored her. "Marriage to Brett agrees with you, Olivia. He knows how to make a woman happy, doesn't he?"

"He knows how to make me happy. I couldn't speak for anyone else." Olivia waited for Kate to step aside, but Kate wasn't about to let her walk away.

"He made me happy, too. For a while."

Meg drew an audible breath, as if she were about to explode, but Olivia put her hand on Meg's arm to silence her. "I'll bet you've never heard the story of Monsieur Crawfish's castle, have you?" Olivia asked Kate.

The question was so outrageous that it was apparent she had caught Kate off guard once more. Before she could answer, Olivia went on. "You see, after all my training as a nanny, I think in children's stories. You'll have to forgive me, but I'll tell it quickly. Monsieur Crawfish was an unhappy crawfish. He had a deep, wide crawfish hole on the banks of Bayou Teche, but every day he'd look over the bayou and see the beautiful plantation house sitting on the other side. He knew crawfish couldn't live in houses, so he decided to build up the entrance to his hole until it was as beautiful and awe-inspiring as any castle in the world. And that's what he did. He spent his life building that castle. Then one day, when he was very old, he finished it. He put the last little bit of mud in place and crawled away to see his masterpiece."

Kate looked bored. "Fairy tales are for children."

Olivia nodded. "There's a bit of child in each of us, and sometimes it comes out at the most unusual times, don't you think? Anyway, let me finish quickly. Unfortunately for Monsieur Crawfish, before he could even admire what he'd done, he saw a shadow moving overhead and he heard the noise of wings. Monsieur Crawfish scurried toward his wonderful, safe hole in the ground, but too late he realized that the entrance had been completely sealed off by his dream castle. The story stops there because Monsieur Crawfish didn't live long enough to tell us how it ended."

Olivia flashed Kate a radiant smile. "I've always thought that if Monsieur Crawfish had lived just a little bit longer,

he might have told us what he'd learned. When life is absolutely perfect as it is, there's no reason to waste even a minute building dream castles. If you do, someday you'll find just how much you've lost, but by then it will be too late to do a thing about it."

"Something to meditate on, isn't it?" Meg added meaningfully. She took Olivia's arm. "Nice talking to you, Kate."

Only Kate's eyes showed her anger. The two women stepped around her and headed toward the banquet hall.

"Well, how'd I do?" Olivia asked when they were some distance away.

"That was done like a pro."

"I hope she understood."

Meg smiled her approval. "Does Brett know how lucky he is?"

"To have me or to have lost Kate?"

"Both!"

"I don't know," Olivia said honestly. "But I know something I didn't know before."

"What's that?"

"I can take care of myself just fine. I'll never have to worry about Kate Parsons or anyone like her again."

Chapter Sixteen

A week after the Bar Association dinner Olivia helped put the finishing touches on a flower arrangement for the academy parlor. Twenty nannies were graduating that night, and in the ironclad tradition of Mary Hopkins herself, everything had to be in perfect order. Loretta worked beside her, and between the two of them the room was taking shape.

"You're not going back to New Orleans before the ceremony, are you?" Loretta neatly stacked gold-embossed diplomas next to a basket of Hopkins Academy emblems the new nannies would be qualified to wear on their maroon blazers after that night.

"No. I asked Brett to come up if he can. I've been cleaning Mary's things out of her apartment. It's ready for me to use now. We can stay here tonight and drive back tomorrow."

"Are you going to rent it? It's a nice apartment. You'd be able to get a good price for it."

Olivia had considered doing just that. She could also convert the apartment into more dormitory space if the school's enrollment increased when the one-year training program began. She hadn't been able to make herself pursue either option, however. The apartment was so convenient. What if... She didn't even want to let her thoughts follow their now-familiar path.

"If I were you," Loretta went on when Olivia didn't answer, "I'd keep it for days like this one. I worry about you driving back and forth every day. Sometimes you look so tired."

Olivia knew she'd been given her cue to say that she wouldn't be doing this much longer, that she'd be selling the academy in just over half a year and could manage fine until then. The problem was that the words wouldn't come. She hadn't been able to talk about selling the academy for weeks. She couldn't even bear to think about it. How long would it be before Brett realized what was happening or what she was feeling?

"I don't know what I'll do with the apartment," she said finally. "It's just one more decision to make."

"What decisions do you have to make, bright eyes?"

Olivia looked up from the flower arrangement and saw Brett standing in the doorway. "Well, hello!" She stuck the final carnation in place and went to greet him.

Brett watched Olivia walking toward him, all grace and style and confidence. In this room, in this building, she was the administrator, the headmistress of the Hopkins Academy for Nanny Development. It hardly seemed fitting to kiss her, but he did anyway.

"You're early." She brushed his hair off his forehead and wished she could brush away the problems between them as easily. "I wasn't expecting you before seven, if you came at all."

"I got off work early. Remember when I told you I was going to cut down on the amount of work I was taking? I've

been doing just that. By the time you sell this place I'll be down to a normal schedule."

By the time you sell this place. Olivia turned away to begin straightening chairs that were already in soldier-straight rows. "Did you eat on the way up?"

"I had a sandwich before I left." Something was bothering Olivia. Brett could see it in the way she held her body and the way she was avoiding his eyes. "Have you had dinner yet?"

"I was going to fix myself something in a few minutes."

"I'll finish whatever has to be done," Loretta volunteered, coming up to greet Brett. "I don't have anything else to do before graduation."

Olivia accepted gratefully. A few minutes later she was unlocking the door to the apartment. The windows had been open all day to let in the breeze, and the apartment smelled like fresh air and sunshine. Olivia had kept some of Mary's furniture, but she had given away the heavier, more somber pieces and added touches of her own. The apartment, like the school, was now a blend of Mary's personality and hers.

"Make yourself comfortable. I'll find us something to eat." Olivia started toward the kitchen, but Brett's arms around her waist stopped her.

"Do you realize you've never given me a real tour of the academy? This is the first time I've even been up to the apartment."

"I didn't think you were interested."

He'd been thinking of the academy as a rival. He should have been thinking of it as part of her life. She had never once complained about his attitude, but he wondered what kind of wedge he'd been driving between them by paying so little attention to something this important to her.

"I want to see the whole place after we eat," he said, letting her go.

"Go ahead and look around the apartment while I figure out what to fix."

She took bread and cheese out of the refrigerator and made sandwiches to toast while Brett wandered through the spacious rooms. In the kitchen he leaned against the door frame and watched her cook. "The apartment's very nice. Have you thought about renting it out?"

"That's what Loretta and I were talking about. I haven't made any decisions yet."

"That's probably wise. If you did rent it, you'd want to be able to guarantee a year's lease, and that could be a problem for the new owners."

"That's true."

Brett heard the lack of enthusiasm in Olivia's voice. She hadn't been herself since he'd arrived. In fact, she hadn't been herself for a while. Something was bothering her. Olivia wasn't moody. She had an internal serenity that kept her above most of life's petty concerns. But something was eating at her now. She'd asked for so little comfort in their months together that he hardly knew how to offer it.

"What's the matter? You're not yourself."

Olivia wanted to blurt out the truth, to finally get her feelings out in the open, but she didn't trust either of them to deal with them. "I'm just tired."

Brett knew she was covering up something. "You don't get enough rest. Every time I come up here I realize how tough the drive must be twice a day."

"It's wearing," she admitted. "But it's worth it."

"You'll be a rich woman when it's over with."

"That's not what I meant." She flipped the sandwiches and the butter sizzled in the pan.

"What did you mean?"

"It's been worth it personally."

"It's been worth the exhaustion and the hassles?"

"It has." Olivia lowered the burner flame and faced him, her arms crossed against her chest. She wondered if she was protecting herself from Brett or trying to be sure her feelings stayed bottled up inside her.

"How?"

"I've learned so much about me, about other people. It's been exciting and challenging. It's been satisfying. I wish..." Her voice trailed off.

"What do you wish?"

"I wish you understood."

And what else had she asked for in all their months of marriage? Nothing. Not his time, not his undivided attention, not even his love. He had gone into marriage believing that it had to be a partnership, but he had never practiced that, not really. If there was a partnership, their roles had been divided along the most chauvinistic of boundaries. She had given; he had received.

Olivia turned back to the stove. Obviously she wasn't going to get an answer.

"I do understand," Brett said quietly. "I haven't wanted to, but I do. These months have been important for you. You've grown. I like the woman you've become."

Olivia knew Brett was trying to show his support. The problem was that he didn't know how much support she needed. He had come to understand how valuable this time had been. What he didn't understand was that she could see into the future and know that the months and the years to come would be valuable, too.

She wanted to keep the Hopkins Academy. She wanted to continue as headmistress indefinitely. Every day, every crisis she solved, every plan she laid, had brought her closer to a decision that could endanger her marriage.

"Olivia?"

She turned off the burner, but she didn't face him. "You didn't want me to grow. You didn't want me to change."

"I've been selfish. I didn't want to sacrifice a minute of your time, much less a year. I'm sorry I've made it so difficult for you."

Hope stirred faintly inside her.

"I'm going to try harder," Brett continued. "I can give you the next months more willingly knowing how important they are to you. When this is over I want your memories to be good ones."

Hope died. Nothing was left except the need to level with him.

"What if it's not over in February? What if I kept the academy, Brett?"

The answer was so plain, he was surprised she had to ask the question. "Then our marriage would be in trouble."

"That sounds like an ultimatum. Be sure you sell the school next February, Olivia, or you'll suffer the consequences."

"Look at me."

She turned slowly, and he was surprised to see that her eyes were glistening with unshed tears. He felt fear slice through him; anger filled the paths it left. "That wasn't just a hypothetical question, was it?"

Olivia knew he finally understood. She'd wanted his understanding, but not this way. "I don't want to sell the academy, Brett. I'll always regret it if I do."

"Is that right?"

His sarcasm hurt worse than anything else would have. Olivia felt a tear trickle down her cheek. For a moment she had almost believed she'd be able to get through to him. He had come so far, but the truth was that he had much farther yet to go. Now he was barred from her by an impenetrable shell. They were back at the beginning.

"Can't we work it out?" she pleaded softly. "I can make any kind of reasonable compromise. I can hire more help, cut down my hours here, work at home more. We could buy a house in Kenner so I wouldn't have so far to commute, but your commute wouldn't be much longer than it is now."

"And would you carry our children back and forth like you carry Folly? Or would you hire a nanny for them? God knows, you'd have your pick, wouldn't you?"

"Brett, I—"

"No," he interrupted. "Let me finish. This is great. You could hire a nanny for our kids while you went off to work. You and I could schedule a few hours together, quality time, I think you called it once. Whatever the nanny couldn't manage, a housekeeper could. And we'd have holidays, wouldn't we? We could make up to each other and the kids for all the time we've spent apart by buying them wonderful, expensive toys. Down the line a ways you could go into analysis to figure out why you were feeling so lonely, so burned out. I could have an affair. If that didn't work, we could reverse it...."

"Stop it!" Olivia put her hands over her ears. "Stop it, Brett."

He strode over to her and yanked her hands to her sides. "Is that what you want for us? That's not what I want. That's not what I wanted when I chose you as my wife."

"I want a partnership," she said, unknowingly echoing his earlier thoughts. "I want you to give, too. I want us to compromise. I want you to love me enough to want what's best for me as well as for yourself."

"You can't change the rules in the middle of the game and expect me to keep right on playing. I'll give you what I can, but don't dream about the impossible."

She felt as if he'd slapped her. But then, she had asked for it by telling him that she wanted him to love her. Was the school the issue at all? Or was it only a tiny part of something much, much larger? Was the real issue the quality of the commitment they'd made to each other?

"What can you give me, then?" she asked past the lump in her throat.

"I can give you what a lot of women would settle for gladly from their husbands: my concern, my attention, my fidelity."

"As long as I play by the original rules?"

He dropped her hands. "I want what I've wanted all along. I've gone along with your taking over the academy, and I'm telling you I'll try to be more supportive until it's sold. That's all I'm going to do. I've compromised."

She made one more appeal. "Can you see that you're not being generous? That you're making my choice for me?"

"No." He stepped back, but he still held her gaze. "No, you get to make the final choice, Olivia. Just be sure you realize exactly what you're going to lose if you choose this place over me."

"And you'll lose very little, won't you? A few months of your life, another failed experiment. Maybe you'll even lose a few nights' sleep. But in the last analysis, if I choose the academy and you leave me, that's all it'll be to you. It won't be like having your heart cut out, will it? Your heart was never mine to keep."

"My heart is my own, and it's a damned good thing it is, isn't it?"

Olivia watched as Brett turned his back to her and headed for the doorway.

The graduation went on that night without him.

A funny thing, marriage. No matter how long you'd been together, some mornings you woke up in bed next to a male stranger. He looked at you, you looked at him, and the only thing you seemed to have in common besides the sheet covering you was the feeling you'd made a terrible mistake. Olivia watched Brett come fully awake on the pillow beside hers, and she wondered how they were going to bridge the gap that had separated them since graduation night.

"Folly's scratching on the door." She tried to smile. "Would you like me to let him out?"

"He's my dog. I'll do it."

Brett sat up and stretched. Olivia watched the play of his muscles under the tan that was deepening from the occasional Saturdays he'd spent fishing in New Iberia. She

wanted to touch him, but she knew her touch wouldn't be welcome. It hadn't been welcome for a week.

"Shouldn't you be up and off by now?" Brett gave her no more than a cursory glance before he stood.

"I have some shopping to do this morning. I'm going to head up to Baton Rouge at noon. It'll probably be late when I get back."

Brett shrugged, as if when she got home was no real concern of his. At the back door he knelt to bury his face in Folly's silky red fur and suffer his exuberant affection. Then he watched as the dog scampered into the courtyard to sniff out the events of the past night.

"Don't you wish we had that much energy?" Olivia belted her robe as she came to stand beside him.

"You used to."

Her voice was wistful. "Actually, I used to be a lot like Folly. I had too much energy and nothing to do with most of it."

"I'll take him for a walk before I go in this morning." Brett moved away to head toward the bathroom for a shower, but Olivia's hand on his arm stopped him. He could feel each separate finger sear his skin. A week without her touch was exactly seven days too long. He pulled away sharply.

"Call in and tell them you'll be late this morning," Olivia pleaded softly. "Let's talk this through, Brett. I don't want to go on this way. Do you?"

For some reason Brett remembered the evening in May when they'd eaten crawfish *étouffée* in the courtyard and then gone inside to make love until they'd both fallen asleep, exhausted, in each other's arms. They had talked that night. Olivia had told him her plans for the academy, and for some reason, for some crazy reason, he hadn't seen through them. He'd been drunk on her intelligence, her sweetness, her sincerity. Only the first hadn't been a lie.

"I don't want to talk," he said, "and I don't want to be late."

"Are we going to grow old together with this between us?"

"Are we going to grow old together?"

Olivia was careful not to touch him again. "There's nothing I want more in the world."

His relief was almost dizzying. She had made her decision. He had won. She had put him first. "Then you're not going to keep the academy?" He faced her for the first time.

Olivia could read his feelings clearly. For a moment she faltered. How easy it would be to say yes, to give in to his demand and be the wife he wanted her to be. In the last analysis, however, she could only be herself. She could only do what she must. For both of them.

"I am going to keep it." She raised her hand to touch him, but she realized her words had destroyed that freedom. Her hand dropped to her side. "I'm going to keep it, but anything else you want from me is yours. Any way you want to work this out will be all right with me. I'll commute from anywhere, cut my hours to the bone, hire as much help as I can afford. And I'll never, never put you second."

"And how much is that promise worth?" He gave a harsh laugh. "As much as the one you made when you said you were only going to keep the academy long enough to fulfill Mary's stipulation?"

"People change. I changed. I didn't realize..."

"You didn't realize what? That you'd find something more important than our marriage? Because that's the choice you just made, bright eyes."

She flinched at the way he said his favorite nickname for her, but he went on, ignoring her reaction.

"Keep the academy, lose me. You can't have both." Brett held up his hand to still her protests. "I've lived my whole life on the empty promises of women. I thought you were

different. I chose you because you were different. I married you because you were different. But you weren't different at all."

"I'm not your mother. I'm not Kate. Can't you see that?" she pleaded.

"I can see a woman who thinks her own fulfillment is more important than her marriage."

"That's not true! I want this for me, but I want it for you, too. Can't you see how much better our marriage is now? If I'm happy, I have more to give you."

"I married you because I wanted us to build something together. I wanted a house and a family and a wife who was there to greet me at night. I didn't—and I *don't*—want a woman who can give me less than that."

"Then you married me for all the wrong reasons," she said, slumping in defeat. "You didn't marry me because you loved me, or because you wanted to grow with me. In fact, you didn't marry *me* at all. You married a fantasy. The real Olivia LeBlanc Terrill is flesh and blood. That's what you can't handle."

"No, I can't handle the real Olivia LeBlanc Terrill," he said, biting off the words, "because the real Olivia LeBlanc Terrill isn't the woman I thought she was. And she's not flesh and blood. She's an ambitious, ruthless manipulator. Hell, I should have stayed with Kate. At least with her it was all out in the open. You're much better at hiding who you really are than she ever was."

"If I've hidden anything it's because you wanted me to." Olivia's voice quivered. "You've never cared enough to want to know what was going on inside me."

"That's right!" As soon as he'd said the words, Brett knew how untrue they were. Even now, when their relationship was hanging by a thin thread, he didn't want to hurt her the way he knew he just had. She had gone visibly pale at his words, and her eyes were overflowing with tears. He

turned away, not wanting to see the damage he'd done. Not wanting to care.

"I'm going to get ready for work. Stay out of my way until I'm gone." The bedroom door slammed behind him.

Olivia felt nausea well up inside her. This hadn't been a fight. It had been a slaughter.

She was outside in the courtyard when she heard the screech of tires as Brett backed the BMW out of the driveway.

The sound seemed like the most mundane of ways to signal the end of a marriage.

Chapter Seventeen

Hello, stranger." Kate Parsons stood in the doorway of Brett's office, a burgundy briefcase the color of her shoes in one hand.

Brett hadn't seen her since the night six weeks before when she'd coldly nodded to him at the Bar Association dinner. She looked much more amiable now. More amiable than the routine wrapping up of the Atkinsons' divorce case should have called for. He stood and gestured to the seat in front of his desk.

"How are you, Kate?"

"As well as can be expected for someone who works too hard and still has too much free time on her hands." She seated herself, pulling her pink pleated skirt over her long legs.

They had been a couple for too long for Brett to miss the subtle invitation in both her words and the way she slid one shapely leg over the other as she made herself comfortable.

It was apparent that Kate had heard he and Olivia were no longer living together and hadn't been for a month.

"I thought Frank was taking care of your free time."

She shrugged. "Frank's my boss."

Brett sat down and shuffled the papers on his desk until he found what he needed. "You really didn't have to make this trip. I could have had these taken over to your office. They're just a few things your client has to sign, nothing that hasn't been agreed on."

Kate looked the papers over and nodded. "They look fine." She slipped them in her briefcase, then sat back to contemplate Brett. "You look tired."

"Unlike you, I've had no free time to fill up."

She smiled her elegant, arrogant smile. "Do you have some now? It's half past five. We could go out to dinner."

"Why?"

"To talk over old times."

"Our old times are hardly worth talking over."

Kate's eyes met his, and Brett thought he detected a flicker at his words. "Some of them were memorable," she said quietly.

Brett was lonely. He needed to get out and, strangely, he didn't want to hurt Kate by saying no. He'd suffered enough in the past month not to want to inflict pain on anyone else. He stood. "Where would you like to go?"

She shrugged. "How about that hole in the wall on Royal with the great gumbo?"

They left their cars parked in a nearby garage and walked to the French Quarter, talking casually about people they knew. Settled in a small booth, they ordered gumbo and a drink apiece.

"I used to love to come here with you," Kate said, reaching for a chunk of French bread.

"That's funny. I thought this place was always my choice."

"I just let you think it was." She offered a piece to him, and he took it.

They sat chewing silently until Kate spoke again. "How's Olivia?"

"I wondered how long it'd take you to ask."

"How long will it take you to answer?"

Brett's smile was thin. How could he answer when he didn't know? He hadn't seen Olivia in a month. He hadn't heard from her in a month. He knew she was in Baton Rouge and physically well; he'd learned that much from a phone call with Myriam. How Olivia felt about him and what she thought about their marriage was a total mystery. Some days he could even pretend to himself that he didn't care.

"She walked out a month ago," he said finally. "But you knew that already."

Kate nodded. "Were you as surprised as I was? She seemed like the till-death-do-us-part type to me."

He wanted to laugh. Kate of all people should know how little effort it took to give that kind of impression. "Olivia wasn't what she seemed."

"Then she was like the rest of us, huh?"

Brett couldn't have put it better himself.

"Just a human being," Kate finished. "I'll bet that was a shock." Her eyes caught Brett's and held them. "You've never been able to stand a woman with noticeable flaws, have you?"

"You mean little flaws like lying and pretending to be what she's not? No, I have a problem with that, Kate."

"You have a problem all right. You put women in the most untenable positions by making unreasonable demands on them; then, when they fail your little tests, you dump them."

He sat back and took a swallow of the beer the waitress had delivered earlier. "This is priceless. You defending Olivia."

Kate waved her hand in the air. "The hell with Olivia. I'm defending myself. I never had the chance before."

"I don't need this now."

"On the contrary, maybe you need it more than you ever did."

Brett lifted his beer to her in a mock toast.

"When we were together," Kate said finally, "I always felt like I had to perform for you. I could never be me, because I knew if I was, you'd be out the door so fast the dust wouldn't settle for weeks. I wasn't right for you, but in my own way I loved you. I wanted to keep you around. That is, I did until it got too hard to keep up the act."

"Which act was that?"

"I'm not marriage material. I don't want kids or a home or a husband to tell me what to do. I'll always put myself first. That's just the way I am. For a while I tried to pretend to myself that it might be different with you, but it really couldn't be. If I'd told you that when I finally realized it, I knew you'd go. So I tried to pretend, to myself, to you, that I could learn to be that way." She shrugged. "It was a lie."

"I know."

"You were the only man I've ever cared about enough to lie that way to."

"Am I supposed to feel honored?"

"I don't know what you're supposed to feel. I don't even know if you feel, period."

Kate sat back while the waitress served their gumbo. Then she leaned forward again. "We were together for two years. Never once in all that time did you ever let me know what was going on inside you."

Brett had never seen Kate get emotional, but she was now. "I wanted to marry you," he said at last. "You knew that."

She dismissed his words with another wave of her hand. "Who cares? You were choosing a roommate, a partner for producing genetically perfect children. Even if you'd de-

clared your undying love, we wouldn't have stayed together, because our needs are different. But no matter what the outcome, I deserved to know how you felt about me."

Brett had never really considered that he might have been at fault, too. Kate's lies and manipulations had been so glaring that he'd never thought about his own part in what had happened.

She seemed to read his mind. "Part of our problems belonged at your doorstep, counselor. I'm willing to take my share of the blame, but for a long time now I've been wanting to tell you that some of the blame was yours, too."

They ate their gumbo in silence.

The meal and conversation ended over a cup of coffee with chicory.

"Are you going to do something about your marriage? Or do you consider yourself a free man?" Kate sipped the last drops in her cup and watched him as if she were going to weigh his answer carefully.

"I'm a married man."

"In name only," she pointed out.

"I still consider myself a married man."

She shrugged. "That's too bad."

Brett hadn't missed the question behind the question. He set his coffee cup down. "What you and I had is finished."

"I know that, but I liked the idea of ending it on a more positive note."

Kate was a beautiful woman, and once she'd been important to him. Brett was surprised that the veiled suggestion they spend the night together had no appeal at all. There was only one woman he wanted to take to bed, and she might as well be on the moon.

"We'd better go," he said, sliding across the booth as if to stand.

"Brett?"

His head turned so he was looking at her again, but his body was poised for flight.

"Did Olivia ever tell you the story of Monsieur Crawfish?"

He frowned. The question wasn't one he'd expected to hear. "Monsieur Crawfish?"

"It's a silly little story about a crawfish who builds his dream castle, then gets eaten by a bird because he's inadvertently covered the entrance to his hole." She smiled her familiar smile. "You really ought to get her to tell it to you someday. She does it with such flair."

The apartment on Bayou St. John seemed empty even though Olivia had taken nothing except her clothes when she left. Even Folly's presence helped very little; the dog just reminded Brett of dreams he'd once had.

The dinner with Kate had been revealing, but it hadn't done anything to make him feel less lonely. After Folly's evening walk and another beer he went out to sit in the courtyard. The ducks had stopped coming to be fed because he had ignored them for so long. He'd gotten out of the habit of buying dried corn; Olivia had always taken care of it. Now he went to look for the ducks with a handful of bread slices. The bayou was as still as the summer night air. Nothing stirred its gleaming surface. He wondered if the ducks had flown north for the summer. It would have been the sensible thing to do.

Brett wanted to fly somewhere, too. The problem was that he would have to take himself wherever he went. There really was no place to go to get away from his thoughts or his feelings.

Feelings. He certainly had them. Kate might doubt it, but if he'd ever had any doubts himself, those doubts had been put firmly to rest. The problem was that he didn't know what those feelings were. All he knew was that something had been seething inside him for a month until he wished he could abandon his body to get away from it. He'd felt this way as a child every time his mother raised his hopes, then

forgot about him; he'd felt this way every time a foster parent decided he had to move on to another home.

He'd made up his mind a long time ago that he'd never feel this way again. Even when he and Kate had gone their separate ways he'd been more disappointed than hurt, more humiliated than angry. Now disappointment and humiliation weren't even in the same universe as the muddled emotions tying his stomach into knots.

The joyful sound of Folly's barking broke Brett's concentration. Folly was becoming annoyingly exuberant now that he was left to his own devices for so much of the day. Brett imagined that even though the owners of the house were seldom at home, eventually they'd be complaining about Folly's behavior. He would probably have to find another home for the dog, or another home for both of them. The Bayou St. John apartment had too many memories, anyway.

"Brett?"

He turned and searched the courtyard with his eyes, but he knew who he would see. Olivia stood on the patio, illuminated only by the soft light of a lamp inside the living room. The soft light didn't matter. He could have been blind; it could have been darkest, deepest night, and he would still have known she was there.

"What are you doing here?"

She walked toward him, and he drank in the graceful sway of her hips as she came closer. "I used to live here."

"That's right. You used to." Had her voice always been this sweet, this musical? He didn't remember. For a moment he felt almost suffocated by the need to remember.

"Now I'm here because I need a lawyer."

Brett knew an excuse when he heard one. He'd been disappointed too many times to hope, but if this wasn't hope trying to push through the ugly, twisting, gut-wrenching mess inside him, what was it? He couldn't even speak because he didn't trust what he might say.

"I need a *good* lawyer," she went on. "This might be a bit complicated. You see, I want to sign over the Hopkins Academy for Nanny Development to someone else, only it's not mine to sign over quite yet. I guess I'll need you to draw up a paper verifying my intent."

"Why?" The word almost strangled him.

"Giving the academy to this person seems like the only solution to my problem." Olivia wanted to touch Brett. In the past month she had dreamed of nothing else, but she couldn't risk having him pull away. She had to be sure he understood everything she was going to say.

"Who is this person?"

"My husband."

Brett turned back to the bayou. Moonlight reflected off its calm surface. He was like the bayou. Nothing could penetrate his surface to uncover the secrets underneath. Kate was like the bayou, too. But Olivia? Olivia wasn't. Olivia was the good earth, warmed by the sun's rays. He wondered how he could ever have thought otherwise.

"And why would you give the academy to your husband?" he asked at last.

For a moment she faltered. What if all the faith and courage that had made her take this step were misplaced? For weeks she had died a little each time she remembered Brett's last words to her. He didn't care about her; he had told her so. She was nothing more than a person he had dispassionately selected to play a role.

Then one morning she had awakened with his name on her lips. Memories of all the wonderful loving things he had done for her in their months together had come flooding back to chase away his words, words that had been spoken out of his own hurt. She had remembered their wedding night and Christmas morning, the night at the Bellemont, the tender look in his eyes when she'd asked him about Kate. There were all the everyday, ordinary moments, too. Moments when she'd caught him looking at her as if he couldn't

quite believe she was there, moments when he'd sensed whatever she needed and given it to her with a warm smile or a kiss. She had been flooded with memories, and she had known, finally, something that Brett didn't even know himself.

Brett loved her. Brett had chosen her as his wife because she was the right woman for him, but not for the reasons he believed. She had been right for him since the very beginning because she had loved him. She was even more right for him now because he loved her. He might never be able to say it. He might never even be able to identify it, but she believed it was true. Just as she now believed he would make the right decision.

"Olivia?"

"I would give the academy to my husband," she said resolutely, "because I trust my husband to do what will be best for us both. If he truly believes our marriage won't last if I stay on as headmistress, then he'll sell it when February comes. But if he comes to realize that the academy is only a small part of my life compared to the part I've reserved for him, then he'll keep it. Either way, the choice must be his to make."

Brett was silent.

"Will you draw up the papers?"

How could he answer?

"I came by earlier tonight, but you weren't here." Olivia wondered why she was chatting as if nothing had happened. She had just laid out her heart and its contents, but Brett wasn't even looking at her. Surely that was the only answer she needed.

Finally he forced himself to speak. "I was having dinner. With Kate."

So the story Olivia had told Kate had been wrong after all. Irrelevantly she decided she'd have to change the ending; Monsieur Crawfish would just have to look harder for his hole. Sometimes it *was* possible to get back what you'd lost

pursuing elusive dreams. Kate had. Too bad it wasn't going to work for Olivia, too. She felt the brush of Folly's fur against her legs as she began to retrace her steps through the courtyard. "I left a few things here that I need. Then I'll be out of your way."

"Why didn't you tell me months ago that you were thinking about keeping the academy?" Brett wondered why he had asked her that now. Did it really matter anymore?

She sighed, and the sound carried across the yards separating them like wind dying after a summer storm. "I didn't know. For a long time I was too frightened to think about it."

"Frightened of me?"

"Frightened you'd walk out on me."

Instead he had forced her out. Brett continued to stare at the water. "And now you've weighed it and decided to leave it up to me?"

"I found," she said softly, "that nothing else mattered as much as you, Brett. I don't know why we couldn't compromise. I don't know why we couldn't find a way to solve this that wouldn't have been so shattering, but I do know one thing. I can do this for you because I love you too much not to do it."

"Then where are you going?"

"If you're eating dinner with Kate these days, there's no place in your life for me."

"We had dinner together so Kate could tell me everything that's wrong with me. It was the first and last time."

"Kate wants you back."

"No, but it wouldn't matter if she did."

Olivia could have believed Brett if his arms had been around her, but the cold emptiness encasing her heart wouldn't be warmed by his words, not when their backs were turned to each other.

"I want you. Does that matter?" she asked. When he didn't answer, her voice broke. "Does anything matter to you? Did you even notice I was gone?"

"I noticed."

She shut her eyes, and her body slumped in defeat. "Just tell me whether you'll do what I asked, and then I'll leave. Don't keep me standing here hoping. I don't deserve this."

He wondered how he ever could have thought Olivia was anything like the other women in his life. Was he so isolated, so ruined by past experiences, that he couldn't recognize love when he saw it? How could he ever have compared her to anyone at all? There was only one Olivia. She was a gift from the gods. She was a gift he had almost thrown away in a childish demand for proof of the love that was so obvious, so tangible, that only a man with none of his five senses could have missed it. Brett's knees were weak with the realization that he had almost lost her. His fault. His own fault.

He turned, and so did she. He saw the droop of her shoulders, the moonlit agony of her expression, the tears that trailed down her cheeks. The twisted mass of emotions inside him broke free. He felt light-headed; his skin felt sensitized to the air around him; his eyes were scratchy and moist. "Olivia." He covered the distance between them in three steps and fiercely wrapped his arms around her. "Don't ever leave me again. Do you hear me? Never!"

She sobbed out her relief against the front of his shirt. If she'd had to give up something, it was nothing compared to this. Her body melted into his. They were two parts of a whole, two parts that had been torn apart. How could she ever have walked out on him? He was every dream she'd ever had.

Brett inhaled the fresh spring scent of her hair; his hands traveled over the rough cotton of the sundress she wore, longing for the feel of her skin. Olivia lifted her face to his and sought his lips. Her own parted at the first contact, and

she lifted her arms to tunnel her fingers through his hair to bring him closer.

She knew he was as hungry for her as she was for him. Their tongues met, and she knew it was only a preliminary. She wanted few preliminaries. She wanted him inside her. She wanted his seed inside her, seed that would flourish and grow into the child he had wanted so much. She wanted that child now. A child to symbolize the love she would give him for the rest of their days together.

He couldn't get close enough. He wanted to be inside her, live inside her. He wanted to fill her and be filled by her sweetness, her love, her passion. He wanted to push her down to the grass by the bayou and take his fill. Instead his mouth broke free of hers, and he lifted her to carry her into the house.

He faltered once. He laid her on the bed, and seeing her there, where he'd wanted to see her for so long, brought back each lonely, pain-filled day of the past month. "Are you sure this is what you want?" he asked, his voice hoarse with desire.

"Yes. Yes!" Olivia sat up and unzipped her dress with unsteady hands, throwing it on the floor beside her. "Hurry!"

They tore off their clothes, and she held her arms out to him. He had forgotten how lushly perfect her body was. She had forgotten the way his broad shoulders contrasted with his slim waist and narrow hips. He had forgotten how her skin felt against his lips, how her body arched under his caresses. She had forgotten how hot he was to her touch, how cold she was without him beside her.

Both had nearly forgotten how good, how right, it was to become one in each other's arms. They made no attempt to savor their reunion. They took what they needed from each other with no concern except to reestablish what they had lost. When he parted her legs, she joyfully surrounded him with them. When he filled her emptiness, she cried out in

ecstasy. Then they gave and took and gave again until there was nothing left to be given or taken. There was only the hope that they would never have to be this demanding, this hungry, again.

Later—a long time later—Olivia felt her breathing slow. She cuddled closer to Brett and sighed. He heard the small sound of satisfaction, and his arms tightened around her until there was nothing between them except a heartbeat.

"I've missed you so much," she whispered, as if saying the words louder might somehow disturb their happiness. "I haven't been able to think about anything except you."

"Why did you stay away so long?"

She had hoped and prayed that he would see she was right and come to her first, but she wasn't going to destroy their newfound happiness by telling him that. Instead she told him part of the truth. "I needed the time to realize what really mattered most to me. I meant what I said about the academy. It's yours now, and your choice come February."

Brett wondered how much more time he would have needed before he'd gone to her instead. She had come to him first, but that was to have been expected. Olivia would always come to him first, not out of weakness, but out of the strength of her love for him. Maybe he would always hold back a little, testing her, waiting, hoping. But the worst of that was over, because he had realized one elemental thing.

One elemental wonderful impossible thing.

"I love you." He stroked her back as he said it. "I love you."

She caught her breath at the sound of the words she had truly never expected to hear. "Do you?" She felt like a small child pleading for reassurance, but she had to be sure. "Do you really?"

"Really." He buried his face in her hair. Someday he would tell her how much she had taught him. He recognized love now, hers, his. And now that his eyes were open to it, he knew he would begin to see it all around him. He

was a man who'd only seen the world in the dreariness of blacks and grays and whites. Now it was full of bright colors and the subtle shadings of pastels. He would never take it for granted. Never.

"We're going to have a good life." Her voice broke, and she was weeping against his chest. "Do you know what this means to me?" she asked through her tears.

He knew. He knew it all. Most of all, he knew what she had been willing to give up. He knew the choices she had been forced to make. Love wasn't supposed to hurt this way, was it? Love gave, just as Olivia had always given to him until she had needed something so badly she had begged him for the right to take it.

He couldn't hold her any closer, but he tried. "Shh, bright eyes. Don't cry." He kissed her hair, her forehead, her wet eyelids.

"I love you so much." She tried to still a month's worth of tears.

"You have to stop so you can hear what I'm going to say."

"You've said everything you ever need to." Little by little she regained control until only her breathing caught, and then that, too, was calm again.

"I don't know why you love me," he began. "I don't know how you could, but if you'll just keep on loving me, I'm going to struggle to be the husband you deserve."

"You're the husband I deserve right now. You don't have to struggle to be anything else."

"I'm not going to draw up any papers for you, Olivia." He kissed away the words forming on her lips. "I'll tell you right now what I want. I want you to keep the academy, but I want you to stop commuting. The firm is talking about opening a branch up in Baton Rouge, and I can run it if I want. We have a number of clients up there, and Lenny feels this is an advantageous time to make the move."

She was wide-eyed with surprise. "Lenny?" she said softly. "You've already spoken to Lenny about it? Before I came back?"

His eyes reflected his shame. "I think I would have come to you eventually. I want to believe I would have. I was just so full of anger. It might have taken months, but I would have come." He paused. "The Baton Rouge office was my idea. Deep inside I believed it was a start toward a reconciliation."

"Neither of us would have to commute?" She touched his cheek. "You'd give up living here for me?"

"I'd like to buy a house up there and settle in. Would you like that?"

"Oh, yes! And I can cut down on my hours." She covered his lips to silence him. "I want to, Brett. We need time together. You've been right about that. And when the children come, I want to spend as much time with them as I can. I can even take them with me to the academy. Mary's apartment will be a perfect place to work out of, and I'll have the best possible child care when I need to be somewhere else."

He smiled and kissed her fingers. "A school full of nannies has its advantages." He pushed her hair away from her face and propped himself on one elbow to be sure he could see her expression. "But, Olivia, the children can wait. I'm going to make sure you don't have to prove your love to me anymore. I can feel it." He touched his chest. "Right here, safe inside me."

Her lips curved up, but her eyes were glistening again. She threaded her fingers through his and pulled his hand to rest on her stomach. "If I'm not mistaken, my love for you is right here, growing in my womb. It's growing there because I want it to."

Brett glowed with warmth as he drank in the beauty of the woman who even now might be carrying his child. Olivia had given—and would give—him everything he had ever

longed for. Now he would spend the rest of his days trying to do the same for her.

"All the right reasons," he said softly.

"The right reasons?"

"Loving, sharing, giving, taking. Why did it take me so long to understand?"

She pulled him down for a slow, wonderful kiss. Loving, sharing, giving, taking. They would have the rest of their life to savor what they had both learned. Tonight was not too soon to start.

*   *   *   *   *

Take 4 Silhouette Desire novels
and a surprise gift
❧ FREE ❧

Then preview 6 brand-new Silhouette Desire novels—delivered to your door as soon as they come off the presses! If you decide to keep them, you pay just $2.24 each*—a 10% saving off the retail price, *with no additional charges for postage and handling!*

Silhouette Desire novels are not for everyone. They are written especially for the woman who wants a more satisfying, more deeply involving reading experience. Silhouette Desire novels take you beyond the others.

Start with 4 Silhouette Desire novels and a surprise gift absolutely FREE. They're yours to keep without obligation. You can always return a shipment and cancel at any time.

Simply fill out and return the coupon today!

* Plus 69¢ postage and handling per shipment in Canada.

Silhouette ❤ Desire®

Clip and mail to: Silhouette Books

In U.S.:	In Canada:
901 Fuhrmann Blvd.	P.O. Box 609
P.O. Box 1867	Fort Erie, Ontario
Buffalo, NY 14269-1867	L2A 5X3

YES!   Please rush me 4 free Silhouette Desire novels and my free surprise gift. Then send me 6 Silhouette Desire novels to preview each month as soon as they come off the presses. Bill me at the low price of $2.24 each*—a 10% saving off the retail price. There is no minimum number of books I must purchase. I can always return a shipment and cancel at any time. Even if I never buy another book from Silhouette Desire, the 4 free novels and surprise gift are mine to keep forever.

* Plus 69¢ postage and handling per shipment in Canada.

225 BPY BP7F

Name _____ (please print)

Address _____ Apt. _____

City _____ State/Prov. _____ Zip/Postal Code _____

This offer is limited to one order per household and not valid to present subscribers. Price is subject to change.   D-SUB-1D

ATTRACTIVE, SPACE SAVING BOOK RACK

Display your most prized novels on this handsome and sturdy book rack. The hand-rubbed walnut finish will blend into your library decor with quiet elegance, providing a practical organizer for your favorite hard-or soft-covered books.

Only $9.95

Approximately 16" x 8" when assembled

Assembles in seconds!

To order, rush your name, address and zip code, along with a check or money order for $10.70* ($9.95 plus 75¢ postage and handling) payable to *Silhouette Books*.

Silhouette Books
Book Rack Offer
901 Fuhrmann Blvd.
P.O. Box 1396
Buffalo, NY 14269-1396

Offer not available in Canada.

BKR-2A

*New York and Iowa residents add appropriate sales tax.